Shattered Soul

Re Della Strada

Book One

Samantha Barrett

My FeFe,

Thank you for changing your ticket my kuz! I knew you loved me. Love you long time my cousin and appreciate you. Now let's get fucking lit.

This one's for you, Keifer Moana!

Note to Reader

Note to reader, this book is a cross over from the Murdoch Mafia & Memento Mori.

You DO NOT need to have read those series before starting this one.

Warning!

This book contains some scenes that may be triggering,
Miscarriage
Loss of sibling
Bully
Suicidal thoughts
Medical manipulation
Drugging
Mental and Physical abuse
Sexual manipulation
Forced Proximity
Kidnapping
Dub con
Torture
Murder

*If you find something triggering that has not been listed please
email authorsamanthabarrett@gmail.com. I do endeavour to
include all triggers but what I may not find triggering others
will so please be kind and reach out to me so I may include
those triggers.*

Prologue

Six years ago...

"Slow down, Lake!" I swipe away the tears that continue to fall and try to see through the haze of them as the rain continues to pelt down like bullets against the windshield.

How could he do this to me?

"He's never chosen me, not once in my entire life, it's always been about his company and what he can earn," I manage to grit out before another sob tears its way out of me. This isn't how tonight should have gone. An hour ago I was happy and getting ready for an amazing night out with my best friend, to go spend the night with my boyfriend and our friends but instead, here I am running away with a broken heart. "I won't marry him!" I scream.

"I know!" my best friend shouts. "Now slow the fuck down or we won't make it there. The storm is bad and you driving like Dominic Toretto doesn't inspire me to be calm."

Despite my depressed state and spiraling inside my own mind, I manage to laugh at her stupid joke. That's the thing with her, she knows me better than I know myself, she can bring me out of the dark space I retreat inside when life gets too hard. She is my person.

I ease off the accelerator, earning a relieved sigh from Wave. "I can't do it, I can't marry him." She reaches over and places her hand on my leg offering me her support.

"I know. All we need to do is get to my house, then we pack our shit and go." I nod unable to speak as tears cascade down my cheeks.

"How do I say goodbye to him?" I choke out. The thought of leaving him behind because I can't marry another is tearing me up inside. I hate my life. I hate that I am being forced to make this fucking choice. All because he got involved with the wrong family and is using this to punish me for falling in love with a *nobody* as he calls him.

"You never have to. He won't let you go without a fight and he loves you so fucking much, Lakeland, that he even breathes in sync with you when you two are together. He is the person who will always choose you! Never doubt him, he will always find you and make sure you choose him because, without you, his soul would be shattered."

"Wave, I need to tell you something—" The words die on my tongue as the car is hit from behind. We both scream and I tighten my hold on the wheel, while managing to keep the car straight without having a panic attack. Fear grips me when the car shunts us again. Wave screams as I bite down on my lip and jerk the wheel to keep us from spinning and going over the bank. Rain continues to pelt down and obscure my view through the windshield.

"Lake, what the fuck is going on?" Wave screams. I chance a glance at her and the fear that is etched into her beautiful features spears me.

"I don't know!" I call back as I glance in the rearview mirror to see the headlights of the other car coming at us again. "Hold on!" I scream as I plant my foot, I just need to cross the bridge and then we will be safe. He knows we're coming and he'll be waiting, they won't let whoever the fuck is doing this hurt us.

"Lake, go faster, they're catching up!"

"I'm going as fast as I can! We just need to get over the bridge—-" Everything happens in slow motion, the car manages to hit the back left fender which sends us spinning. We have no traction on the road and it feels like we are aquaplaning. I try to correct the car and get us straight but I over-correct—slamming on the brakes does nothing. Our screams fill the inside of the car as we near the guardrail of the bridge. Fear grips me in its clutches the closer we get to the edge.

"Lakeland!" Wave screams as the front of the car smashes through the rail, and the nose of the car hangs over the edge. I try to remain still but Wave thrashes in her seat trying to open her door. I feel the car shift as the back wheels begin to slip, I lift the handbrake and keep my foot on the brake hoping that will stop the car from going over the edge and plummeting into the water below.

"Wave, stop fucking moving or we're going to fall over the edge!" I scream loud enough that she hears me over her own screams. She slowly begins to calm and turns to me with tears trekking down her cheeks, but it's the look of terror in her eyes that sparks my anxiety. I have no idea what happened or why this is happening to us but I know we can't stay here, the headlights from the car creep toward us slowly. "We need to get out of here." She attempts to move so I rush to add. "Slowly."

She nods, I see it in her body language and the way her hands shake that she is in fight or flight mode. "My door is jammed, I can't get out." Panic is evident in her tone but I remain calm to try to ease her worry.

"Okay, can you climb over the back?" Her bottom lip trembles as she shakes her head.

"Lake, you climb out and I'll follow you."

I shake my head. "No. I need to stay on the brake so the car won't move."

"It's front wheel drive Lakeland, your foot on the brake isn't doing shit, now fucking move before they come back." I look out the window and the car is coming toward us but what scares me the most is the fact they are just crawling toward us at a snail's pace.

"Okay, once I'm out, you climb straight over and we run."

"Okay," she says barely above a whisper. I fight through my fear and gently grip the handle and ease it open but freeze when the car slips forward. "Slowly!" My heart is racing so fucking fast and it is taking everything inside me not to break down and cry. This time when I open the door, the car doesn't move.

"Unclip my seatbelt slowly." Wave does as I ask and we both wait with bated breath to see what happens, when nothing happens I slowly ease my foot off the brake and shift my body the car creaks and slips forward as I'm halfway out.

"Tell my brother I love him!" Wave screams, then I'm pushed the remainder of the way out, landing on my hands and knees. I push to my feet and spin around to meet the terrified eyes of my best friend who is slipping over the edge. I grab onto the car and try to hold it so she can escape but it keeps slipping.

"Jump out now!" I scream as the front of the car begins to tilt toward the water.

"My leg's stuck. I love you, Lakeland. Now fucking run before he finds you." Gut curdling screams tear out of me as the car slips through my fingers and goes over the edge, leaving behind the ghost of my best friend's screams.

"Waverly," I cry out, I attempt to move toward the edge but the sound of the engine revving behind me draws my attention. I manage to spin around in time to see the headlights coming straight at me. I'm paralyzed by fear and unable to move, my legs won't work. I stand here, welcoming the end. The only regret I have is not telling him, I should have told him earlier but I was scared and now he will never know. Closing my eyes I stand here and brace for what is to come. A scream rips from me as the car collides with my body sending me sailing through the air. Pain courses through every inch of me as black spots dance in my vision. Before the darkness can take me, I look up into the eyes of a man I never thought would betray me. I welcome the blackness and pray I never wake up to live in this fucking nightmare.

Chapter One

You need to start shifting this weight out to the distros." I look up from my phone to see Xander walking into my office —the fucker never knocks. He drops into the seat in front of my desk and kicks his fucking feet up on the edge of it, then scrolls through his goddamn phone.

"You want me to shoot you, don't you?" The fucker flicks his gaze to me and smirks.

"What's eating your ass today?" I'm not in the mood for his bullshit right now so instead I toss him my cell. He catches it and stares down at the screen. I watch as his face morphs from amused to dead-ass serious. "What the fuck?" he breathes out.

"Exactly." He snaps his gaze back to me, then drops his feet to the floor and places my phone on the desk.

"How the fuck did this happen?" I shake my head, utterly lost for words. Waking this morning, the last thing I expected to see on the news was the announcement of Lakeland Deveraux's engagement to Giovani Dario. Percy has just declared war with the Re Della Strada by doing this as Lakeland was originally promised to Roberto Da Luca, the previous head of this family. The girl was only sixteen at the fucking time. I had no idea who he was back then or who I even was until shit changed and I became who I am because of her.

"Gio works alongside the fucking Irish, he even has ties to the English," I growl.

"So, those fuckers we have a treaty with are going behind our backs and still doing business through our fucking borders?" The anger is evident in Xander's tone and I don't blame him. We should have killed Percy Deveraux six years ago and ended all of this but the slimy fucker's daughter made a deal for her family. I may be a lot of things but I never break my word. Now, the bastard has aligned himself with my rival and it appears he is trying to unite himself through marriage for extra protection. He already tried to sell her off once before and now it appears he is trying to do it again to solidify his place in this underworld.

"Yes. We can't fucking touch them. If we do, it will be an all-out war and right now we can't fucking have that. We need to be wise about how we deal with this. When we meet with the families in a couple months for the induction of the *Memento Mori*, we'll deal with Ian and Karl after that." Before Xander can respond, Taylan walks in with a pissed off look on his face. I know everything about these two, I can gauge their moods just from a look or from their body language. They can read me just as good, that's what happens when you all grow up together and make a vow to never abandon each other. "What is it?" Tay grinds his teeth and clenches his fists at his sides, trying to calm himself enough so he can speak. Out of the three of us, Taylan is the one with the worst temper. He's easy going and is a complete and utter ladies' man but once you get on his bad side, there is no coming back.

"Gio just ambushed our guys and raided the stock house."

"Motherfucker!" I roar as I shove back from my desk and begin to pace the length of my office, scrubbing a hand down my face. This is just adding salt to the fucking wound this morning. Learning about Lakeland's engagement to him was bad enough but to add this fucking shit on top is a kick in the dick. "Any casualties?"

"Mase called it in and said six were taken out, four injured and the other five of our guys managed to pop at least eight of their guys," Tay answers.

"Any alive for questioning?" Xander asks.

"Yeah, we got two of the fuckers. Mase is bringing them here now." I shoot my boys a dark smile. Taylan wiggles his brows in excitement knowing we are about to extract our pound of flesh from these fuckers. The three of us are a little fucked up from bullshit in our pasts, now we use every opportunity to torture as an outlet.

My mom wasn't a shitty mother, she is great and she is the only parent the three of us have ever known. Xander's parents abandoned him, Tay's stepfather used to beat him when he would drink so he came to live with us as well. "Let's go, fuckers, Mase should be here by now." Xander and I both nod as we follow after Tay. On our way to the basement my mom spots us from her place at the kitchen counter and clears her throat.

"That can wait five minutes." I fight the urge to roll my eyes and tell her it can't but when both my boys make their way toward her, I begrudgingly follow after them. We each place a kiss on her cheek before standing on the opposite side of the counter waiting to hear what she has to say. "I saw the news, Knox." My spine stiffens.

"And?" I grit out, her eyes narrow slightly.

"Don't take that tone with me, it may work on your men but I am not them." Feeling like a dick for biting her head off I mumble an apology and grunt when Xander elbows me in the side. I shoot the fucker a glare but he matches it with one of his own, warning me not to fuck with Mom again or we'll be throwing hands. I fucking love how both of them are so protective over her and would lay down their lives without a second thought for the woman who raised them. "Giovani is old enough to be that girl's father. What are you going to do about it?"

Anger thrums through me, so I take some calming breaths before I answer. "Nothing. She made her bed and now she can lay in the flea infested fucking thing."

Mom's eyes fill with anguish. I tear my gaze from hers unable to see that look in her eyes. "Knox–"

"I got shit to do. Lakeland isn't my fucking problem anymore," I force out through clenched teeth. As I make my exit heading straight for the basement, bloodlust courses through me. The need to inflict pain on these fuckers takes control of me as I descend the stairs to see Mase and a couple of my other guys strapping them to the metal chairs that are placed on top of a clear plastic sheet. Upon my entry, the two fuckers look toward me, the fear I see in their shit colored eyes feeds the fucking monster inside me that thirsts for blood.

"Boss, these are the only two survivors," Mase says as he comes to stand beside me while we wait for the others to finish strapping these fuckers down.

"How much did they get away with?" I ask, not taking my eyes off my victims. He hesitates so I turn to face him making sure he can see the rage in my eyes. "Need I remind you of the laws of the R.D.S?" I grit out.

Mase shakes his head. "No, sir. They managed to take over half of the powder and the entirety of the arms." I grind my teeth so fucking hard that they begin to ache. The guns those fuckers stole were supposed to be shipped to Bishop Murdoch. I managed to secure a deal with him in the hopes that a working relationship with the Murdochs would somehow come in handy one day. They normally deal with another family but I made a promise to double their quota and at a better rate but now, I may have just fucked us. Mase is one of our best guys and I know he is shitting himself, worried about what I will do to him for this fuck up but I'm nothing like Roberto. I will never harm my men and expect them to remain loyal to me. This shit is part of the job and more common these days thanks to Giovani being pissed that

I was recognized by the other families as the head of Canada and offered a seat at the table with the other heads and he wasn't.

"Scout all of Giovani's known haunts and I want men following his brother. If anyone is going to fuck up and lead us straight to where they are hiding the guns it's Christiano," Xander says as he enters the room. Mase nods and motions for his guys to follow him out the back door leaving me, Xander and Taylan alone with these spineless pieces of shit.

Reaching up, I grip the back of my shirt and yank it over my head, tossing it to the side before moving to stand in front of these bastards. Their gazes dart between the three of us when Tay hands me a pair of brass knuckles. Slipping them on my right hand, I clench and unclench my hand as I crack my neck side to side.

"He's going to kill you bitches!" the fucker on the left shouts and without pause I dart forward so fast he has no time to prepare for the force of my jab. He roars in pain and rocks back in his chair, whimpering as he spits out a couple of teeth. His buddy starts to pale and that's when I know he is the weaker of the two—he'll squeal soon enough. That is where Gio is a dumb cunt. These men are prepared to rat him out because of how he treats them. My men risk their lives for me so I think it's only right I compensate each of them fairly and look after not only them but their families as well.

Tay doesn't wait for my go ahead as he rushes forward and begins to land punch after punch on the pussy to the right. Xander and I share a look before we step forward and go hit for hit on the bastard in front of us. I would have loved to break out the tools and peel their skin from their bones but I can already smell the stench of piss permeating the air, these cunts wouldn't survive that so we are left to dole out a good old beating.

"Please!" the one behind me screams. I take one last jab at our guy before turning back to Tay's guy. My brows raise at the sight of him. Tay truly fucked him up. I shoot my friend a loaded look and shake my head.

"Taylan, how many times have I told you to use your fists and not slice and dice our guests?" Tay stands there covered in blood while gripping the hilt of his favorite knife, his chest rising and falling in quick succession. I focus back on the rat. His arms, chest and thighs are littered with cuts, even his face has a few but the one that stands out the most is the gaping hole on his cheek that is gushing blood. I cluck my tongue and chuckle. "Did he make you hold your mouth open while he stabbed your cheek to see if he could get the blade through the other side?"

The little bitch has tears streaming down his face. "Y-yes, please, I'll tell you whatever you want to know." Xander comes to stand beside me and rests his elbow on my shoulder acting bored.

"But how would we know you're telling the truth? For all we know you could just be bullshitting us so Tay won't keep slicing you." His eyes widen and he shakes his head.

"I won't lie, I swear, please. I owe the Dario family nothing, all I ask is a swift death." Xander, Tay and I all share a look making sure to keep our masks of disbelief in place, knowing he will start spewing details freely if we make him sweat it out for a few seconds and sure enough, it takes him all of ten seconds before he tells us everything. "Gio ordered us to take the stash to the new place." That draws my attention.

"What new place?" I snap.

His trembling intensifies under the pressure of all our stares. "H-he said to take everything to the place in Winnipeg." I keep my anger from taking over at the mention of Winnipeg. I can feel Tay and Xander's gazes on me but I ignore them as I give our rat my full attention.

"He's taking the guns and coke to Percy Deveraux, isn't he?" Surprise covers his features but he nods, clearly stunned that I managed to put that shit together. I turn my back to him as I focus back on my guys. The fact Gio has made a move as bold as this is a fucking insult. Winnipeg is part of my territory, he controls Ontario over to Quebec. The fact he is ballsy enough to cross into my own territory and have a deal with the Deveraux's means he's preparing for a takeover. I see unease on each of my friends' faces. We haven't been there in six years and now we don't have a choice.

"Just let this go, leave the past alone, brother," Xander implores me.

"We don't get those guns back, we go to war with the Murdochs. We can't fight Gio and the Murdochs at the same time. Bishop would team up with Gio just to obliterate us. We fly to Calgary tonight with our men then we go after Percy and take back what is ours," I growl.

"And what about *her*?" Tay pushes, I inhale sharply knowing there is a chance I will see her but I swore I would never let that shit cloud my judgment.

"We put her down like we would any other bitch," I force out through clenched teeth.

Chapter Two

Lakeland

There is nothing worse than not feeling chosen.

I'm never the first, second, or even third choice. Never have been and never will be. I like to fool myself into thinking I'm okay with that, I'm used to it but the truth is, I'm not. It stings so fucking badly. People crave love and hearing those three stupid words from their significant other, but not me. I want them to tell me that they would choose me no matter what. I want them to want me before anyone else. I want that feeling of knowing that I am their person, their one and only. Love comes and goes but finding your person doesn't fade, ever.

I wish I could have that but given what my last name is and who my father is, I have no chance of finding that one person that sets my soul ablaze inside me.

"Daydreaming again?" I shake my head and push away

those silly thoughts as I smile at my sister when she claims the seat across from me. Riverland Deveraux is stunning, she puts no effort into her appearance at all, she just wakes up and deems herself ready. Her long black lashes enhance her moss-green eyes. Her brown hair is piled into a messy bun atop her head but it's her style that gives her that edgy look. She has such a skater vibe about her and she constantly wears a pissed off look on her face. I hate that I can't remember why she decided to change.

"Yeah, it's the only way I'm gonna be able to get through this," I mutter bitterly. God, I wish taking over my dad's empire didn't mean I had to marry some egotistical prick who thinks he is a prize to women. Giovani is a pig.

"I'm sorry, Lake." River drops her gaze to her lap and guilt gnaws at me. I know if she could trade places with me she would.

"It's not your fault. I'd rather it be me than you anyway." I force cheer into my tone but River sees through my bullshit and pins me with a look that has my walls crumbling. I let her see the heartache and loathing I feel for my situation.

"Why do you allow him to do this to you?" Before she can continue, the front door opens and we both tense. I shoot my sister a worried look. She isn't supposed to be here. Dad kicked her out a couple of years ago after they had a nasty fight. She tried to take me with her but he stopped it and had his men throw my sister out. I cried for weeks and begged him for months to change his mind and allow her back but even if he had, I don't think she would come back. As Dad enters the room the smile vanishes from his face when he spots his eldest daughter.

"What the fuck do you think you are doing in my house?" he shouts. I push to my feet, ready to intervene but I'm too late.

"If I recall, this is my mother's house and you just live in it." Dad's lips thin and his eyes blaze with anger, my head begins to throb like it usually does when my emotions heighten. I fight through the pain as best I can to block my dad from reaching my sister when he moves forward.

"Daddy, please," I beg. He grips my shoulders and shoves me aside. I scream out for him to leave River alone and not to touch her but it's no use. I watch as he backhands her and sends her tumbling to the floor. My vision turns hazy as pain explodes inside my head. I cry out when it becomes too much then quickly bite my lip to silence my screams.

"Come on, you old cunt. Touch me again and I'll put a bullet between your fucking eyes." I snap my eyes open and gasp. River has a gun pointed at our father, her cheek bruised and her lip split. Tears fill my eyes at the sight of her injuries.

"You have thirty seconds to get the fuck out of my house before I kill you," Dad grits out through clenched teeth. River keeps her gun pointed at him and never turns her back as she slowly edges toward me and holds out her free hand. I stare at it in confusion.

"Lakeland, this is your chance to be free, you won't get another one. Come with me now, please." I dart my gaze from her to my father who is shaking silently with anger until his gaze collides with mine.

"Don't even think about it. You gave your word to Giovani. You will marry him for this family and do your job." I flinch at the cold tone and hesitate for a second longer before I place my hand in hers and allow her to pull me to my feet. "You walk out that fucking door and I will hunt both you worthless bitches down and murder you with my bare hands." His threat sends a cold shiver down my spine.

"We'll take our chances, you sadistic fuck!" Without warning River fires the gun and then blinding pain explodes inside my head as I pass out.

I come to, groaning and clutching my head. It feels like a band is playing heavy metal inside it. I fucking hate that I have these severe migraines. The doctor Dad took me to said it's common. I have no idea what the fuck could be common about these things since I know no one who suffers from them this badly.

I haven't been allowed out of the house unless it's with my father for years and I have no cellphone or access to the internet, hence why the only way to see my sister is if she sneaks into the house.

"Take your time, Lake." She may have whispered the words but it feels as if she shouted them. I hate that this is a common occurrence. I pass out whenever my stress levels are heightened. I slowly blink my eyes open and whimper when the stabbing pain in the back of my head intensifies. "Here,"

River says as she gently slips her arm behind my shoulders and sits me up, handing me some pills and a glass of water. I hope she thought to bring my medication with her, without those pills my headaches are always present. I hate how they make me feel like a zombie but they are the only things that keep the pain at bay. I smile my thanks as I down the pain killers and look around.

We're clearly not at my father's house anymore. From the size of the room and the fact there is a tiny bathroom off to the side, I would assume we are in a rundown motel. The wallpaper is peeling and the ceiling is yellowed from guests smoking in the rooms. God, I hope this isn't one of those rooms you rent by the hour!

"Where are we?" I croak out.

"Not far enough away. As soon as you are okay to travel we need to leave." Her words have the events of earlier rushing back to me. I gasp and shoot her a worried look.

"What happened, Riverland? You had a gun? Oh my God, he is going to kill us both!" My hysteria begins to rise the longer it takes for her to answer me.

"Calm down, you passed out and I got you out of there."

"How did you get me out?" My sister may be a badass but there is no way she was able to carry me out and keep our father at bay.

"Colson helped me carry you out." My jaw unhinges and she rolls her eyes.

"Colson?" I squeak.

"Yes." I shake my head, unable to comprehend what she is saying. Aside from Wallace, Colson is my dad's second most trusted man and not to mention Wallace's son and grew up with us. "Colson has seen what we had to put up with for years and when I reached out to him a couple of months ago he didn't hesitate to offer his help."

"Dad is going to kill him!" I whisper.

"He can't because he is here with us, keeping watch outside." A whoosh of air escapes me, this is a lot to digest.

"What are we going to do, River? We have nowhere to go, no friends, no money—"

"Don't worry about all of that, Lake. We have each other and that is all that matters. I swear I will never let that bastard hurt you again." Her every word is laced with hatred but I feel like there is a double meaning to what she is saying. "We need to get going. Are you able to move?"

I nod and accept her help to stand when she offers. I make quick work of using the restroom, then splash some water on my face before staring at my reflection in the mirror. My hair is a mess of knots, so I use the elastic on my wrist to twist it into a messy bun like my sisters. I pinch my cheeks to give them a bit of color and sigh. My green eyes are lifeless and my brown hair has no shine to it, I don't know what the fuck is wrong with me but I feel like a huge part of me is missing and I can't figure out why.

"Lake, we need to move," I hear River call from the other side of the door. I quickly exit the bathroom and follow her downstairs to the parking lot, only to cringe when I see an old man leading a woman around my age to one of the rooms on the lower level—this is definitely one of those places that rents rooms by the hour. A shudder of revulsion runs through me as I climb into the back of the car. Colson shoots me a welcoming smile as I buckle in.

We've been driving for about an hour and night has fallen but I still haven't said anything since muttering a greeting to Colson. He rides shotgun next to River and they are both tense, constantly checking the mirrors to make sure we aren't being followed. I can't stop taking in the view outside my window. It feels so strange to be outside without my dad beside me. At first I summed it up to him being a worried parent and wanting to keep me safe but after a while, I figured out it was just his way of trying to control me. I'm the sick child, he would say. If only I wasn't such a burden and more like River, I would be the perfect daughter, he had said.

I don't know what I did to make my father hate me so much. Growing up I remember him being kind, caring and loving to us and our mom before she passed away, but everything after our mom's death feels hazy. I can't recall much and she has been gone for nearly seven years now.

"Do we have a destination?" Colson asks, breaking the silence. I haven't spoken to him in a long time. The last time I recall actually seeing him and having a conversation was around the time my mom passed away. Dad wouldn't let any of the young guards near me. The only men allowed around me were old and of course, I had the maids watching my every move and dictating what I could and couldn't eat. Dad would never allow me to have fast food, he'd say if I got fat I would be worth nothing.

"I'll take the first shift driving then we can switch. I only want to stop for gas and that's it. We need to get to Calgary." I reel back.

"Calgary?" I practically shout, earning a scowl from my sister in the rearview mirror.

"Yes. We need to put as much distance between us and Winnipeg as we can. It's a thirteen-hour drive but we don't have a choice. Percy will have all the airports locked down and we need to get out of Giovani's territory as fast as we can." Her words have a pit forming in my gut.

"If Gio or Dad find us, they will kill us," I mutter.

"Percy won't kill *you*, he needs you to keep his deal with Gio." Colson's words offer me no comfort.

"What deal?" River asks.

"Percy is marrying Lake to Gio in order to form an alliance against the Re Della Strada. Gio gets Lake and Percy's finance companies throughout the US and Canada to clean money while Percy's debt with Gio gets wiped and he makes millions."

"Percy's broke, isn't he?" My eyes widen at River's question.

"He ran your mother's family's companies into the ground. He made some sketchy investments and owes Gio a shit load of cash. Percy was lucky to walk away with his life but given what La–. Percy had something that Gio wanted and knew it would piss Knox off, so he gave your father a way out."

"Who is Knox and what is the Re Della Strada?" I ask, interrupting their conversation. Colson shifts in his seat and turns back to face me. His warm brown eyes are filled with sympathy and that confuses me.

"Knox Bronson is the leader of the Re Della Strada and the head of the Da Luca family." It takes a second for that to register inside my head, then I'm gasping.

"Oh my God, he's the guy that is at war with Gio. Dad hates him and the Da Luca family." Knox is the man who ran me down. Dad had business dealings with him and six years ago their deal went sour and Knox came after me as revenge against my father.

Colson nods. "They aren't known as the Da Luca family now, they go by the Re Della Strada. Percy has something that means... a lot to Knox and was willing to sell that to Gio in the name of revenge."

"Why does Dad hate this man so much? I know they had a deal that went bad years ago, hence my accident," I say bitterly. Colson and River share a weird look. River subtly shakes her head and Colson straightens gazing out the window without answering me. "Someone answer me!" I snap.

River sighs. "Lakeland, believe it or not, Percy promised you to someone else before Gio but that plan was ruined when that man was murdered."

"You're lying," I bite back.

Her shoulders hunch as she meets my gaze in the rearview mirror. "Percy had promised you to Roberto Da Luca when you were sixteen." I hear the truth in her words. Horror fills me with the notion that my father was planning to sell me off to some mafia Don at the tender age of a child.

"If he wasn't... taken out, then Percy would have gone through with it."

"Why was he murdered?" I mutter in shock.

"His daughter was murdered. Someone who loved his daughter very much sought out revenge and killed him when he found out that he was trying to pimp her out as a child before her mother ran away and kept both her children safe."

Chapter Three

Knox

"We need eyes on Percy and his men before we make a move," I say to the men who are gathered in the foyer of my Calgary mansion. Fourteen of our captains are present with all their teams on standby awaiting orders. Taylan, Xander and I always plan out shit rather than running in half-cocked. I refuse to be one of those Don's who have no regard for their men's safety. I trust my inner circle and captains enough to know they will always have my back and never betray me.

"Can I make a suggestion, sir?" I motion for Floyd to continue. "I would like to suggest that we send men to the border of Ontario and have men positioned in case Gio tries to cross into our turf." I look to Xander and Tay who both nod their heads in agreement.

"Take two teams with you and alert me when you are in

position." Floyd nods. "Keep me updated," I call out as he exits the room with Stu and Cohen following after him.

"I want to know if Percy or Gio or any of them board a plane." Tristan nods and heads toward the back of the house where we have all the computers set up for him and his team.

"The rest of you, I want you to scout out Percy and his men and watch them. I want to know his routine and what he is up to. I want a man inside and the cunt's house bugged. If we have to take his trifling-ass cunt of a daughter for leverage against him and Gio, then do it." I grit my teeth in annoyance when my men shoot me surprised looks. "Did I fucking stutter?" They all mumble their apologies before rushing out of the room, leaving me, Xander and Taylan alone.

"You didn't need to bite their heads off." Ignoring Xander I head for the wet bar in the next room. Being back here and this close to Winnipeg is fucking with my head. I pour myself two fingers of Jameson and down it before refilling the glass, Tay snatches it off me.

"What the fuck man?" I snap.

His icy glare holds a weight to it but I'm not in the right headspace to unpack that look right now.

"You need to sort your shit out, we are here to get the fucking guns, then we're out. We don't even have to step foot in that place. This is the closest we have to get, Knox." His words hit me like a ton of bricks and some of the tension flees my body as I nod.

"We know this is hard but you have our word that Percy won't get away this time," Xander enforces.

"He's got friends in high places, his death won't go unnoticed by them or the media," I add.

"We'll make it look like an accident. We'll overdose the fucker and shoot him with a bad batch." I want to rebuke what Taylan says but I also know I can't kill him outright or torture the cunt within an inch of his life. She is the person I want to watch bleed out, her selfishness robbed me of the person I loved most.

"He dies for the part that he played in this. Once he's gone, we move on to taking out Gio and wiping him and his scum from this country. I want this dealt with swiftly so we can get the fuck out of here before I break the deal I made with River and kill that cunt."

We've been stuck here for five days.

Tay and Xander are just as annoyed as I am that this is taking so long but Percy isn't keeping a normal schedule like we thought. He's locked down his security detail tighter than a virgin's pussy so getting a man inside to bug his house has become a fucking problem.

"Something is up," I announce. Tay and Xan look at me over the lids of their laptops. I lean back in my chair and run my gaze over the office. Out of all the houses I now own, this is the one I hate the most. He spent so much fucking time here and was mere hours away and never once came looking for us.

"What do you mean?" I lull my head to the side and meet Xander's questioning gaze.

"Something is up with Percy. There is no way he keeps this much of a fucked up schedule and not go into his office daily. The cunt has a finance company and apparently he also owns a few real estate companies." We just learned from Tristan that Percy has been busy expanding his empire, which is fucking hard to do when you're broke. That's how we know Gio is the one funding these expansions. "He hasn't left his house during normal business hours all week. We need to find out why."

"Maybe he's sick?" Both Xander and I pin Tay with a deadpan look that has the fucker smiling. "Hey, you both are the biggest bitches I know when you're sick and always claim to have the 'man flu' so don't fucking look at me like that." Xan and I both snicker but don't comment. Taylan always gives us shit whenever we're sick, claiming we aren't real men because we milk it.

"Should I get Floyd and his team to move in closer?" I shake my head.

"Nah, we keep eyes on him and figure out what the fuck is going on. We need to find a way to bug his phone and find out how deep he is in with Gio." Both my boys nod just as my phone rings. I grit my teeth when I see Bishop Murdoch's name flash across my screen. I shoot the guys a loaded look before picking it up and placing it on speaker.

"Bishop," I say in lieu of greeting.

A growl comes through the phone before he even utters a word letting me know he's pissed.

"I gave you a chance to form a working relationship with us and you are three fucking days late on the shipment." I keep my cool and try to fix this before we end up at war.

"I know—"

"If you fucking know then you best have a solution, boy. I am not the fucking man you want to get on the wrong side of." His threat is clear but it rubs me the wrong fucking way and has me shutting down all rational thought as I start to think like a Don and not a man trying to broker peace and form an alliance.

"I'm well aware of who the fuck you are, Bishop. I also know that much like me, you understand that certain situations can go wrong," I grit out.

I hear a scuffle on his end of the phone, the three of us share a loaded look before another voice comes through the phone.

"Knox Bronson, this is King, Bishop's underboss." Before I can respond Taylan snatches the phone off the top of my desk. Xander and I both try to reach for it and stop him but the fucker just smiles and responds.

"King, this is Taylan Carter. I am the underboss for the Re Della Strada formally known as the Da Luca family."

"Where the fuck is your Don?" Taylan doesn't miss a beat.

"I thought it best that I come to you underboss to underboss and not bullshit you." Tension rattles me to my core as I implore my best friend with my eyes not to do this. Xander is shaking his head and mouthing that he is going to fuck Tay up.

"Speak."

"We had a slight setback. Giovani Dario did a snatch and grab on our stash house and stole your guns. We are enroute now to reclaim those guns and finish that fucker for good. As a show of our goodwill and to prove to you and your Don that we are serious about this working out and want to continue this arrangement, we offer this first shipment to you at our own cost." My eyes widen in outrage. "We also offer the next three shipments to you at half the usual cost and can guarantee that they will be on time." Xander throws his hands in the air and begins pacing the length of my office.

"And when can we expect this first shipment?" King asks after a beat of silence. Taylan shoots me a wink and smirks.

"You can expect it to arrive at your port in two days' time." That's it. I rush around the desk, ready to tackle this fucker and beat the shit out of him but Xander stops me.

"This is your final chance," I hear Bishop grit out in the background before he ends the call.

"You motherfucker!" I roar as I fight against Xander's hold to get to Taylan.

"Calm the fuck down, you dickhead," Tay snaps. Xan whistles through his teeth knowing I'm about to fuck up our best friend for that.

"We can't fucking deliver shit!" Xander snaps.

Tay rolls his eyes. "You can't but I can." Xan and I exchange a look before he steps aside and we both stand here looking at Taylan.

"Explain," I grit out.

The fucker smirks and makes his way around my desk

and drops down into *my* seat kicking his feet up on the edge. My eye twitches at the sight and it takes everything inside me not to leap over there and pound his fucking smug face in.

"Simple, I knew we had a shit load riding on this deal so when we figured out that Gio took it, I made sure to have another shipment procured and ready to go." Shock ripples through me.

"You did what now?" Surprise is clear in Xander's tone.

"I stepped up and did what we needed to so that Knox could focus and deal with what the fuck being back here does to him." Guilt washes over me. I feel like a cunt for both my boys having to step in and handle shit because I've been a fucking headcase. "At least with the threat of war off our backs we can take our time and end shit with Percy and Gio. I know taking the hit for the next three shipments is going to be fucking hard but I gave Donny the go ahead to start cutting the product back home and distributing it as fast as we can. We'll lose money on the guns but we can make it back from the coke and the pills, I know we can." Xander and I stand here silently staring at Taylan in a whole new light. He is the one to goof off and make a joke about everything. Normally it's Xander and me that have to deal with all the hard shit and the decisions like this, but the fact he just saved our asses and even had a backup plan is fucking genius.

"I think you just got my dick hard," Xander says.

"I aim to please, my brother," Tay says without missing a beat.

"Thank you," I mutter. Tay shoots me a pitying look.

"No thanks needed. We're brothers and this family is everything to me. I dick around a lot but I also know when I need to step up. You and Xan have a lot of shit on your plates so it was the least I could do."

"You saved our asses, you know that, right?" He nods and shoots me a wink.

"I also have something else to confess."

"What did you do now, Taylan?" Xan grits out. I prepare myself for him to tell me he knocked some chick up or that he crashed another one of my cars.

"I didn't do shit but I think I know why Percy is being weird."

That piques my attention. "What do you know?" I press.

"This whole time none of the guys have reported seeing either Lakeland or Riverland at their father's house. I think Percy's baby girls have flown the coop and he is floundering trying to find Gio's bride-to-be. I mean, without Lakeland his deal with Gio would fall through because we all know Gio wanting Lakeland is only to get back at you." My brows raise. I mull over his words for a moment... and it actually makes sense.

"Have Tristan do a search for them. I want to know for sure that they did run before I pull the men and go after the heiresses." Xan nods and rushes from the room to do as I ask. Taylan looks at me with a strange expression on his face. "What?"

He pushes to his feet and holds my gaze as he speaks. "You think being here is hard, what do you think it's going to do to you when you come face to face with Lakeland Deveraux?" The air rushes out of me. I close my eyes and remind myself why I do this and why I became the Don of the Re Della Strada. All of this is for her. I had a deal with River but given the fact her father broke it, I am within my rights to finally go after her cunt of a sister.

"Lakeland is nothing to me. We find her and her sister and use them to draw out Gio and Percy."

"And then what?"

My nostrils flare in irritation. "Then I extract my pound of flesh from the bitch who thought she could break me... but only *after* I have killed her father and Gio."

Chapter Four

Lakeland

We've been in Calgary for over a week now and River has confined me to this shitty-ass motel room. There is only so much you can watch on TV without any cable. Colson handed me a phone but it's one that has no access to the internet and can only text or call. I snort out a laugh. It's not like I have any friends to call or someone who will be worrying about me. I'm no one's person and as hard as that hits me in my feels, I know I have to power through it. River and Colson have been going out every day since we got here, trying to find help as she called it. By help she means someone who can get us fake documents to cross the border into the US until we can get enough money together to hop our asses on a plane and get the fuck out of Dodge.

When I hear the room door unlock, I don't bother getting up from my position on the bed, choosing to remain sprawled out.

"Get up, we need to move now!" At the panicked shriek from my sister I leap to my feet. "Grab your shit, we need to leave now," she snaps again. I have nothing but the meager possessions we bought at Walmart, so it only takes me a few seconds to snatch the plastic bag off the floor before she is gripping my arm and pulling me out the door after her. It takes everything I have not to trip down the stairs after her.

"What's going on?" I ask once we hit the first floor and she begins to run, forcing me to follow her lead. I spot Colson in the car across the lot. As we near the car the sound of tires screeching draws my attention and I see a Cadillac Escalade drifting into the motel parking lot.

"Get the fuck in the car!" River screams, shaking me out of my stupor. I yank the door open and jump in the back seat and before I can even close the door, Colson is peeling out of the lot trying to escape the Cadillac that is gaining on us. He pulls onto the main road without even looking, drawing a scream from me when I see an eighteen-wheeler jamming its brakes on. Horns honk but it doesn't deter the wannabe Dominic Toretto, who weaves in and out of traffic at break-neck speed.

"Get the gun out of the glove compartment and shoot when they get close." Terror fills me when I watch my sister follow Colson's instructions.

"River—"

She cuts my protest off. "Shut up, Lakeland. We either take them the fuck out or we are as good as dead."

"You can't kill our father!" I snap before Colson takes a

sharp turn and I'm thrown into the door with a grunt. I rush to secure my seatbelt and pray to God that we don't die in some high speed car chase.

"At this point I would rather it be our father chasing us than *him*." Before I can question her more, she rolls her window down and leans her upper body out with the gun raised and fires off two shots. I cover my ears and scream. "Get us the fuck out of here, Cole. There are too many people out to keep firing."

"You want to fucking drive?" he snaps back at my sister.

"If he catches us, he is going to kill her."

Me? Fear thrums inside me.

"He won't touch her," Cole grits out.

"I won't let him take her," River says with such conviction that it sends a shiver down my spine. Ignoring the remainder of their conversation, I peer out the back window at the white Escalade chasing us down. They are only a couple car spaces away when Colson takes another sharp turn. The seatbelt yanks me back against the seat with a grunt. "They're gaining on us, Cole." He curses and pushes the car to go faster. As we hit some back streets that have zero freaking traffic, I watch the car close in on us. Dread forms in the pit of my stomach as the white car comes up beside us. The windows are tinted so dark I can't see who is inside the car. I scream when the bastard rams us from the side. Colson curses loudly before returning the favor and slamming our car into theirs.

"Take a fucking shot, Riverland!" he roars as we

continue smack into each other. River lifts the gun but in order for her to fire at them she would have to fire across Colson. She aims the gun but growls in frustration.

"I can't get a clean fucking shot and I'm not risking hitting you to get to those fuckers."

"Fuck!" Colson shouts before he slams on the brakes sending us all lurching forward. When the car finally stops skidding, I pop my head up to see a barricade of cars in front of us blocking the road. Men stand behind all the cars with guns trained on us. Colson slams the car into reverse but quickly slams on the brake again when the sounds of vehicles behind us skidding to a stop penetrates the air. "We're trapped," he grits out as I look out the windshield to see three guys standing in front of us with their arms crossed over their chests. They were the ones chasing us down.

"Get us the fuck out of here," River barks. I look around and see we have no way out, the road is blocked. Colson looks at my sister with a look of regret and she growls before turning to me. "You stay the fuck in the car, no matter what you see or hear you stay in the car!" Before I can protest she is getting out of the car with Cole hot on her heels. Fuck this! I follow after them. I am not a coward and will not let my big sister fight my battles. At the sound of my approach River spins around, her eyes wide with fear. "Get out of here now!" she screams before turning back to the three men with her gun raised. Colson has his aimed at them as well but my breath lodges in my throat at the sight of the three guys pointing guns at my sister and Cole. I rush to my sister's side, but she pushes me behind her and shields me from the men's view.

"Let her go and you can have us," Colson says.

"You mean nothing to me," the guy on the end says. I peer around my sister's shoulder to get a better look. The guy on the end looks like he should be off fighting the Hulk, his black hair is a mess atop his head. The five o'clock shadow that dusts his face adds to his edgy look, but his brown eyes hold no warmth in them.

"You're full of shit, Xander," River snaps back. I reel back in shock that she knows these guys.

"Your bark is bigger than your bite, Riv," the guy on the other end says. Unlike his buddy, he doesn't hold a dark edge. His blue eyes spark with mischief and the casual way in which he dresses makes him look like he has a boy next door type of vibe. He catches me staring and shoots me a wink before running a hand through his brown hair.

"She comes with us and you live." I stifle a gasp at the sound of the guy in the middle's voice—it sends a shiver down my spine. I've heard that voice in my dreams. I run my gaze over him. I can tell without anyone needing to alert me that he is the leader of this... gang. Power wafts off him in waves, the clothes he wears are nothing but a mask. The Converse, blue jeans and black shirt may make him seem approachable but the sneer on his full lips would have men running in the opposite direction. Unlike his friends, he has dusty blond hair that is just the right length to give you something to tug on. His green eyes draw you in but even from this distance I can see the haunted look inside them. There is no mercy in his gaze as he flicks it to me. I feel nothing but deep seated hatred. My lips part in a gasp as I get locked in his eyes and not knowing why he would look at me with utter disdain when he doesn't even know me!

But why does he seem so familiar?

"You are not taking my sister, Knox." A strangled sound escapes me at the mention of his name. I awoke in the hospital six years ago not knowing how I ended up there. My father had to tell me what happened. I was run off the road by a local thug by the name of Knox Bronson all because my father refused to help him with his company. Dad has told me for years that this man has been coming after him and trying to tarnish his reputation.

His gaze is still locked on mine when he answers River. "How many shots need to be fired before you give her up?" He doesn't give River a chance to answer before he fires a shot. Colson roars in pain as he drops to his knees clutching his thigh. I drop down beside him and apply pressure to his wound.

"You're gonna be okay, Cole," I say, pain is etched into his features.

"You son of a bitch!" my sister screams.

"I'm telling Mom you said that." The blue-eyed one says with a smile.

"Fuck off, Taylan," River grits out as another shot rings out. I scream when I feel the bullet whizz past me and lodge itself in Cole's shoulder, sending him sprawling backward. I don't think as I jump on top of him and press my hand against his shoulder. I ignore the sounds of footsteps closing in around us as I continue to use my thigh to press against his leg wound and then use my hands to keep pressure on his shoulder. Me straddling him like this puts me in a compromising position but I don't care. Colson will not die because of me!

"You're gonna be okay." He grunts but I can tell he doesn't believe a word coming out of my mouth.

"You need to run, Lake," he mutters. I shake my head, refusing to run and leave them behind. "He will kill you," he says low enough for only me to hear.

"Why?" I whisper.

He smiles sadly. "Because all great wars start over the love of a woman." Before I can figure out what the fuck that means, another shot rings out but this one comes from my sister.

"Try that shit again and the next shot goes straight through her fucking head." I peer over my shoulder to see Knox's gun trained on me while the other two have theirs on my sister. A grunt from the other side draws my attention. A man lays on the ground clutching his stomach.

River just fucking shot him!

"You have three seconds to step aside or I kill you and that fucker before I take her. Either way you look at this, Deveraux, I'm still walking out of here with that bitch. It's up to you whether or not you are breathing when I do." Knox's words wash over me, sending anger coursing through my body. My sister is stubborn and there is no doubt in my mind that she would choose death over allowing these low life thugs to get their grimy hands on me.

"Look after her," I whisper to Colson before I climb to my feet. He tries to grab for me but I step out of his reach. River keeps her gun trained on the thugs as she turns her head to me, her green eyes implore me to not do it but I won't allow her to be hurt because of me.

My gaze remains on my sister as I speak to them. "I'll go with you if you give your word that you will allow my sister and Colson to leave unharmed?"

"Lakeland, no—"

"You don't make any fucking demands, bitch!" Knox roars. If he thinks his callous words hurt me, then he has another thing coming. My father calls me many different names and none of them are the one on my birth certificate.

"Put the gun down," I urge her. She shakes her head but the sight of unshed tears in her eyes is what prompts me into action. I reach out and grip the gun. She reluctantly lets it go. I hold it out to the thugs as my sister wraps me in a tight embrace.

"I'll never stop coming for you. I'll find you wherever they take you. Stay strong and never let him break you—" A scream tears out of me when I'm pulled back by my hair. River screams and tries to reach for me but Taylan and Xander are there holding her back. Knox uses his other hand to pry the gun from my hand, as he drags me through the barricade of cars to a black SUV at the back. "I'll fucking kill you, Bronson!" River screams as I'm shoved roughly into the back seat. I quickly scurry to the other side and turn to face the devil who stares at me with pure malice.

"Your sister already did that." His words confuse the fuck out of me. I press myself flush against the door when he climbs in next to me, the moment the door closes I feel claustrophobic. "Feel chosen yet, kitten?" I suck in a sharp intake of air as shock ripples through me, then blinding-hot pain erupts inside my head.

Chapter Five

Knox

I watch her with a frown as she clutches her head in her hands letting out a scream so fucking loud I recoil into the door. If this bitch thinks faking agony is getting her ass out of this, she is dead ass wrong. She owes me a pound of flesh. I swore I would never touch her as long as that fucker kept to his side and stayed out of my way. For years I wanted to hunt her down and ruin her like she did me. The only thing that saved her from me was my memories, without those she would have been dead years ago. Clearly fate chose a different route for her and now that I have her in my grasp, she won't be going anywhere until I get the fucking answer and the reason why she did what she did!

"Make it stop!" she screams out as she hunches over yanking on the strands of her hair. Taylan and Xander open their doors ready to climb in but when Lakeland lets out another harrowing scream, they pause.

"What the fuck is wrong with her?" Tay asks.

"Bitch is faking," I snarl. She throws herself back against the door screaming. But this time I can hear the pain in that scream. My eyes narrow at the sight of blood dripping from her nose. Without thinking I reach out and grip the back of her neck hauling her to me, her eyes snap open.

"Make it stop!" she screams right in my face. It's not her words that have me tensing, it's her eyes, the whites of them can no longer be seen, they are bloodshot. "Help me!" she cries out before her eyes roll into the back of her head she slumps forward against me. I sit here stiff and unmoving with her draped over me, her face buried in my chest.

"What the fuck was that?" Taylan mutters, the distress in his voice is mimicked by Xander when he speaks.

"She wasn't faking that shit, Knox." I look to my two best friends to see worry etched into their features. I push my hatred for her aside for a second as I speak.

"Get Corey to take that fucker to the hospital. Make sure he stays with him so he doesn't snitch, then bring me River-land." They both nod and rush off to do as I asked. I stare down at her, hating that my hand itches to run my fingers through her long brown hair. I remember the feeling of her silky strands wrapped around my fist as I fucked her from behind, the sounds she would make had me going crazy. Grinding my teeth, I shake that thought away just as the back door opens and Xander shoves River inside. she opens her mouth ready to fight but at the sight of her sister passed out on top of me all the fight flees her.

"Lake," she whispers as she reaches for her sister and

pulls her backward so Lakeland is resting against her chest. She shifts her around so she can position her more comfortably, wipes away the blood with the hem of her shirt and brushes the strands of hair from her face. "You're gonna be okay, I got you, Lay," she whispers before pinning me with a scornful look as Tay and Xan climb in. "What did you do to her?"

I say nothing not owing her a fucking thing. Xander drives us away from the scene where our guys will cleanup and make it look like nothing happened. Tristan will already be wiping every camera and any reports to the cops from the system before we even get home. When River curses, I look down to see Lake's nose has started bleeding again. She tries to use her shirt to stop the flow of blood but it does nothing. I huff as I pull my shirt over my head and toss it to her, the bitch doesn't say a thing as she uses it to press against her sister's nose and tilts her head back slightly to stop the bleeding.

"Put her legs on your lap," she barks.

"Get fucked," I grit out.

"You want her blood all over your seats?" I shrug.

"Don't care, I'll buy another one tomorrow after I torch this one to dispose of your bodies." Her eyes brim with hatred.

"You are a fucking asshole, you know that?"

"At least I own what I am. Can you and the whore in your lap say the same thing?" Her jaw locks and she wisely remains silent going back to tending to the bitch.

We've been driving for what seems like a couple hours

and I'm getting pissed off at how long it's taking to get back to the house. The bitch keeps jolting and annoying the fuck out of me. River constantly checks her pulse and opens her eyes every so often using her phone torch to make sure she is reacting to the light.

"How did you find us?" she asks after pocketing her phone.

"When you're on the run you shouldn't go to public places with cameras," Tay says not bothering to mask the sarcasm in his voice.

"Why were you even looking for us, Knox. We had a deal." I snap my head to her and growl, making sure she can see the full brunt of my rage.

"I honored that fucking deal!" River doesn't flinch away. "Your bitch-ass daddy crossed the line and broke it first. I agreed to leave her breathing because of the past the four of us shared. I know what happened that fucking night—"

"No, you fucking don't!" she screams.

"She killed my sister!" I roar. At the mention of Waverly, she recoils and drops her gaze back to her sister. My chest rises and falls rapidly as I try to regain my composure but it's fucking hard when I can't help but stare down at the reason for every ounce of pain I have felt for years.

"She didn't kill, Wave," she whispers after a minute of tension filled silence. I cut a glance to her to see her running her fingers through her sisters hair.

"Who the fuck did then?" I grit out. "She left my sister in that car as she jumped out like a coward and saved herself."

River slowly lifts her gaze to me. "I'm telling you, Knox, shit didn't happen the way you thought it did."

"She was fucking drunk and speeding in the rain! My sister paid the price for that bitches meltdown over being promised to Roberto. She could have called me and I would have stopped it," I snarl.

"She wasn't drunk!" Taylan shifts in his seat to stare at River. I search her gaze trying to detect her lie. "She. Wasn't. Drunk," she says again, making sure we hear what she is saying.

"Start fucking talking now before I say fuck it to you ever being our fourth wheel and kill you now," Tay sneers as he points his gun at River. She pays him no mind as she stares at me.

"Percy lied and had her blood switched at the hospital. I only found out when I broke into his safe a few years back and found the real accident report and the paperwork from the hospital." My brows draw in. "Knox, there was another car there that night."

"Bullshit, you're fucking lying you bitch to cover for your sister. We went to the scene and there were no other tire tracks." Riv ignores Xan as she pushes on.

"I'm telling you the truth, there was someone else there that night."

I scoff. "If that were the case, why the fuck did the cunt hide away from me? That bitch claimed to have loved me and even told me I was her person," I say sarcastically. Tay and Xan both chuckle but River glares at each of us. Before she can answer, the cunt in question begins to stir in her lap, groaning in pain.

"Take it easy, deep breaths and try to breathe through the pain, Lay," River says. You can tell she has said that same speech often. Lake keeps her eyes closed as she reaches out and grabs my arm, using it as a crutch as she pulls herself up. She's so fucking close I can feel her breath fanning across my face. "You may want to back up," River mutters. A whimper escapes Lake before she slowly begins to blink her eyes open, it takes her a couple seconds to adjust and the moment her eyes finally focus and she realizes how fucking close she is her eyes widen for a second before she flinches in pain and slams them closed again, slumping forward. I try to shift out of reach of but it's fucking futile, I have nowhere to go, so she ends up with her face in the crook of my neck.

When River coughs to mask a laugh and I shoot the bitch a look promising pain, my attention is drawn back to the other bitch when she lays her hands flat against my chest and pushes herself back. This time she seems more alert as she looks to the front. Tay wags his brows at her, she cringes and scrunches her face before looking back to me. Earlier she looked at me with fear but now... I see nothing.

"Who are you?" she whispers. I search her gaze trying to figure what fucking game she is playing but her eyes, they don't lie. I see the truth, she doesn't recognize me. I divert my gaze over her shoulder to her sister, who looks guilty.

"Do you believe me now?" she mutters. I turn back to Lakeland to see her running her gaze over every inch of my exposed skin. She reaches out with her pointer finger and traces the tattoos that cover my body. She squints trying to get a better look at them in the dim light. Feeling utterly robbed and angry by this new revelation, I grip her wrist, halting her movements when she gets too close to one tattoo in particular. She cuts her gaze to me and stills. I see no flicker of emotion except confusion.

"Don't ever fucking touch me again," I snarl right in her face before shoving her back into her sister. River shoots me a scathing look while Lakeland just seems... more confused. I tear my gaze from both of them and look out the window. I refuse to allow both of these bitches to trick me. They get each other and have no idea what it feels like to lose your sibling, your only friend, your partner through life. I lost my sister because I let her cloud my mind and trick me. Losing Wave was just the start of figuring out everything she lied about—she knew the fucking truth and never once uttered a single fucking word.

Chapter Six

Lakeland

The moment the car stopped in front of the largest log cabin style house I have ever seen, Knox gripped me by my hair and dragged me out of the car kicking and screaming, not caring that I fell to my knees and hurt myself. I had no choice but to quickly find my footing or risk him dragging me the entire way. My sister was held back by his friends. I see men patrolling the grounds but none of them spare me a glance or even a second look as their boss drags me like a caveman, he doesn't pause when the front door is opened for us. He continues to drag me after him like a disobedient dog, when we reach the stairs I trip and fall. He growls and rather than give me a moment to get my feet under me he just uses my hair to drag me up the stairs. I scream out and tears cascade down my cheeks as the pain in my scalp becomes too much.

"Please, stop!" I cry out as I scramble to get on my feet.

"You're as fucking useless as an ashtray on a motorcycle,"

I hear him sneer as he tightens his grip and ignores my protests. The hair that has fallen into my face obscures my view. I stumble behind him blindly. A shriek leaves me when I'm yanked forward and crash into the side of a large bed. I push off the side and swipe the hair from my eyes as I turn and face the bastard. He stands there shirtless with his tattoos on display. I'm powerless to stop my eyes from dropping lower. His jeans sit low enough on his hips that I can see that infamous V that women cry over and wish their boyfriends had. I avert my gaze and meet his sinister stare. I push through the fear that is strangling me.

"I'll kill you if you touch my sister," I vow, only to flinch in pain when a sharp stabbing begins to pulse at the base of my skull. I need my medication.

His upper lip pulls back in a snarl. "I'll kill you both without batting an eye, you little bitch." I have no time to mull over the meaning of his words before his hand is around my throat and I'm forced backward. I'm arched over the side of the bed with him right in my face. I claw at his arm, trying to get him off me but he doesn't budge. I kick out with my legs only for him to trap them between his much larger ones. My vision becomes foggy as spots begin to dance in the corner of my eyes. I strike out and slap him so hard my hand stings and vibrates from the force of it. My grip on his arm slackens as I feel myself drifting into unconsciousness. Before I can pass out, he releases me and jerks back.

I drop to my hands and knees, gasping for air as tears leak from my eyes. I'm light headed and feel nauseous. I gag and begin to cough as I sway, my arms give out and I fall to the wooden floor, sobbing. I don't look up when his shoes enter my line of sight. I flinch away when he crouches in front of me, the dark chuckle that escapes him has me preparing for him to lash out and strike me, I'm no stranger to taking a beating.

"When you think it's over, it will have only just begun," he says quietly. I shift my head back along the ground and stare up into his eyes only to see disgust and loathing in their depths.

"Why are you doing this?" I croak out.

"Because I want to watch you break and fall apart. I want to destroy you. You are going to beg for me to kill you by the time I am finished with you. Shower's through there, when I get back you better be clean and ready to take whatever the fuck I give you." Tremors wreak havoc over my body at his innuendo. I say nothing as he pushes to his feet and leaves me here on the floor, closing and locking the door behind him. The moment I can't hear his footsteps I let the sobs I was holding back free, then curling into a ball on the ground, I allow the tears to flow unchecked.

I feel utterly helpless. I'm not like my sister in the sense she is a badass and gives zero fucks. Ever since the accident I haven't felt like myself. Six years have passed and I still feel like I'm missing a huge part of my life and no one seems to understand that. Any time I asked Dad about what happened, he would brush me off or get angry. I was never allowed to attend doctor's appointments on my own. He had to always be by my side, never allowing me to ask any questions. I've asked River and every time she would just shut down and say she's sorry. My life has been a series of cluster-fucks one after another and I can't fucking live like this anymore!

"Get up." I snap my eyes open to see Taylan standing in the doorway with a bitter look on his face. My body protests as I gingerly climb to my feet. He nods and moves around the room with familiarity. He stands in front of me a minute later holding a fresh towel and shirt. "I suggest you get in the shower, kitten. He's in a bad way and you don't need to push him more than you already have." The tinge of sadness that coats his tone confuses me.

"I haven't done anything to him," I rasp out, his eyes narrow before gripping my chin and lifting my head to expose my neck.

He growls in disapproval at the sight, I no doubt have bruises. "He do that?" I look away. "Answer me."

"It won't change the outcome, what's done is done," I say bitterly.

"Nothing is set in stone, Lakeland. Things can change but you have to want them to. Don't cower behind your sister, you were never meant to be a sheep, you were always meant to be the shepherd." I study him and take in the way he stares at me like he knows me. It fucking baffles me how he thinks he can speak about me like he knows something I don't.

"You don't know me." He smiles, his dimples are on full display and I'm sure those weapons garner him a lot of atten-tion from the ladies. He tentatively reaches out and brushes his fingers along my cheek. I gasp as a feeling of longing hits me in the chest.

"Lakeland Deveraux, I know you better than you know yourself right now, kitten." His softly spoken words have my pulse thumping. The longer I stare up into his eyes, the more I feel like there is something I'm missing.

"Get away from her, Taylan." Both Taylan and I jolt in shock. His hand drops back to his side as he turns around to face an angry Knox who stands in the doorway looking like an unhinged tanned God.

"You gonna choke me too?" Knox's eyes narrow at his friend.

"Stay out of it. She isn't who the fuck you think she is, get out." Taylan's shoulders bunch, I must be out of my fucking mind because I reach out and place my hand on his arm drawing his attention back to me.

"Thank you for the towel." His brows furrow for a second before he nods and leaves, shoulder checking Knox on the way past. Not wanting him to unleash his wrath on me again I hastily make my way toward the bathroom across the room. I try to close the door behind me but Knox shoves it open, causing me to stumble backward and catch myself on the edge of the counter.

"It stays open." I want to argue but the dark look in his eyes has me swallowing down my retort. I place the shirt and towel on the counter as I turn my back to him. I feel utterly violated knowing he is watching me. My hands tremble as I grip my shirt, pulling it over my head while forcing myself not to cry. I have road rash scars down my side from my accident. I've struggled with being okay with the way my body looks. I have more scars down the sides of my legs due to breaking them from the impact of the hit and run. I shakily reach behind me and unclasp my bra, dropping it next to my shirt. It takes me a full minute before I work up the courage to unbutton my cargo pants. I want to curse him out and demand he get the fuck out or scream for my sister but I don't do either of those things, instead I strip down to my thong. I feel his gaze on me as I bend and push my panties down, kicking them to the side.

I keep my back to him as I shuffle toward the shower, it has frosted glass which I am grateful for. He will be able to see my silhouette but that's it. I practically slam the glass door closed behind me and release the breath I didn't know I was holding. I turn the shower on and gasp when the cold water hits me. I jump out of its trajectory only to smack into a warm body. I scream and spin around so fast I nearly lose my footing, but manage to catch myself on the built in shelf. The ice-cold water pelts my back but I can't feel the sting of the cold as I stare up at Knox.

"What are you doing in here?" I screech as I wrap an arm across my breasts and use my hand to cover my pussy. I force my eyes to remain on his. I'm disgusted in myself for wanting to check him out after everything he has done to me. He runs his gaze over my body, taking his time to document every detail and not caring about the fact he has no right to see me like this.

"You could stand to lose ten pounds." My jaw unhinges. I hate that his nasty remark has old insecurities rushing to the surface. I know I'm not a stick figure like my sister or many other girls my age, unlike them I have hips and an ass. It doesn't help that I've been a double D since freshman year at high school. Girls would call me all types of names because boys would always stare at my ass or tits. They hated the fact their boyfriends would openly check me out thinking I would spread my legs for the team. Dumb bitches, their disgusting boyfriends are the reason I've chosen not to spread my legs at all. I refuse to allow my first time to be meaningless.

"And you could stand to get Botox on those crows' feet." The words flew out of my mouth before I could stop them. His arm lifts as if to grab me and instinct takes over. I smack it away and shove him against his chest but he doesn't budge. We become a flurry of shouts and flailing arms as he keeps coming for me while I fight him off. He manages to catch my wrist and uses it to spin me around and slam me against the tiled wall. I cry out as my head bounces off the wall. He bends my arm halfway up my back, drawing a cry of pain from me as I rise to my tiptoes.

"You ever fucking touch me again and I'll snap your fucking arm." Tears prick the backs of my eyes but I refuse to allow this asshole the satisfaction of seeing them fall. I try to breathe through the fucking pain, refusing to submit. I won't allow the likes of this fucker to break me. I did not escape one tyrant to wind up at the mercy of another.

"Fuck. You," I grit out through clenched teeth, my bravado fleeing when he drops his hold on my arm only to plaster himself against my back. I bite down on my lip to keep the whimper from escaping when I feel his hard cock pressed against my back. Gripping the back of my neck he forces my face to the side. I take deep breaths through my nose and watch him out of the corner of my eye. I stiffen when he leans forward and buries his face in the crook of my neck. I don't know what I expected him to do but it sure as fuck wasn't for him to bite me. "Fuck!" I scream so loud my own ears ring when I feel his teeth puncture my skin. Unable to keep the tears back as I thrash against him, trying to dislodge his bite, but it's futile. I whimper when he releases me. Using his free hand to run his fingers over the bite mark, he gathers the droplets of blood before smearing it over my lips.

"Next time, I'll use your blood to lube my cock up before I slam it into your ass." His threat hangs in the air and horror fills me, knowing he isn't making idle threats. "Now, wash me." He sneers as he pushes me harder into the wall before stepping back.

Chapter Seven

Knox

Her bottom lip trembles as she shakily turns to face me, keeping her head down and eyes on her feet. I refuse to bend or allow her a chance to think without me being in her face and reminding her of what she did. I want her thoughts to be plagued by me. Every waking moment I want her tearing herself apart over what she did. Her sister tried to spit some bullshit earlier but I'm not buying what the fuck she is selling. Her story is so farfetched. Lakeland is just a good fucking actress, she deserves an Oscar for the way she fooled me. She can't fake the scars that mar her body, you wouldn't know she had so many hidden beneath her clothing. I never even suspected she had them. She turns to the side and reaches out to grab the sponge from the shelf and squirts some soap on it. She turns to me, keeping her eyes on my chest.

I see the way she is warring within herself. Part of her

wants to do it just to get it over with but the other part, that part wants to tell me to go fuck myself. I wait silently for her to make her mind up. I personally hope she chooses the latter, I would relish in making her scream. I want to feel her bones breaking beneath my hand, I want to see her eyes filled with terror knowing I am the one who is going to end her sorry-ass excuse of a life.

"You act like you've never done this before." She jolts at the sound of my voice and without thinking reaches out to glide the sponge across my chest. A satisfied smirk tugs at the corners of my mouth, this is going to be easier than I thought. Before she at least had a bit of—no, scratch that, she had a mountain load of fight in her but it seems she's acting like she *forgot* about that too. Her hand trembles as she reaches out to grip my own. I watch her with keenness, refusing to relax around her or allow my guard down. She washes that arm before doing the same to the other, then clears her throat.

"C-can you turn around?"

"So you can stab me in the back while I'm not looking again?" I bite out.

She shakes her head and darts her tongue out to moisten those full fucking lips. I may be raging and hate her but the sight of her curvaceous body and the way her perfect tits rise and fall with each breath has my cock standing to attention. She thought keeping her back to me as she undressed would deter me... Wrong, bitch. I've always loved her plump ass and watching it bounce up and down on my cock while she rode me.

"No," she says with slightly more determination but she still refuses to avert her gaze from the center of my chest.

"You don't command me and there is no fucking way I would ever turn my back on a snake like you. Now, kneel." For the first time, she finally meets my stare, her eyes spitting fire. I see it in her features, she wants to fight and refuse me. I bend until we are eye to eye, leaving a sliver of space between us. I hear her sharp intake of breath. "Kneel." Her nostrils flare in indignation.

"You're sick." She growls as she slowly lowers to her knees.

"You'd like to think so, wouldn't you?" Her jaw works side to side as she fights to keep her retort to herself. Her lips thin as she tears her gaze from mine only to come face to face with my cock. Her eyes widen at the sight of it being fully erect, her throat bobbing as she swallows audibly. I had planned to force her to clean me and that was it, but now with the way she is looking at my dick I decide to change my plan. I tangle my hand in her hair, she hisses but remains silent as I grip my cock in my hand. A shudder rolls through me as I pump myself and a groan slips free as I continue to stroke myself.

The sight of her cheeks flushing with heat and the way she gnaws on her bottom lip proves this bitch is a thirsty cunt and would suck my cock willingly if given the chance. I keep my gaze on her as I continue to stroke myself, her breaths are coming in short rapid pants. I'd bet good money that her dirty cunt is wet. Using my grip on her hair I force her head back and relish in the grunt that comes from her rotten mouth. I slap my cock on her lips, drawing a wide-eyed stare from her. She opens her mouth to curse me out no doubt but I don't give her a chance, I force my cock inside. A groan pulls from me as the feeling of her warm wet mouth swallows me.

"You bite it, you'll fucking regret it," I warn. Tears fill her eyes as I continue to take what the fuck I want from her. Seeing tears streak down her cheeks as she gags around me only fuels my need. A fire begins to burn low in my stomach as I feel my balls tighten with the need to come. Holding her in place, I force my cock all the way to the back of her throat. Her hands slap against my thighs as she chokes but all her fight does is turn me on. At the last second, I pull free and stroke myself hard and fast. She gasps for air and coughs but that doesn't stop me. I throw my head back and roar out my release as jets of cum land on her face and hair. A strangled sob comes from her as I gaze down at the picture I've painted. Releasing my cock, I smear my cum all over her face. She swings her head side to side and tries to shove me away but it's pointless. I make sure to cover every inch of her face and even smear it in her hair.

"Stop!" she screams. I keep my grip on her hair as I crouch down in front of her, grabbing her chin forcing her to look at me.

"You are nothing, you're a pathetic waste of space. All you will ever be good for is a place to sink my cock into and even then that was the worst blow job I've ever had in my life."

"You're cock seemed to like what it saw though." Her eyes widened in surprise at her outburst.

"My cock wasn't hard for you, it was hard because I was thinking about the many ways I'm going to fuck your sister." I shove her away from me as I stalk out of the shower. The sound of her crying follows me into the bedroom only to find Xander standing next to the window. Gritting my teeth, I grab a pair of sweats out of the dresser and yank them on. "What do you want?" He turns away from the window to run his gaze over me, the look of disdain in his eyes pisses me off. I know him and Taylan don't agree with what the fuck I'm doing but they don't get a say, not in this. I'm the fucking Don and if I have to remind my two best friends of that, then so fucking be it.

"Don't fall for her bullshit. I want to see the bitch broken and nothing more than a shell of the girl she once was." Surprised that he is on my side, I nod.

"I want her begging for death before I finally end it the same way she ended Wave. She won't survive this, you have my word." Xander seems to relax at my declaration.

"We move on her father and take Gio out before getting rid of her." I bristle at the demand but don't say anything. I've always valued and trusted his and Tay's opinions or suggestions of certain things but he needs to also remember that I call the fucking shots.

"Anything else?"

"She staying here with you?"

"You got a problem with that?" I grit out. He shakes his head and moves to exit the room but pauses at the sight of

Lakeland in the bathroom doorway wearing one of my shirts. Her eyes are puffy and red from the tears, my hand print is bruised around her neck. He narrows his eyes and sneers at her with hatred. Her brows furrow and her head cocks to the side as she stares at him. I can see the confusion in her eyes. After a minute, Xan storms out of the room, slamming the door behind himself. Lake seems to snap out of whatever the fuck that was and shakes her head before flicking her gaze to the bed. I scoff before grabbing a pillow and a throw blanket off the end and toss it on the ground. "Try and escape and I'll break your legs. Fight me and I'll break your sister's to teach you a lesson." Her bottom lip trembles, causing disgust to roll through me. "You keep crying and I'll give you a fucking reason to shed tears. Harden the fuck up, Lakeland, you brought this on yourself."

It's been hours since I shut the lights off and still I can't fucking sleep. Lakeland seems to have no fucking trouble though! Her constant sleep talking and panting keeps me up. When she starts to whimper in her sleep, I growl. This has to be a fucking joke. I lean over and turn the bedside lamp on, ready to rip the bitch a new asshole for daring to keep me up. When I look down at her I'm surprised to see tears trailing down her cheeks. Actress or not, there is no way she can fake the pain etched on her face.

"Come back," she murmurs softly through her tears. A

crease forms on my face as I begin to wonder who the fuck she is dreaming about. I don't give a shit if she has nightmares so long as I'm the star of them and the one inflicting the pain but I know for a fact, this dream isn't about me because she would never tell me to come back. "I tried," she whimpers. I debate leaving her to continue moaning in her sleep or continue to listen, hoping she'll say more but the sound of footsteps has me climbing out of bed and following the sound downstairs. I know for a fact it isn't one of the guys because they never make a sound, it was one of the things we taught ourselves when we took over. I move silently through the house. I spot the light in the kitchen and head there ready to lay waste to whoever the fuck it is. None of my men or the maids stay in the main house.

Rounding the corner, I rush in ready to tackle the fucker, only to slam to a halt at the sight of the culprit drinking milk from the carton! River startles at the sight of me and spits milk everywhere.

"What the fuck, Knox?" she snaps as if she has the fucking right to be drinking *my* milk and walking around *my* house like she isn't a fucking prisoner! When I take in what she is wearing, I roll my eyes at the shirt that is clearly not hers and definitely one of the guys.

"Which one are you fucking?" I ask as I lean my hip against the counter and cross my arms over my chest, watching her as she wipes down the spilt milk. She pauses and snaps her head up to shoot me a filthy look before returning to her task.

"Not you, so why does it matter?" I could never figure

out which one of the guys she was sleeping with. When I asked Tay and Xan, they both just shrugged and refused to answer me.

"Why are you walking around my house like you have a right?" She dumps the cloth in the sink and mimics my position on the other side of the counter.

"Because you and I both know that the three of you still can't bring yourself to hurt me. I've been here mere hours and already your best friends are tripping over their feet and falling into my vagina." I shudder with disgust at the mental picture she is painting.

"You're worse than a fucking guy, you know that?" She shrugs and purses her lips.

"Maybe. I've never lied about what I want or who I am. I don't do commitment and never will, you all know this. Now, how about we stop with the bullshit small talk and trying to figure out whose cock was inside me ten minutes ago and remove the elephant in the room, shall we?"

"Jesus Christ, River!" I grit out as I scrub a hand down my face in frustration. Out of all the women in the world, we could have possibly formed a bond. Of course, it had to be one without a filter and a personality as fucked up as a serial killer. "How the fuck do you not have a cock swinging between your legs with the amount of big dick energy you put out?"

Without missing a beat the bitch claps back, "Because I prefer to suck cock not stroke one out in the shower and plus, I have really long fingers so it makes it easy for me to hit my own G-spot."

I refuse to acknowledge that shit!

"I'm going to bed. Get the fuck out of my kitchen." Before I can move an inch she fires back at me.

"I'll leave when you tell me what you plan to do with my sister?" My eyes narrow in warning but she ignores it. "I know you are livid and want her to suffer but believe me when I tell you that she has been suffering, silently for years without knowing why."

"Clearly, she hated you six years ago and now you both seem fucking chummy." Her lip twitches, it's always been her tell whenever she's getting angry.

"She never hated me, we're sisters and we tend to fight because of Percy filling her head with shit. I'm not lying to you she really did—"

"I don't fucking care!" I roar as I slam my palms down on the marble counter. River reels back, dropping her arms to her sides. "I hate her, I fucking hate her!"

"I know—"

"You know nothing!" I shout. "You have no idea how I fucking feel. That night changed everything for me. I didn't want this shit or to be the boss. All I wanted was to live a normal life and one day make enough money to give the girl I had fallen for a life she deserved, but look how fucking well that turned out. All she had to do was come to me and I would have fixed everything. I could have saved my sister but that selfish bitch ruined everything."

I keep my gaze on River as she moves around the counter to come stand before me with a pitying look in her eyes that grates on my fucking nerves. I don't need her pity. I may not have wanted this life but I wouldn't give it up now that I have everything. I'm not weak or worrying about how to help my mother pay the bills, I own a fucking country.

"Knox," she whispers my name as she wraps her arms around me, causing me to stiffen in surprise. This bitch isn't the type to be affectionate or offer anyone a shoulder to cry on. After a minute my rage slowly starts to ease and I find my arms lifting on their own accord to return her embrace. "I'm sorry all this happened to you but you have to know that this isn't who you really are. In the absence of light, darkness will prevail. Don't let this darkness consume you and change who you are."

Shoving her away from me, I sneer at the angry look in her eyes. "You think you can come back into my life after six years and mumble some mumbo jumbo bullshit then all will be right in the world?" I scoff and push on before she can answer. "You made your choice six years ago. It's clear to me now that we meant nothing to you. All we were to you was some punk kids your father hated and you used us to get on his nerves, nothing more."

"Fuck you, I loved the three of you like brothers—"

"Bullshit!" I snarl as I get right in her face. "You ran like a scared little bitch."

"My sister was in the hospital for months, what did you want me to do?"

"Have the fucking guts to come to *my* sisters funeral!" I shout so fucking loud I know I would have woken the others. River stumbles backward, looking pale. "I trusted you. I let you in and welcomed you as one of us, only for you to turn your back on us like we were nothing the moment your father demanded you to. You may be fucking Tay and Xan but that doesn't mean we are friends. By the time I am done with your sister, you will hate me as much as I hate the both of you." I turn, not caring what the fuck she has to say but the cunts words have me tensing.

"There's a fine line between love and hate and you, Knox Bronson, still love my sister."

"Never said I didn't," I snarl.

Chapter Eight

Lakeland

I come to with a groan. My eyes are puffy and feel swollen from all the crying yesterday and my back is aching from sleeping on the hardwood floor. I slowly sit up, grunting when my back cracks. My head feels foggy from all the headaches yesterday but I push through the pain and climb to my feet needing to use the bathroom. A quick scan of the room has relief flooding through me that he isn't here. After relieving myself, I splash some water on my face and help myself to the toothbrush, not caring who it belongs to. Once I finish I stare at myself in the mirror and cringe.

Why me?

It's the thought that has plagued me for years. I reach up and part my hair at the back, running my fingers over the scar. My head was cracked open from the accident and I needed emergency surgery but the details of that night still elude me to this day. All I know is what my father has told me. I hate that I have to rely on someone else's version of the events when they weren't even there. Whenever I think about that night, a pit always forms in my stomach and if I push too hard to try to remember, my head begins to throb like it does when I stress too much.

"Hungry?" I jolt and spin around to see Taylan standing in the doorway with a smirk on his face.

"Am I allowed to eat?" The sarcasm is thick in my voice and I don't feel an ounce of guilt for it. Taylan doesn't comment on my snarky attitude, instead he grips my hand and drags me after him. "I don't want to eat!" I snap as he drags me down the stairs, ignoring my protests. I stumble over my own feet but he doesn't seem to notice or care. "Where is my sister?" Taylan still refuses to answer me as we round a corner, my protests stopping at the sight of my sister sitting at the counter smiling as she talks to... Xander?

"Help yourself, babe," Taylan says as he releases me and grabs a plate from the stack at the end of the counter, which has a full range of different foods. It takes a second before River realizes I'm even standing here. Her gaze runs over me, her lips pinch but she says nothing when she turns back to Xander and continues her conversation. Anger thrums through me. How the fuck is she so calm and collected when we have been kidnapped!

"River—" The words die on my tongue when I'm shoulder checked from behind and stumble forward, catching myself on the edge of the counter at the last minute.

"She doesn't eat with us." My nostrils flare as I turn to

see Knox grabbing a plate and loading it full of food while acting like I'm not even here!

"Knox, stop being a dick," Taylan defends.

"You feed her, I punish her while you watch," he says with a shrug. I look to my sister for some sort of help or at the least a pitying look, but she keeps her fucking eyes glued to her plate and that's all it takes for me to snap. I swipe the stack of plates off the counter and relish in the shocked gasps of the four of them. They all stand there staring at me.

"Fuck you all!" I scream directly at Knox before turning to my sister, her eyes are wide and her mouth is open in surprise. "I expected more from you but I guess all it took was for one of them to dust the cobwebs out of your snatch for you to turn against me. Shame on you, Riverland!" I turn on my heel ready to escape and cry alone in my kidnapper's room. A scream tears out of me when I'm yanked back by my hair. Refusing to allow this bastard to manhandle me again, I fight back. Spinning around, I swing my arms and relish in the grunt that comes from him when I manage to land a decent slap to his face. "You fucking asshole, I hate you!" I scream.

He keeps one hand tangled in my hair, while his other wraps around my throat as he slams me against the wall. I grunt as my head bounces off it.

"Knox!" The warning that comes from Taylan is clear but as I look up into his eyes I can tell he isn't listening to his friend.

"Let him break the bitch," Xander growls.

"That's my fucking sister," I hear River say but it's too

late to come to my defense now. Knox and I stand here in a glare off, his face so close I can taste his breath on my lips and suddenly I'm grateful that I brushed my teeth. I frown at my own stupid inner thoughts. "Let her go." He ignores my sister as he presses in closer until I feel the hard outlines of his muscles pressed against me causing me to suck in a sharp breath.

"You have three seconds to get your ass in my room before I snap your fucking neck." I swallow audibly at his whispered words. My mouth feels like it's full of cotton as I dart my tongue out to moisten my lips.

"Snap it, you'd be doing me a favor." His eyes widen and his nostril flare at the same time as his upper lip pulls back in a snarl. Without an ounce of hesitation or warning I'm flung over his shoulder caveman style. I scream when I feel the cool air against my bare ass as he stalks out of the kitchen, meeting my sister's worried gaze for a second before he rounds the corner.

"Knox, she can't—"

"Shut the fuck up, Taylan, she's mine," Knox snaps as he takes the stairs two at a time. I grunt each time, wincing in pain from his shoulder knocking against my stomach. Once we reach his bedroom, he kicks the door shut and locks it. Fear rushes through me and before I can dwell on it too much, I'm tossed from his shoulder. A scream tears from me but is silenced the moment I bounce on the bed. I don't get a second to recover before he lunges at me. I kick, scratch, slap and scream but it does nothing but entice him. He grips my arms and holds them above my head, then straddles my lap using his weight to keep my legs pinned beneath him.

"Go to hell, you bastard!"

"You sent me there six years ago, bitch," he snaps back as I watch in horror as he reaches down and begins to unfasten his belt with one hand.

"No, stop, you can't..." Tears prick the backs of my eyes as he pops the button on his jeans and yanks the zipper down as he shifts down my legs and tugs my shirt up exposing my bare pussy. "P-please," I beg as the first tear escapes. I try to fight him. He forces my legs open and settles himself between them, then pushes his jeans down and I whimper at the sight of his hard cock tenting the front of his boxers. He leans forward, pressing it against my pussy. I try to shift away but he's too strong. When he yanks my shirt up further exposing my breasts, I scream and fight harder but all that seems to do is bring a smile to his face.

"I tell ya what." At the sound of his voice I still and scowl up at him through my tear-filled gaze. "I won't sink my cock into you on one condition."

I search his eyes trying to decipher what his game is but I come up blank. "Name it?"

"If I check and find you wet for me, I'm going to fuck you." I gasp. "But, if I check and find you are as dry as a nun's pussy, then you can just blow me as punishment," he says it like either option is a reward for me. I grind my teeth so hard my jaw begins to ache. "Make your choice, Lay." My brows furrow at the use of my nickname coming from him. A prickling sensation travels down my spine as a flash of a memory plays in my mind.

Knox presses a soft kiss to my lips and smiles lovingly at me as he runs his fingers through my hair. "I'm yours, Lay."

I roll my eyes. "I allow Tay and Xan to call me Lay, you are only allowed to call me baby or kitten."

My back arches off the bed bringing me flush with him as I suck in a rugged breath. My eyes are wide as I stare up at him. He frowns down at me as I continue to stare at him. He releases my hands and without thought I grip the front of his shirt and pull him to me until there is a sliver of space between us. I feel his breaths coming is fast succession. He doesn't move an inch, allowing me to come to terms with whatever the fuck that just was.

"You called me Lay?" I whisper. His breathing turns erratic, I see the war he battles internally through his green eyes.

"So?"

Unsure if I have lost my mind or if the fear of this whole situation has finally sent me bat shit crazy, I take a chance and pray my fucked up mind isn't playing tricks on me.

"You don't call me Lay, you call me... kitten," I whisper, it takes half a second for his face to harden, then his hand is around my throat and the other is forcing its way between my legs.

"I knew you were a lying, bitch," he grits out as he pushes a finger through my folds. I slam my eyes closed, not needing to hear him say the words. I already know what comes next and I am beyond disgusted with myself. "What do you know, my point is proven," he growls when I feel him smear my wetness across my lips. I snap my eyes open and glare at him. Whatever protest I was about to scream at him dies when he captures my lips, groaning at the taste of my arousal when he swipes his tongue along my bottom lip. I fight against my body's reaction to give into him and melt into the mattress. My body and mind are at war with each other.

The grip I have on his shirt tightens as his tongue forces its way past my lips. The moment his taste invades my senses, it consumes me. Without consent, my body relaxes beneath him as he continues to kiss me, his hand trailing up my side causes gooseflesh to erupt all over my skin. He trails his fingers across my nipple, drawing a gasp from me which shamefully turns to a moan when he twirls it between his fingers. Knox breaks our kiss. I'm breathless and panting but he doesn't seem affected like I am. He licks a trail down my neck, nipping at the tender flesh between my neck and shoulder. I shudder beneath his touch when he pinches my nipple. The moment his lips wrap around my nipple, a cry tears from me as my back arches off the bed. My mind is no longer in control as my body takes over. My fingers tangle in his hair as I try to keep him there sucking and lapping at my nipple.

He releases it with a wet pop before switching sides. Embarrassing sounds come from me and I hate myself a little more each time knowing this is wrong—he wants to rape me and has already hurt me!

He pulls back, staring down at me with lust brimming his eyes.

"I don't do rape, Lakeland, and believe me, I would have kept my word if you were dry." My eyes widen, I must have said that shit aloud! "It's not rape when you're willing." I open my mouth to deny him but he pushes on. "The fact that your pussy juice has soaked the front of my boxers tells me whatever you were about to say is bullshit. I'm fucking you regardless of what your mouth says." Shame washes over me when he rests back on his haunches and I see the front of his gray boxers are in fact drenched in my arousal.

"I don't like you!" I grit out.

"I hate you but my cock doesn't seem to agree with my head." I snort because fucking ditto! My bravado flees when he pushes his boxers down and his cock springs free. The tip is glistening with pre-cum, my breathing turning ragged the longer I stare at it. My fear spikes and without warning, the words fly out of my mouth before I can stop them...

"I'm a virgin!"

Chapter Nine

I freeze, then look back at her ready to call her on her bullshit, but the moment our gazes collide I see her fear. I get her being scared and playing on it just to piss me off but this look is different. Her cheeks are rosy and her eyes are hazy with need but there is also a hint of fear lurking in the depths of those captivating eyes.

"Virgin?" I question.

She bites her lip and nods. "Yes."

"Not for long," I growl, playing along. I don't know what the fuck this bullshit her and Riverland are playing at, but until one of them cracks and starts telling me the truth, then this is how she will be treated. She will be my pet and treated like a dog until she can learn to obey her master and speak the truth when she is fucking told. Her bottom lips quivers as I grip my cock and run it through her slick folds. I want to taste her and reacquaint myself with her taste but this isn't about her pleasure, this is about teaching her a fucking lesson for acting out and thinking she can have a say over anything in this house—*my* house.

"Please," she whimpers. Ignoring her protest I line myself up with her entrance and push inside her slowly, her face contorts in pain. I grit my teeth and grunt as I force myself inside her tight cunt. Fuck, she does feel a like a virgin. Her pussy is strangling the fuck out of my cock and almost making me believe her bullshit excuse, except for that fact that I was the one who already took her virginity years ago.

"This means nothing to me but means everything to you. I'm going to enjoy taking this moment from you." Tears roll down her cheeks as I continue to push inside her tight little body. The moment I'm fully sheathed inside her, I groan.

Home.

I push that stupid thought aside and give her a minute to adjust. As more tears continue to fall, I get pissed off at the sight of them. I may be a cold heartless bastard but I'm no rapist. I meant what I said, if she were dry I would never have fucked her. She turns her head to meet my gaze, the look in her eyes has my breath lodging in my throat.

Hate.

Good, I want her to hate me as much as I fucking hate her. I want her misery and pain. If she knew a fraction of the pain I have been living with for these years, she would be begging me to end her miserable life.

"I hate you," she mutters.

"The feeling is mutual... kitten." Her brows raise but

before she can respond, I claim her lips in a kiss that is pure dominance as I begin to move inside her. It takes her a couple minutes before she begins to kiss me back and suddenly a heady moan comes from her. I swallow it, loving the fact that even though her mind is screaming at her that it is wrong and she should be fighting, her body is submitting to me. Maybe what River said is true but even if it is, her body still remembers me and the way I can make her feel. I bite down on her lip hard enough to draw blood. She whimpers but I don't release it until she quits struggling. She's going to learn quickly, the more she fights the worse the pain will be, submit and the pain will lessen, simple.

"Holy shit," she cries out as she breaks the kiss. I push back and lift her legs, resting them on my shoulders needing to be deeper inside her. I brace my arms on either side of her head and thrust into her at a ruthless pace keeping my gaze above her head, not wanting to look at her face. Her pussy begins to clamp down on my cock. I want to deny her this orgasm but I know her coming on my dick will haunt her more than me denying her this release..

"Come, Lakeland," I growl as her eyes meet mine.

"Oh my God," she screams out.

"I am your God," I snarl as she shatters beneath me screaming my name. I don't ease up, I continue to fuck her hard as I chase my own release, but I can't stand the sight of her fucking face! I pull out of her and flip her onto her stomach, ignoring her protests. Lining my cock up with her pussy I slam inside her without remorse. She screams out in pain but I don't care or even slow my pace as I thrust inside her, chasing my own release. She tries to turn her head and peer at me over her shoulder. Gripping her hair, I force her face into the comforter as I fuck her. I throw my head back and bite down on my tongue to keep from roaring her name as I come deep inside her tight, wet little pussy.

The only sounds that can be heard are the harsh breaths coming from me and the soft whimpers from her. Suddenly the reality of what just happened slams into me. Not wanting this to seem more than what it was—a fuck—I pull out of her, not missing her wince. Ignoring her completely, I pull my pants up, tucking my cock back inside but pause at the sight of blood coating it. I dart my gaze between her legs and relish in the sight of blood smeared between her thighs. I hadn't plan to be that rough but I'm not mad about it.

"Get used to cleaning your blood off the sheets, you'll be doing it often," I snarl. I feel her gaze boring into the back of my head the whole time. I make sure to lock the door behind myself, not wanting fucking Taylan to go in and pacify her.

The moment I enter the kitchen I can feel the weight of their stares. I grab my plate that I discarded earlier and move to claim a seat at the table. For one split second I felt sated and calm, everything inside my mind was quiet until I looked down and saw her. I know without a doubt she is upstairs crying her eyes out and wondering what the fuck just happened—her feelings and wants, not even her fucking needs are my concern.

"Well, you feel better now you got to hear her scream your name because myself, I feel like I need to bleach my ears after hearing my own sister come!" I ignore River as I spear some eggs and bacon and shovel it into my mouth, her judgment means nothing to me. I spy her and Xander out of the corner of my eye and finally get my answer. It isn't Taylan fucking her, it's Xander. I've never seen Xan with many girls even as a teenager. He was the guy in the back glaring at anyone with a pussy that came near him. For years, the only girl he would let near him was Wave and when Lakeland came along, it took him a couple months before he would even speak to her. I know this shit is hard on him. Xander isn't like most people, it takes years for him to trust and just as long to love them. Losing my sister really did a number on him and I'm not sure why exactly.

"Boss?" I dart my gaze up from my plate to see Tristan standing at the other end of the table with an iPad in his hands.

"What is it?"

"I think we have a location on Percy." I climb to my feet and follow after him with Xander, Taylan and fucking River following after me. Ignoring the three of them, I move to stand behind Tristan as he sits in front of his computer and types away on his keyboard before bringing up a map and pointing to a location with a red dot. "We managed to get a tracker on his car." I pat him on the shoulder, surprised at how well Tristan has done. He was only recently promoted to capo and seems to be excelling fucking well.

"Where is he?" Xander asks.

Darting my gaze to him I smirk. "In the city, the dumb fuck has come to us without even knowing it."

We're parked down the street from the house Percy has rented in his assistants name, rookie fucking error. So far all we have counted is four men, his assistant and that's it. We haven't laid eyes on Percy himself yet. It seems he was traveling light. If he was hiding our stash for Gio, he should be guarding that not staying out here. I push that thought aside for a moment as I check in with Mase.

ME

Where are you with locating Christiano?

MASE

Been following him to most of the strip clubs around Canada but he has yet to make contact with his brother.

ME

You bugged his phone?

MASE

Paid a local escort to amuse him and snatch his phone while he was distracted.

ME

Keep me updated, I want to move on Gio as soon as we can.

MASE

On it boss.

"We need to move in," Tay says, recapturing my attention as I pocket my phone. A knot in my gut tells me that something is off.

"How long have we been here?" I ask no one in particular.

"About three hours, boss," Floyd answers. I keep my gaze on the house as I mull over his words. The moment Tristan managed to ping his location, he pulled our men back from the borders, they broke every speed limit to get back here for the takedown.

"Knox, what are you thinking?" Xander hedges, clearly picking up on my reluctance to move in. I watch as the assistant passes by the large bay window again but this time when she looks up, I see the apprehension in her features.

"Fuck," I snap before darting my gaze to Xander in the front seat. "Get the fuck back to the house now, this was a decoy." Xander's eyes widen for a second before he grunts and slams his foot down on the gas. Floyd radios our men that are scattered out around the house and the street to fall back and head back to the house.

"Are you sure?" Taylan questions from his spot beside me.

"Percy isn't at the house, he knew we were onto him. This was a decoy!" I grit out.

"How?" Floyd asks as he peers around his seat to look at me.

"We have a fucking rat in our midst." His eyes darken, there is nothing more my men hate than a snitch.

"Any guesses who?" Xan asks as he jerks the wheel and has us skidding around a corner.

"There is only one fucking person who isn't with us right now that knew our plan and would have something to gain from throwing us off Percy's trail. I'm going to kill that fucking cunt." Bloodlust courses through me as I clench my fists at my sides. He called all our men back from Gio's borders opening them up for the fucker to slip through with ease.

"He'll come for Lakeland to honor his deal with Gio," Tay says, I nod.

"He plans to ship her off to the Dario family in return for safe passage out of the country," Xan adds.

"Giovani Dario only wants Lakeland because of who she is—was to me. This isn't about Percy and settling his debt with Gio, it is about Gio getting back at me for killing his brother. This is personal." I knew from the moment her engagement was announced to him that this was all about revenge. I will fucking gut her and skin the bitch alive before I watch that cunt touch a single hair on her head. Xander's phone rings and he fishes it out of his pocket, frowning at the screen a second before he answers it and places it on speaker.

"Yeah?" he answers.

"Your fucking house is over run with Dario soldiers!" River shouts into the phone. I hear gunshots in the background and her cursing before she screams out, "You touch my fucking sister and I'll gut you where you stand!" The blood in my veins turns to ice when I hear Lakeland scream in the background before the line goes dead. We're still thirty minutes from the house and there is no telling what those spineless women-hating bastards will do to her! I close my eyes and try to calm myself, my heart beating so fucking fast that I begin to feel dizzy.

I hate her.

I want her dead.

She means nothing to me.

I keep repeating that shit over and over in my head, I want to be the one to break her and see her crumble to nothing beneath my feet, but the thought of someone else touching her has my trigger finger itching and the need to peel skin from bone thrumming inside me. The car is filled with tension and I can tell my boys are amped up and ready to lay into some fuckers the moment we get back. Xander drives like a bat out of hell, taking sharp turns that have us gripping the *oh shit* handle so we don't slam into each other.

A mile out from the house, I reach into the back and grab the duffle bag filled with guns and place it on the seat between Taylan and me, I pull out the bulletproof vests and toss one to him then hand Floyd his and Xander's. We may be the mafia but that doesn't mean we are stupid and go into a gun fight unprotected if we can help it. I pull guns out and hand them to the guys, Xander snatches one from Floyd's lap. The noise of magazines dropping out are the only sounds as we check our mags and make sure we are fully loaded. I flick the safety on two of my guns as I shove them into my waistband and grab another four mags from the bag and stuff them in the slots on my vest. I double check the mag on the gun in my hand before flicking the safety off as we screech around the corner, bringing us onto our street.

"Fuck," Tay mutters at the sight in front of us. Cars are scattered all over the street, the sound of gunshots and screams can be heard through the car. Rather than feeling fear like a normal person, all I feel is excitement. I never feel more alive than when I'm about to put my life on the line. There is a fine line between being suicidal and living for the thrill of is this my last moment. Xander plants his foot and rams into the Dodge pickup blocking the street before we throw our doors open and join in the fight.

Chapter Ten

Lakeland

I lay here numb, staring up at the ceiling for hours like it holds the answers to the questions swirling in my mind. I allowed him to defile my body, I didn't even put up a fight when that stupid flashback or whatever the fuck it was played through my mind instead. I clung to him. I don't know what is happening to me, my headaches are always present now that I am not on my medication. I worry with how often they are coming on that I won't be able to cope with the pain. I have noticed though that without taking my medication, my mind doesn't seem as cloudy.

I hate that I allowed him inside me and I even came. The reminder has a sob escaping my mouth. I tried to quiet the sound by burying my face in the blanket but the moment I rolled onto my side, I felt the slickness between my thighs.

"No." I gasp in horror as I sit up to see his cum coating

my inner thighs, but that isn't the worst part, I see my blood and shake with silent tears.

He stole my virginity.

He robbed me of that special moment and I didn't even fight him, I allowed him to use me all because I had a stupid thought or whatever the hell you want to call it. I'm a weak pathetic fucking whore! I drag myself off the bed and refuse to look back at the ruined sheets. A hiss escapes me as I take a step, feeling the ghost of him inside me. He wasn't gentle, he took me brutally and didn't give an ounce of care to how I would feel. Ignoring the throbbing pain between my legs and burning ache, I stagger to the bathroom needing to rid myself of his touch.

Once in the shower I scrub until my skin is crimson and raw. I gently clean between my legs and slam my eyes closed when the burning sensation from the water intensifies. I'm no expert but from the pain I am in I know he tore me. The realization has a whimper bubbling out of me. I try to fight back the tears and refuse to allow him to reduce me to a sobbing mess, but it's a fucking struggle. I feel so weak compared to him, he can overpower me and take what he wants without consequence, and the fact my own sister sat by and did nothing to defend me or even help has a stabbing pain blooming in my chest. A rhythmic tapping on the bedroom door snaps me out of my pity fest. I switch off the shower and hastily wrap a towel around my body.

I wait a minute to see if someone will enter but when no one does I sigh gratefully. I don't think I could face anyone right now after what happened. There is no doubt in my mind that they all heard me. Disgust rolls through me and I feel bile rise in my throat. I swallow it down and fight the urge to vomit.

"Lake?" I grit my teeth at the sound of my sister's voice coming from the other side of the door. Ignoring her incessant knocking, I help myself to his clothes in the dresser and pull out a black shirt and find a pair of sweats that are way too large for me to the point I have to roll them at the waist four times to fit! "I know you can hear me!" she shouts, I ignore her again. I turn to the bed and flinch at the sight of the specks of blood on the white sheets. Not wanting the reminder, I snatch the sheets off the bed and dump them in the corner of the room. I shoot them a glare and stomp my foot as if they are the reason I am in a shitty mood. "Lakeland, you can't ignore me all day."

"Yes, the fuck I can," I mutter angrily to myself as I stomp around the room aimlessly, trying to find something to occupy my mind so I don't spiral.

"I know you're mad." I snort, mad is a fucking understatement. "But I need to tell you something, Lake, and I need you to understand that what you have been told about the accident is a lie." I freeze at the mention of my accident. I know exactly what happened. Dad told me it was Knox Bronson that ran me down that night. "Knox didn't do it, Lake."

Clenching my fists at my sides, I glare at the door. How could she say something like that when she was by my side every single day that I was in the hospital! She saw how I struggled through rehabilitation and dealing with the scars that now mar my body. Jesus, I can't even wear a swimsuit without them being on fucking display for the world to see. I have struggled to accept and love my body for years now. Thanks to that horrible night, I suffer from constant headaches due to stress and if I overdo it, I wind up with a migraine that ends up causing me to black out, which is why I have to take medication daily.

"The story Dad told you is a lie."

Unable to keep quiet any longer I lash out. "You're a fucking liar!" I scream at the closed door. "You're saying that because you're screwing them!"

"Pot meet kettle, sister. From what I heard, you went to pound town with Knox!" I recoil in self-loathing. I want to deny her claim and scream she is wrong but it wasn't like he forced me.

"Go away, River," I mumble bitterly as I make way over to the bed and drop down onto the edge in a huff.

I hear her sigh and know that she isn't going anywhere. "Lake, I'm sorry. I shouldn't have said that." Rolling my eyes I remain silent, waiting to hear what else she has to say. "Look, I know this is hard for you to believe but Dad lied to you."

"Why would he lie to me? You were there when he told me what happened and so were the doctors. What the hell do you have to gain out of this bullshit story?" I can't keep the anger from my tone and right now, I don't care to try. She is dredging up shit from my past that she knows hurts me. I have no memory of the night of the accident, that whole day is blank for me. I had to rely on my father and sister to help explain why the hell I was in the hospital. I was scared, confused and in a really dark place for a long time as I came to terms with the fact my life had changed forever because of some man's grudge against my father.

"Because he didn't want you to know the truth. I had to lie to you, Lake, and I hated doing it but if I didn't he threatened to... kill you."

"Six years later and now you finally think it's a good idea to come clean about this?" Sarcasm laces each of my words. "Dad had no reason to lie to me. I know Knox tried to kill me because of some business deal that went wrong with Dad—"

"Knox was the reason for the accident but he never caused it. He would never have hurt you, Lakeland, because he—" She's cut off by the sounds of gunshots and men screaming. Panic flares inside me.

"River, what's going on?" Hysteria rises inside me as I'm locked in a fucking room while shots are being fired.

"Stay here and hide. Don't make a fucking sound until I come for you, okay. I love you, little sister." A lump forms in my throat as fear grips me in its clutches, robbing me of air and thought. The stabbing sensation in the back of my head snaps me out of my meltdown.

"Love you too," I whisper so quietly I know she wouldn't have heard. I look around the room trying to find a weapon or anything to defend myself with. The noise outside the door has my blood running cold. I hear screams and more shots, suddenly I don't feel so angry about being locked in this room. I find nothing as I yank the drawers open and rummage through his clothes, checking the closet all I find is nothing! When I walk back into the room my eyes are glued to a framed painting on the far wall.

Fuck it.

I snag a shirt from the dresser and stalk across the room, I grab the picture off the wall and throw it on the ground jumping back so the glass doesn't cut my feet. I toss the frame out of the way and using the shirt, I wrap it around the largest piece so I don't cut my hand. I hope I don't have to use it but I will not go down willingly. I have a conversation with my sister I need to finish.

I hide inside the closet hoping no one comes in here. I'm crouched down behind the door with my back against the wall. I've been in this position so long that my legs are numb but I'm too scared to move or even make a sound. I can still hear fighting downstairs and screams. I heard footsteps earlier and began to panic, thinking they would burst in here but then I heard a gunshot and a loud thud. Whoever came up here is no doubt dead and rather than feel sick with the thought, I'm grateful.

"Check that one at the end!" I hear some shout, my breathing turns erratic as I hear someone jiggling the door handle.

"It's locked," he calls back to the other guy.

"Then bust the fucking thing down and find her!" the guy shouts. My blood turns to ice, he said *her*. They're here for me. When I hear the wood splinter, I cover my mouth with my hand to silence the sob. Fear can either rule and paralyze you, or it can become your greatest motivator. Right now I'm not sure I'm the latter.

"You in here, bitch?" I hear him taunt as he moves around the bedroom. I hear the glass outside the bathroom crunch beneath his shoe and the dark chuckle that escapes him sends a shiver down my spine. "Should have cleaned up after yourself." I hear the floorboards creak as he makes his way toward the closet. I grip the shard tighter and pray to God I don't freeze but fight my way out of this.

I see his shadow in the doorway and breathe through my nose to keep as quiet as possible. The moment he steps in I brace myself, then push every ounce of emotion down inside so I can focus on this moment. He passes the open door and without hesitation I dart my arm out and lodge the glass into the side of his thigh. He roars in pain and stumbles away as I push to my feet and make my escape. I get two steps into the bedroom before I'm tackled from behind and land on the hard floor with an oomph. My head bounces off the wooden floor boards and I see black spots for a second before he grips the back of my head and slams my face into the floor again.

"You stupid cunt!" I groan in pain and feel a wet substance dripping down my top lip. My vision blurs and I groan as he rolls me onto my back. The breath is knocked out of me when he rests his full weight on my stomach. I try to focus on his face but my vision is still fuzzy. "You're gonna pay for that," he grits out. I cry out in agony when his fist collides with my cheek. I make out his fist coming at my face again and manage to cover my face with my arms, pain shoots down my forearm.

"Get the fuck off me!" I scream as I try to thrust my hips to throw him off but he's huge. Grunts and groans come from me as he continues to punch my arms, I can't even claw his face because I run the risk of him knocking me out if I move my arms.

"Your daddy didn't say we had to bring you back alive." Hearing those words from his disgusting mouth fills me with anguish. My father really does hate us for leaving. He wraps his hands around my neck and squeezes. I drop my arms and begin slapping, clawing, punching, I do anything I can to get him to release me. The sinister smile on his face is not the last thing I am going to see, I refuse to allow that. I feel my strength waning as I fight to get free but it's futile. I spot the shard of glass still embedded in the side of his thigh, without thinking I yank it free. He throws his head back and roars in pain, dropping his grip on my neck. I push up and ram it into the side of his neck.

"Fuck you!" I scream. His eyes are wide and filled with disbelief. He sways backward and I use his own size against him as I shove his chest and crab crawl away from him. My back slams into the dresser, then I draw my knees up and wrap my arms around them as I watch him and he watches me. He yanks the shard free and tries to cover the wound with his hand but it won't save him. He sputters and gurgles on his own blood before he finally collapses, his soulless vacant eyes staring directly at me. I feel his blood soaking through my shirt and dripping down my cheek but I don't have it within myself to move an inch.

If someone else comes in, I'm fucked. I have no strength left to fight off another attacker. I know his buddy was up here with him and I worry he will come investigate what his friend was shouting about but still, I can't move.

I just killed someone!

Chapter Eleven

Knox

It takes us no time to gain entry to the house, most of the bastards fled as soon as they saw us coming. Bodies litter the floor of the lower level. Guilt swarms through me when I see two of my maids laying in a pool of their own blood, but that isn't what makes me sick—it's the sight of their pants around their ankles and their torn panties stuffed into their mouths.

They raped them.

Grinding my teeth, I motion for Xander to clear the bottom floor with Floyd while I take Taylan and a couple others with me. I need to find Lakeland and make sure her father didn't fucking take her. The moment we hit the second floor Taylan branches off to the left while I go right toward my room. The sight of my door busted open has all rational thought fleeing as I race toward the room and skid to a stop at the threshold at the sight of some fucker dead on my floor. Movement out of the corner of my eye catches my attention.

"Lakeland," I breathe out at the sight of her covered in blood and huddled against my dresser. At the sound of her name she snaps her head toward me. I expect to see anger, fear or *something* in her eyes but all I see is... nothing, she looks slightly unhinged.

"He was going to kill me," she mutters before tearing her gaze from mine and staring at the body in front of her. I stow my gun in my waistband and slowly make my way toward her, keeping a small amount of space between us as I crouch down beside her. "He wanted to hurt me." I don't know if she is trying to convince me of that or herself. What I do notice are the bruises on her face, arms and even the hand prints around her fucking throat. Only I am allowed to mark her, not that son of a bitch.

"You defended yourself," I say. She frowns and cocks her head to the side but still won't look at me.

"He was going to kill me," she mutters.

I reach out to her only for her to flinch and shift away. She finally looks at me and gone is the hollow look in her eyes only to be replaced by fear.

"He was going to kill me!" she screams just as Taylan enters the room. I peer over my shoulder to see him dismiss the other guys before coming to stand beside me. He smiles comfortingly at Lake before snatching the blanket from the bed and tossing it over the fucker beside her. She keeps her focus on the both of us, barely blinking.

"You did what any woman in your position would have

done, Lay." She shakes her head denying what Tay is saying but he pushes on, slowly closing the space between them as he speaks. "You were strong. You were brave. You were resourceful and resilient. You didn't cower in fear and allow him to brutalize you. You fought back and guess what?" He crouches down in front of her forcing me to shift so I can see her face. Her brows furrow as she stares up at him. "You won." Her bottom lip begins to tremble.

"He hurt me, I didn't have a choice," she chokes out before sobs wrack her body. Taylan wraps his arms around her tiny frame and pulls her flush against him, holding her tightly. She clutches the sides of his shirt in a vice-like grip as if she's afraid he'll disappear.

"You made the right choice, Lay," he mumbles as he places a kiss to the top of her head. Seeing him comfort her rubs me the wrong way.

"Clean her up then bring her downstairs," I say in a cold tone as I push to stand. She pulls back from Taylan and stares up with worry etched into her features.

"Where's my sister?" she asks with concern thick in her tone. I attempt to respond but I don't get the chance. She shoves Taylan back. He lands on his ass with a grunt as she races from the room. Growling I chase after the little shit. She nearly tumbles down the stairs a couple times at the sight of the bodies but it's only when she reaches the landing that she comes to a halt and gasps. Following her line of sight I find the reasons for her sudden pause. "They were my father's men and they hurt those innocent women," she speaks quietly but the disgust and anger is clear in her tone.

"Your father and his men will pay the price for what they did to Laura and Sophie." I motion to two of my men to cover up the maids. They may have been disrespected in their final moments but I will make damn sure they are treated with the utmost respect in death. I won't allow their murders to be in vain. We watch as Thomas and Patrick lay some sheets over each of their bodies.

"Stop!" Lakeland snaps. They freeze and turn to me waiting for my orders. She moves toward the women. I hold my hand up, telling them to wait. She kneels in front of Laura and gently strokes her hair back from her face, her eyes are open and stare vacantly ahead. Lakeland removes her panties from her mouth and looks up to Patrick nodding for him to cover her. "I'm so sorry for what happened to you," she whispers as she moves onto Sophie. Unlike Laura, her eyes are closed. Lake tugs her panties free and then jerks back when Sophie gasps. I dart forward and place two fingers against her neck and when I feel it, I turn to Thomas.

"Get her to a hospital now and don't leave her fucking side for a single second. You piss in a cup if you have to." He nods and scoops her up in his arms before dashing out of the house with Patrick hot on his heels.

"Knox." I tug Lakeland to her feet and pull her behind me as I go in search of Xander. I find him in Tristan's makeshift office at the back of the house. The sight before me turns my arms to lead and my blood to ice. Lakeland yanks free of my hold and darts in front of me before I can stop her from seeing the gruesome sight.

"Nooooooo!" she screams so fucking loud it jolts me out

of my shock as she races around the desk and drops to her knees in front of her sister, who is strapped to a chair with a bloody note *nailed* in the center of her chest that reads, *A sibling for a sibling, boy, you're next.* River's face is bloody and bruised, her head hangs forward limply. Lake tries to free her sister from the binds as Xander stands there staring at River like he's looking at a ghost. "Hang on, sister. I'll get you out. Hold on, okay." Lakeland sobs. "Someone fucking help me!" she screams.

I move forward and pull my knife free from its sheath at my side and slice through the ropes. River falls forward. Lakeland catches her and shifts as she slides along the ground so her sister is resting between her legs. She rests River's head against her shoulder and brushes her hair back. Blood is dried to her face and it's clear those cunts tied her down and beat the shit out of her before delivering the final blow, this was a message that Percy and Gio are willing to do whatever it takes to take me down.

The note that is nailed to her chest is from Gio. He's coming after me for taking the top spot from him and for killing his useless sack of shit of a brother.

"It's okay, you're gonna be okay," Lake chokes out as she continues to stroke her sisters hair. "I choose you Riverland, I fucking choose you. Do you hear me?" Recoiling at her words, I stare down at her. River said she couldn't remember anything but she remembers *my* words! "You can't leave me, you can't fucking leave me because I need you." Sobs claw their way out of her. She hiccups and clutches her sister tighter, placing kisses on the side of her head.

"River," Taylan whispers brokenly as he enters the room staring down at the Deveraux sisters. He drops to his knees beside them and reaches out to touch River but Lake bats his hand away, glaring at him.

"Don't fucking touch her. Call an ambulance now!" Tay's features contort in pain but it's not his, he's feeling what she's going through. He isn't the only one. The sight of her holding her sister's body brings up feelings and memories I thought I had buried. A quick glance at Xander tells me he isn't seeing River either. We're both seeing a scene from six years ago that paved the way for us.

"It'll be quicker if I drive you." Lake frowns for a second and gnaws on her lip debating if she should trust Tay.

"I don't think–." Taylan pins me with a look over his shoulder that has me closing my mouth.

"You of all people should know she needs this. You can worry about being an asshole and breaking her after this but right now, we need to help her so she can get through this." His words hit their mark. Sighing, I nod my head. Before Tay or I can grab Riverland, Xander pushes us both away as he crouches in front of the girls and grips Lake's face between his hands, forcing her to meet his stare.

"You're going to let her go so I can carry her out of here." Her tears fall rapidly as she shakes her head.

"No, she's strong she can—"

He cuts her off. "Every man here either knows her or has heard stories about your sister. None of them will view her as weak, you have my word." My brows raise. Xander never gives his word to anyone. "I don't know if what she told us about you is true but if it is, then listen carefully, Lakeland." Her brows draw in as she gulps loudly. "Your sister was one of our best friends. We love her like you do now, so give her to me so we can take her to the hospital where you will hear from the doctors what you already know to be true."

"She's not dead," she says with such conviction that I almost believe her. Xander just nods but says nothing as he gently scoops River into his arms, her body limp, her arm flopping to the side. I reach out and gently place it on her stomach, then run my hand over her head.

"Go get em, killer," I whisper. That was something River used to say to me all the time when we were kids. I never understood what it meant but it just kind of became our thing. Tay wraps an arm around Lake's shoulders as the three of us follow behind Xander. When the guys see who he is carrying, those who knew River from our earlier days in school bow their heads and those who didn't get the chance to know the spitfire that is Riverland Deveraux, still bow their heads in respect for the woman who they can clearly see means a shitload to me and the guys.

She meant a lot to all of us.

Watching Xander climb into the backseat with her body in his arms has pain flaring to life inside my chest. The sound of Lake's sobs draws my attention to her. I motion for Taylan to get in the car, at the look on my face he doesn't argue and does as he's told. I grip her shoulders and force her to face me.

"Look at me," I say in a firm tone. She whimpers and slowly lifts her tear-filled gaze back to me. The pain I see in her eyes mimics the pain I feel daily. "I know what it's like to lose a sister. The pain you feel inside, latch onto it."

"Why?"

"Because that pain is going to be the only thing that gets you through this." She shakes her head trying to deny me but I push on. "You are going to learn some harsh fucking truths. Learn to channel that pain into anger because your whole world is about to come crumbling down leaving you no choice but to live in *my* world."

Chapter Twelve

Lakeland

Numb...

I have no other word to describe how I feel.

Lost. My soul is shattered.

Maybe that is another way to describe the situation. Since arriving at the hospital hours ago that's all I have felt. Before the doctors could wheel my sister away, Knox snatched the note off her chest. I had forgotten all about that and I don't even have it in me to ask what it says, nothing on that paper can or will change what happened. The doctors were gone for mere minutes before one of them came back out to us in the waiting room. The moment he removed his surgical cap, I stood up and walked away. There is only one reason why they remove those caps and I refused to hear the words come out of his mouth.

Everything else passed by in a blur after that, one minute I was in the waiting room then the next I had the doctor's poking and prodding me, a CT scan done and questions hurled at me. I answer each of them on autopilot not really hearing what they say and honestly I don't care to know, I want to remain in this state of nothingness. Nothing hurts here, I don't feel anything. The only thing I do register through this whole fucking ordeal is that Knox has been with me every second. Taylan and Xander are nowhere to be found and I can't even remember when they disappeared.

I watch as the doctor enters the room and looks to me sadly before turning back to Knox, who is sitting across the room with his gaze fixed on me. I watch his features change from confusion, sadness, anger and finally murderous as the doctor tells him something.

"What the fuck do you mean there is no record of her?" he snaps. The doctor looks shaken and swallows clearly nervous.

"There is no record of her ever being in a hospital six years ago," he answers.

"You saw the fucking scars on her body." I scrunch my face and frown when I look down to see I'm in a hospital gown—I don't recall changing.

"I know, which is why I believe someone had her records scrubbed, Mr. Bronson. My team is working to figure it out —" Knox climbs to his feet, silencing the doctor.

"Don't waste your time, I know who the fuck did it. Wipe any record you have of her or us being here." The doctor nods and quickly scurries from the room as Knox makes his way to me. My legs dangle over the edge of the bed. He pushes his way between them, gripping the back of my neck, forcing my head back to stare up at him. "It appears there may be some truth to what your sister said if your father had your records scrubbed." I cock my head to the side, trying to decipher what he means. "Get changed." He steps back but when I don't show any sign of moving he grits his teeth and scrubs a hand down his face, clearly frustrated.

Gripping my waist, he hoists me off the bed. Once he's sure I'm steady on my feet, he releases me only to turn me so my back is to him. I feel him pull the strings of the gown. I don't protest when he pushes the gown down my arms, then slowly turns me to face him again. I should be screaming and shouting but what's the point, he's stronger than me and showed that by taking advantage of me. Men always seem to have the upper hand because we are less, we are viewed as weak, we are the objects they can take whatever they fucking like from, we're nothing but something to entertain themselves with when they please.

He grabs a handful of clothes from the end of the bed that I didn't notice. I wish I had the strength to snort or laugh when he kneels before me and taps my leg so he slips the jeans on, he does the same to the other side and I move on autopilot. It does surprise me when he fastens the button that they are in my size. Next he does the laces on the sneakers that he slips on my feet. He tugs a shirt over my head—this is in my size as well—then next he pulls a hoodie over my head and tugs the hood up. It feels weird to wear clothes that fit. I'm not even bothered about the fact I'm not wearing panties or a bra. It's not like either of those things would stop him from fucking me when he wanted to.

He grips my hand and interlocks his fingers with mine. A zapping sensation travels down my spine and a slight thud begins in the base of my skull as I stare at our intertwined fingers. If I was in the right frame of mind I would have asked the doctors for a prescription for my medication. Knox doesn't seem to notice or if he does, he says nothing as he leads me from the room. I pay no mind to my surroundings as I let him blindly lead me to wherever the hell it is we are going. I just don't have it in me to care.

We reach the parking lot and he places me in the passenger seat, securing my seatbelt before rounding the car himself. I stare out the window in a daze as he drives. I see everything and nothing at the same time. I know time is passing but I feel stuck, almost like I'm in a time loop and I don't want to break that circle, I want to live in this moment forever. I look at the sky and wonder when it changed from darkness to light. That thought continues to circulate in my mind for a while until the sound of Knox's phone ringing pulls me from my thoughts.

"Yeah?" he says.

"Where are you?" Comes through the Bluetooth system in the car.

"A couple hours out still, why?" he answers.

"We know who the rat is."

"I already know it's Tristan," he growls.

"Percy crossed the border and is in Gio's turf. It looks like Dario soldiers were the ones to help Percy." At the mention of my father's name anger courses through me.

"Percy will die." My voice is scratchy and hoarse. Knox

snaps his gaze to me and the strange look on his face, he shakes his head and focuses back on the road.

"We'll be there soon. Get everything ready, I want to move on those cunts before they have a chance to hide," Knox snarls before he ends the call. Silence stretches between us as he continues to drive. I see him out of the corner of my eye white knuckling the steering wheel, his face a picture of unfiltered rage.

I must have fallen asleep. I wake to Knox shaking me and the scent of greasy food hitting my senses. My stomach lets out a hideous rumble. Blinking my eyes open, I turn in his direction. He hands me a burger and fries, my mouth watering at the sight. I mumble a thanks and devour them, not caring that I can feel his gaze on me the whole time. I spy a large drink in the center, without asking I snatch it and down half of it before finishing off the last of my fries. I turn to Knox attempting to hand him my trash but he just sits there staring at me with a look of equal parts distaste and mirth. Rolling my eyes, I toss the wrappers onto his lap and go back to staring out the window. I gasp when I feel something soft hit the side of my head. Peering down, I see my wrappers on my lap. Slowly turning back to Knox, I meet his scowl with one of my own.

"Get your ass out of the car and put it in trash." Gathering the wrappers, I toss them back at him, the shock is evident on his face.

"Fuck. You," I seethe. He drops his own burger to gather the wrappers to no doubt throw at me, so I lean over to grab his half eaten burger, then toss it right in his face. It takes two seconds before he's reaching for me. I fight the fucker and scream at him as I smack his hands away. I feel like I'm a woman possessed but releasing this pent up anger inside me feels too good to stop.

"Lakeland!" Ignoring his warning I continue to scratch, punch and hit him anywhere I can.

"Fuck you, fuck you, fuck you!" I scream as I try to get closer but my seatbelt keeps me restrained. "You're a bastard. You're a life ruining fuck. I fucking hate you!" I manage to slap him across his annoying face and feel proud. I continue to hit him without mercy, not realizing that tears have started to fall down my cheeks. My arms grow heavy and my movements turn sluggish, its then that I notice he is no longer fighting back but weathering my blows, allowing me to hurt him. "I hate you," I choke out as I weakly beat my fists against his chest.

"I know." Is all he says before he unclips my seatbelt and drags me from my seat to sit in his lap. I try to get free but he just bands his arms around me, securing my own at my sides and holding me against his chest. Without consent, anguished sobs claw their way free and tear my chest open as the loss of my sister truly begins to sink in. Knox's hold shifts from restraining to comforting as he rubs up and down my back, while cupping my face and holding it against his chest as I grip his shirt in a tight hold and cling to his forearm.

"He took her from me." I feel him deflate beneath me. It's the first time since seeing my sister I have allowed myself to accept the fact that she isn't coming back, she won't be my hero anymore. She was my best friend, my person, the one and only person I have chosen! Before I can stop myself, I shift and turn so I'm straddling my asshole kidnapper, locking my arms around his neck and burying my face into the crook of it, sobbing. He doesn't push me away, but holds me as I use him to find comfort in someone other than myself. Sometimes you just need someone to hold you while you break down and right now, that person happens to be the prick who hurt me.

The moment I feel his fingers tangle in my hair, I wait for the pain that normally accompanies his touch but it doesn't come. He uses his hold on me to draw me in closer as he buries his face in my hair.

"I understand what you are feeling." I slowly untangle myself and lean back as much as I can without honking the horn. I search his gaze trying to decipher his meaning. "Losing a sibling, someone who is your exact other half, the person that shares the same DNA make up as you is the worst type of pain. Losing a parent is hard but they were only half of you, a sibling is the exact same. That's why it hurts so much more because they are you essentially but with a different soul."

"My soul is shattered," I whisper brokenly.

"Shattered souls are something that can never be fully repaired, they are something we can mend over time but there will always be cracks in it. The imperfections of a shattered soul can be beautiful." My mouth is ajar in surprise, I've never heard Knox speak so... lovingly before, he's never shown me any type of kindness, only pain and fear.

"You say you know how I'm feeling, how? Was your

sister murdered as well?" I brace myself for him to lash out and scream at me or throw me from his lap and demand I shut the fuck up. Surprise ripples through me when he allows me to see the pain in his eyes, he doesn't mask it or shield his emotions from me.

"I lost my sister suddenly like you. Losing her shattered my soul and I've never been able to patch that thing back together." I gasp.

"I'm sorry," I blurt out without thinking. Hatred and understanding war in his eyes, causing me to tense.

"Yeah," He mutters. Feeling slightly awkward now, I move to return to my seat only for him to grip my waist and hold me in place. I peer down at him in confusion but remain silent as he works through whatever it is he is trying to say. "The vengeance you seek for the life stolen from you is something I can relate to."

"I don't understand."

He inhales sharply. "I know what it feels like to want to tear the beating heart from the cunt that stole the life of the person you loved most. It can consume you and change who you are as a person because all you have is your vengeance."

"I don't care," I growl, he nods solemnly.

"Then vengeance is what you shall have."

"What about you?"

He frowns. "What?"

Swallowing, I force myself to be brave and ask, "What about your vengeance? Did my father steal your sister from you as well, is that why you took me?" When a sad smile tugs at the edge of his mouth I tense. He slowly reaches out to me as if he's going to cup my cheek only for him to pause midair and drop it.

"I'm starting to think he had a part in taking my sister from me but he also took someone equally as important from me and for that, I plan to make him suffer and if what I suspect is true, then he won't die quickly."

"Good, I want him to suffer for taking both our sisters from us."

"Riverland and Waverly—" My head begins to pound instantly as he said that name. I clutch it and grit my teeth as I try to ride out the pain but I'm so accustomed to these pains now that I know, I am seconds from blacking out. I need my medication!

Chapter Thirteen

Knox

I watch as she grabs her head and hunches forward grunting in pain. Call me a heartless fuck if you want but I watch in fascination. The moment I said Waverly's name her eyes glazed over and then she began holding her head in pain. Either she is an amazing fucking actress or my hunch is correct.

"Ahhh," she cries out a second before she flops forward. I grunt from the impact of her headbutting my chin. I try to shake her just to be sure and when she doesn't flinch or make a sound, I know she is knocked out.

When something is said or she sees something that reminds her of the past she gets these headaches. Percy told her it was from stress but it isn't. It's her mind trying to help her remember but she fights it all the time. I think the pills he's been feeding her for years are what keeps her from remembering anything from the past.

River's words play out in my mind as I climb out of the car and gently lay Lakeland in the back seat before climbing behind the wheel and heading to our new location that is a few miles from the border of Gio's territory. There is a reason I left this fucker alive but now, not even she can save him from what comes next. I dial my mom's number as I hit the road, she picks up on the fifth ring.

"I'm so sorry, Knox." Sighing I run a hand through my hair.

"Xander already told you?" I ask.

"No, Tay rang and filled me in. He said Xander wanted to ride alone with River," she says quietly. "I think Xander loved her."

I nod even though I know she can't see me. "Yeah, in his own way I think he did."

"What do you plan to do, Son?"

A whoosh of air escapes me. "Percy is with Gio."

Silence ensues for a minute before she finally speaks. "Knox—"

"He isn't getting away again. I know he helped you with me and Wave when that cunt took off and left you but I won't let him live again. He crossed the line when he agreed to the engagement with Lakeland. I'm taking him out."

"I figured you would say that. Taylan also told me she is with you." Unlike me, she doesn't hate or blame Lakeland for what happened. She has always fought for her innocence and tried to get me to see reason but the police reports detailed everything. But now, with her hospital records being wiped, I'm not so sure. She thinks because of what I said that her father killed my sister and that's why I hate her and that motherfucker has her believing that I am the one that ran her down.

"Yeah, she's asleep in the back."

"What are you going to do with her, Knox? I don't want to see you hurting yourself by hurting her. She is a good girl, Son."

"I don't know what I'm going to do, Mom. I... I don't know what the fuck to do with her right now."

I can hear the smile in her voice as she speaks. "That girl has always managed to cloud your thoughts and force you to rethink things without having to say a word."

"Stop," I growl.

"I'm speaking the truth. Now you listen to me, Knoxville Bronson." I tense at hearing my real name from her, she only uses it when she's serious. "I may be tender toward Gio for what he did for me and you kids but, if you find out he had anything to do with hurting River or... if you find out he hurt your... if he hurt my baby–" A whimper escapes her. Closing my eyes for a second, I force my own emotions to remain in check. "You bring that son of a bitch back to me. Do you hear me? If he hurt my little girl, you bring that bastard back to me, am I clear?" A smile crests across my face. My mom is a badass. People think because of who my father was that I get my ruthlessness from him. They're fucking wrong, that shit is all from my mom.

"You have my word."

"I choose you, Son."

"I choose you, Mom." I end the call. I never said I love

you as a kid. Mom said it was because I watched other kids say it to their fathers and refused to say it to anyone because of that. So one day she started to say she chose me. After a while, Wave and I both started saying it back and that saying became our thing until I said it to someone else and it seems she recalls those three words. Hearing her say them to her sister today floored me. I forgot all about her knowing them, so hearing her say them sent me back down memory lane to the first night I said it to her.

"You're it for me, Lakeland Deveraux. I choose you forever."

"What does that mean?" she whispered, nothing but love shining in her eyes as I cupped her cheek and leaned forward, resting my head against hers as I breathed her in.

"People always say I love you but love never lasts. I don't want to be the person you love, I want to be the person you choose because being chosen by someone means they are your person. They are the person you fight for, live for and if it comes to it, you die for them. So, I choose you, kitten."

When we reach the new house, dusk is starting to set and Lake is still knocked out in the back seat. I carefully lift her out of the car and look around to see my men scattered around the house and yard. Walking to the front door it's opened from the inside before I even have to knock or say a word. I take two steps inside before Taylan is on me and looking at the girl in my arms with worry.

"She passed out after one of those headache things," I say before he can ask.

"What triggered it?" he asks.

"I said Waverly's name." His shocked gaze meets mine before he nods.

"We need to figure out why the fuck she keeps blacking out, it's not normal, brother. Second room on the right is yours," he says as he points in the direction of the rooms. This is the first time we've been to this house since acquiring it six years ago. The room is nothing special, it's small. The house itself isn't even large, but what is perfect about this house is we own the two beside it and the three on the opposite side of the street from it. I lay her gently on the bed and remove her sneakers before pulling the throw blanket over her. Before I can do something stupid like climb in beside her, I leave and close the door quietly behind myself and head into the lounge room where I find Floyd, Xan, Tay, Patrick and Thomas.

"I thought I told you to stay with—" Xander cuts me off before I can finish going at Thomas.

"She didn't make it."

"Fuck," I growl tugging on the strands of my hair, I man up and ask Xander. "Where is River?" His face hardens at the mention of her, I know he's mad and I get it but we need to deal with this now.

"We called Jerry and paid off the mortician at the local funeral home to fuck off for a couple days. Jerry just got to her about an hour ago. He'll take care of her and prep her for... her farewell," Taylan answers. I nod. Jerry is our Mortician on staff and the only one we trust to handle our fallen soldiers.

"Once he's finished with River, I want him back home to take care of Laura, Sophie and the rest of our men. All their funeral costs will be covered by us and their families are to be taken care of." I look at Patrick as I finish. "I want you to organize the transportation of the fallen and oversee the arrangements for their families. When you get home, call my mom and she will notify the families and sort out taking care of them." Patrick nods and leaves immediately. Next I turn to Floyd who stands straight under the pressure of my gaze. "I need another hacker, find me one within the next two hours. When we get Tristan back, he is to be given the full rat treatment, he will face each of us and the men." He nods. "An invitation will be sent to each of the fallen's families as well. They will be given a chance to claim a pound of flesh from the rat that cost them their loved ones."

I turn and walk out of there, needing to place a call that is going to wound my pride but I know through the grapevine and from experience that he is the best at what he does. "Knox, hold up." I pause and turn to see Taylan and Xander coming after me. I motion for them to follow me out the back and claim one of the old wooden seats, they both stand and lean against the railing as they look at me expectantly. Sighing, I lean back in my chair and stab a hand through my hair.

"What happened at the hospital?" Xander asks. I lull my head back and stare up at the sky as I answer.

"They ran tests on her. I was waiting for them to come back and tell me that River's story was bullshit and she was drunk the night of the accident but..."

"But what?" Tay presses. I look between the both of them before answering.

"All her medical records from six years ago don't exist, there is no trace of her ever being in the hospital." They both frown and exchange a look before looking back to me.

"What the fuck does that mean? River said she was in the hospital for months," Tay breathes out.

"It means there may be some truth to what River said and she wasn't drunk." I nod my agreement. "Lakeland thinks Knox or one of our guys ran her down because that's what she was told... but what if those are both just bullshit and the truth is the most farfetched story, the story her own sister told us?"

"I'm not saying I believe it but I'm going to call Knight Murdoch and ask for his help."

"Why?" Xander snaps.

"What the hell for?" Taylan grits out.

"Because the last hacker we had was a fucking rat and I know for a fact that Knight is the best at what he does. Do you know how much that guy gets paid from other families to find shit out? He is one of Bishop's greatest assets. I'd say it's because of him that Bishop is always a step ahead of everyone else." Neither of them look happy about my idea but we are out of options. "I need to know the truth about that night. I need to know if the girl I fell in love with did kill my sister because she is a selfish bitch or not." The anguish in my tone has both of them nodding.

"Do it."

"Put it on speaker," They say unison. Nodding my head, I pull my phone from my pocket and dial Knight's number. It rings for so long I begin to think he won't answer but when he finally does he isn't happy.

"Who the fuck is this and how the fuck did you get this number?" he grits out.

"Knight Murdoch?" I ask.

"Who the fuck is asking?"

"My name is Knox Bronson and I am—"

"I know who the fuck you are, Knox, what do you want?" Both Xander and Taylan frown at my phone but remain silent.

"I need your help. I'm willing to pay whatever it costs—"

He cuts me off again and it's starting to annoy the fuck out of me. "What's it for and don't bullshit me because I'll find out the truth either way." I grit my teeth, I was hoping to give him the basics without baring it all to him. I look at my boys and they both nod encouragingly.

"I need you to recover hospital files on a woman named Lakeland Deveraux from six years ago."

"Why?" I take a deep breath and remind myself that this is the only way to know the truth, even if it's from someone I don't know or trust.

"Because the police reports say she was drunk on the night an accident occurred and I need to know the truth."

"I need more kid, what accident?"

"Fuck." I blow out a loud exhale. "Fine, I need the files from the hospital and to know if the police reports were forged because my sister died that night."

"Who is the girl you want the information on?"

Closing my eyes, I answer him. "She was my girlfriend and I need to know if she killed my sister." A gasp from the doorway draws all our attention to see Lakeland standing there, her face pale and her eyes wide.

"Give me forty-eight hours and meet me in Jersey City." I nod even though he can't see me as I keep my gaze on Lakeland. "Knox?"

"Y-yeah?" I mutter distractedly while staring at Lakeland.

"I wouldn't hurt the girl until you know the facts. Been there, done that and regret it."

"Hmm." Is all I manage to say before he ends the call.

"Lay, let us explain," Taylan tries to appeal to her but she isn't hearing a word he is saying, she turns and runs back inside. I give chase only to slam to a halt inches away from her when she snatches a knife from the butcher's block. Tay and Xander slam into my back, sending me staggering forward. I manage to stop an inch from the tip of her blade.

"Put the knife down," I grit out through clenched teeth.

Chapter Fourteen

*"She was my girlfriend and I need to know if she killed my
sister."*

I stare at him, praying that what he said is a lie but the
look on his face gives away the fact he isn't talking out of his
ass. I can see the familiarity in his eyes as he looks at me, I see
it in his friend's gazes as well. I'm so fucking confused. I
thought my sister was lying to me but clearly she wasn't and
everyone knows the truth except me.

"Were you all laughing at me?" Knox's face contorts in
confusion. I look to the other two assholes who look just as
perplexed. "I bet you were all having a great big fucking
laugh at my expense!" I scream. I hear others enter the
kitchen behind me but don't take my eyes off the three in
front of me.

"Stand down, no one is to touch her," Knox growls as he
stands to his full height eyeing whoever it is over my head

before slowly bringing his gaze back to me. "You are going to put that fucking knife down right now or—"

"Or fucking what?" I taunt, his eyes narrow.

"If I have to take it from you, I won't be gentle about it." The warning is clear but right now, I don't care. Everything is fucked up. My sister is gone, the past six years of my life are apparently a lie and the guy I have been dreaming about killing for the past couple of days is supposedly my ex-boyfriend.

"Nothing with you is gentle," I sound hysterical to my own ears and I give zero fucks as I wave the knife in Knox's direction forcing him to jump back a step.

"Final warning, Lake."

"Fuck you, Knox, you're a fucking liar and a bastard. Nothing more you do to me can hurt more than what you have already done." He tries to mask it but I see the flicker of regret in his eyes before he hardens his features again. "Kill me, beat me, do whatever the fuck you want because clearly no one seems to give a fuck about what I want or need." I toss the knife at him and stalk out of the room, brushing past the men that block the exit. They try to shift out of the way as fast as they can. With nowhere else to go, I head back to the bedroom I woke up in and slam the door closed angrily. I feel tears prick the backs of my eyes but I refuse to let them fall.

I focus on the anger I feel toward my father and for what happened to my sister. I'm angry at her for lying to me for years, when she could have come clean but she said Percy would have killed me if she told the truth. My mind is a clusterfuck and I can't seem to think straight right now. How the hell did my life get so fucked up? Sure, I was alone most of the time and confined to the house but I grew to find comfort in solitude. When River would visit it would brighten my whole day and put a real smile on my face. Thinking about her has my heart aching, she was my hero. I wrap my arms around myself and move to the window that overlooks the street. I see men walking up and down the footpath, trying to look natural but it's obvious to me they are Knox's soldiers.

"I need answers." I keep my back to him and ignore his presence. "I have to know the truth about that night."

Scoffing, I shake my head. "You're not asking my permission, you're telling me what you're doing so why bother coming in here?"

"I know you need to know the truth as well." He sounds closer but I still refuse to face him. He's nothing but a gangster and a liar, no better than my father. I refuse to be the victim. I won't allow either of these fucking men to control my life. I may need answers but I can find out the truth on my own, I can't trust either of them to be honest with me.

"Don't try to make what you did seem right by masking it like you are doing me a favor, from the moment you kidnapped me and shot my friend—"

"Who is alive and fine by the way."

I ignore his interruption and carry on. "You could have come clean, you should have told me the truth."

"Fine." I feel his breath hit the back of my neck and I shiver, my body wanting to lean into him but I fight against the pull I feel toward him. "You want the truth, here it is. When I took you, I planned to break you mentally, emotionally and then physically. I wanted you to hate yourself so fucking much that you would take a blade to your own throat and save me the trouble." I won't lie, that thought has crossed my mind many times over the last couple of years as I sink deeper into the dark hole of depression.

"Do it then," I force out through clenched teeth.

Gripping my shoulders, he forces me to face him. I glare at the bastard. "Oh, I had fucking planned to and even began the process until your sister told us a story. I paid it no mind until I saw the look in your eyes as I was about to fuck you." Disgust rolls through me at the memory of his hands on me and the way he used my own body against me. His fingers trail down my arms slowly. "After that, I started to think maybe her story did hold some merit."

His hands find their way under my shirt and when he touches my bare skin, I suck in a sharp breath, then try to pull free of his hold but he doesn't allow it.

"Let me go."

"I did but your father broke the deal I made with your sister."

Ignoring how his hands trail up my body like he has the right to touch me, I ask, "What deal?"

The moment his hands skim the sides of my breasts I gulp and his eyes darken. "I would never seek vengeance against you so long as your father never steps out of line again and you remain out of my city for good. You were only granted that mercy because of who your sister was to us. Killing you meant going through her and I couldn't deal with losing another person I loved." His thumbs skim over my nipples. I shudder under his touch and try to remain focused and remember that I hate him but it's hard to do when he's teasing me like this.

"What did my father do to make you hate him so much?" His eyes darken further as he yanks me flush against him. I can feel his hard cock through his jeans pressed against my stomach.

"He tried to take you from me. You were supposed to tell me what he did that night but you never made it to my house." I feel the throbbing pain begin in the back of my skull and slam my eyes closed, willing the pain to stay away. He's right, I do need answers. I gasp when I feel his lips grazing the side of my neck and snap my eyes open.

"What are you doing?" I breathe out.

"Distracting you," he says, like it's supposed to make sense to me.

"No, I don't want you," I growl. He kisses the side of my neck before drawing back and resting his forehead against mine.

"Your mind doesn't want you to want me but I guarantee you that your pussy wants to repeat my cock slamming inside it."

"Does not! You already stole my virginity—"

"I didn't steal shit, Lakeland." The anger that laces his tone gives me pause, his gaze bores into mine. "You gave me that gift years ago, it was already mine and I cherished it because *you* gave it to me. What happened between us earlier was a reminder. You can call me a bastard and lie to yourself about hating me and you may just believe it, but your body doesn't because it knows it belongs to me."

"I don't belong to anyone."

"I'll let you believe that for now. When I get the copy of your medical records and they say what I think they might, all plans are out the fucking window and I'm taking down every motherfucker that tore you from me. I'm a cold heartless son of a bitch and you've seen firsthand the lengths I'm willing to go through to get what I want." I open my mouth to argue but he pushes on. "We're both covered in blood and need to shower, you try to fight me on this and I won't be gentle. Be a good girl and do as you're fucking told and I'll reward you." The ache in the base of my skull begins to beat again hearing him call me a good girl.

My nostrils flare, I'm ready to give him a piece of my mind until he pinches my nipples between his fingers, drawing a shocked gasp from me. He uses that to his advantage and slams his lips down on mine, his tongue slipping inside my mouth with ease. I plan to bite the fucking thing until the taste of him overrides my senses and I find myself kissing him back eagerly, only for the bastard to jerk back and smirk at me.

"Shower. Now."

"Argh, you're such a fucking ass," I snap as I stalk toward the closed door on the opposite side of the room.

"That's the closet." Humor is thick in his tone as I slam the fucking door closed and glare at his stupid smirking face. "Bathroom is across the hall, it's a shared one." If I had something to throw at his bipolar ass I would, his mood changes are giving me whiplash. I stalk across the hall to the bath-room and try to slam the door behind me. He catches it as he enters and closes it behind himself.

"Get out," I snarl. He ignores me as he flicks the lock, then yanks his shirt over his head. The sight of all his ink distracts me. I run my eyes over it greedily but that seems to annoy him.

"Clothes off now." I stomp my foot and turn. Giving him my back, I yank my hoodie and shirt over my head. I feel his gaze rake over my exposed skin and fight the shiver from breaking free as I begin to undo my jeans. It's stupid because he's already seen me naked and yet I'm still nervous. Actually, according to him he's seen me naked a few times now. I hate that I don't know if what he says is true or not. I try to think back only for the pain in my head to return, I groan. "Stop thinking. Lose the fucking pants now or I'll do it."

I push through the stabbing pain in my head and shove the jeans down my legs, then take a deep breath ignoring him all together as I step into the tiny shower stall and turn it on. I plaster myself against the far wall hoping to keep as much space between us as I can but the moment he steps in, the shower feels like it's shrunk. I keep my gaze on the wall as I wait for the water to heat. Knox doesn't seem to care that he is openly staring at my body like he has the fucking right to. Even if what he says is true and I can't remember ever being with him, he should fucking respect that and get the hell away from me, but he won't because he is a controlling prick.

"You can make this easy on yourself." I give him the best fuck off side eye I can before I go back to staring at the wall hoping this shower will fucking heat up faster. "Hard way it is then," he growls before he grips my hair, tugging on the strands and forcing me to face him. He narrows his eyes at the sight of the scowl on my face and yanks my hair harder drawing a hiss of pain from me. "Your face is saying what your mouth refuses to."

"Oh, no my mouth can say you're a cunt just fine." His eyes spark with indignation but in the boldest of moves I have ever made in my life I strike out and grab his cock. His hold on my hair drops and he grunts as I crush his dick and balls, making him rise to his tiptoes.

"You are going to pay for this," he grits out through clenched teeth.

"I've paid for enough already. You think you have the right to be mad?" I squeeze harder, drawing a loud curse from him. "You have no right. If what you and my sister have said is true then I'm the only one who gets to be fucking mad. Six years of my life has been a waste and a fucking lie!"

"Fuck. Let go, Lakeland." Pain laces his words but fuck him and his heavy handed bullshit.

"I have you by the balls literally and you are going to do as I say." His jaw locks and I see he wants to hurt me but he's too fucking scared I'll rip his cock off if he makes a wrong move.

"Name it."

"I want to see my sister." His forehead crinkles and his brows draw in.

"What?" Sighing, I release my hold on him and step back. I honestly expected him to beat the shit out of me or scream or something but no, he just stands there staring at me.

"I want to see my sister," I say barely above a whisper. He cups his dick and grunts in pain, shooting me a filthy look. When he doesn't respond, I step under the spray and pray the drain swallows me like it does the water. Tilting my head back, I let the water cascade down my face, relaxing slightly until I feel his lips on my exposed neck and his body plastered to my front. I keep my eyes closed and step back out of the spray thinking he will release me—stupid me, of course he doesn't. He licks a trail down my neck and nips at my collar bone as I finally open my eyes. I grip his shoulders ready to push him away, when he grabs my waist at the same time.

"I'm not stopping," he growls against my skin. Is he a mind reader? I'm about to tell him to fuck off until he captures my nipple in his mouth and a heady moan escapes me without consent. My grip on his shoulders turns from firm to lax as my head lulls back against the shower wall. When he flicks his tongue over the enlarged peak a shudder rolls through me.

"Knox," I whine, not sure if I'm saying his name to get him to stop or because I want to beg him to continue. He bites down softly and I gasp as I press up onto my tiptoes. He releases it with a wet pop and places a soft kiss on it before changing sides but this time, he flicks his gaze up to me as he swirls his tongue across the peak, drawing a strangled moan from me. My hand fists in his hair as I pull him in closer, my mind and body are at war again but him sucking on my nipples has my pussy tingling.

He slips his hand between my thighs and I tense when I feel his fingers slip through my folds. A soft growl escapes him when he feels how wet I am. He swirls his finger around my entrance gathering my wetness and uses that on my clit.

"Fuck," I cry out at the first touch. I feel him smirk against my nipple only I can't find it within myself to care as long as he keeps touching me like this. Five minutes ago my mind was overloaded with thoughts and worry, but right now all I can focus on is him and the way he is touching me and the feelings he is bringing to life inside me. Knox releases my nipple but never stops circling my clit. He captures my lips in a kiss that robs me of breath, his tongue tangling with mine in a fight for control. It takes him all of a few seconds before he is the clear victor. I feel my orgasm cresting and wrap my arms around his neck in case my legs give out but the bastard uses that to his advantage and pulls his hand free only to grip my waist and lift me. Instinctively I lock my legs around him, not wanting to fall.

"Don't fight this, it's going to happen so accept it and thank me for the distraction when I have you seeing stars." I have no reply as he lines his cock up with my entrance. I tense in anticipation of the pain but he distracts me by kissing me again. I get so lost in his taste that I barely register the sting of his cock slowly pushing inside me, inch by glorious fucking inch, until he is fully sheathed inside me. We both break apart and groan at the feeling. Last time wasn't like this—it was rough, unwanted and stolen but this time, I want it. I need him to distract me and make me feel something other than this hollowness inside my chest. I want him to help me breathe again. "Fuck, you're so tight, Lay." He moans.

"Make me forget." Three little words seem to change something inside him, his blissed-out look morphs into one of pure hunger, he almost looks savage as his hold on me turns punishing. He draws almost all the way out before slamming inside me again. I cry out, not giving a fuck who hears me as long as he keeps going and doesn't stop. "Knox, fuck–"

"Shut the fuck up and take this dick like a good girl." I bite down on my lip and take what he gives, loving the way he fills me. The fact he isn't gentle or handles me softly only turns me on more. I can feel myself growing wetter with each thrust—fuck it feels so good. He growls as he pulls out of me and drops me to my feet. I'm about to scream at him for stopping until he spins me around to face the wall and grabs my hips. "Hands flat against the wall and spread your legs." The hunger in his tone has me eagerly obeying. "Still the same."

"What?" I don't push him for an answer as he thrusts inside me. I scream out. Fuck, this angle feels so different, he feels deeper and... Jesus, when he pulls almost all the way out and slams back into me I nearly see stars.

"The only way to get you to submit is by fucking you." His words don't register as I feel my orgasm building. I try to latch onto it, needing to come so badly that I would do anything he asks as long as he makes me shatter.

"Yes, like that, make me come," I cry out. His hold on my waist turning almost violent as he fucks me deeper, harder than before, forcing me to push back against him or risk headbutting the wall. "Oh my God."

"I told you before, I am your fucking God. Now come," he snarls in my ear before biting down on my shoulder and reaching around me to pinch my clit between his fingers. I come so fucking hard that my legs give out and my vision turns black as I scream his name until my throat is hoarse. His arm around my waist is the only thing keeping me standing as he continues to fuck me ruthlessly, chasing his own release. I feel my pussy clamping down on his cock trying to hold him inside me and that's what it takes for him to let go and come deep inside me.

"Fuck, Lake," he roars out, the sound of my name coming from him as he shatters sends a delicious shiver down my spine. "Fuck, I hope your sister was telling the truth, it will break me to kill you."

Chapter Fifteen

Knox

I slipped up earlier, I never should have told her it would break me to kill her.

If it turns out that she did end my sister's life because she was a drunk coward and left her in that car while she fled, I will skin her alive and deal with the repercussions later. After showering, I found her some clothes and dragged her out to the living room where she has sat silently for the past hour while Tay cooked dinner. By cooking dinner, I mean he picked up the phone and ordered Chinese, then sent one of the guys to pick it up. He's plating it all up while Xander and I lean against the counter sipping a beer each.

"Jerry called while you were... busy." I shoot Taylan a warning glare to shut his fucking mouth, the bastard just smirks. I look over at Lakeland who is still staring at the TV screen, it's obvious she is lost in her own thoughts. "What are you going to do when you meet up with Knight?"

"What are you trying to play at here?" I snap at my best friend who looks taken back by my pissed off tone.

"What do you mean?"

"Ever since I brought her back you have played the savior and tried to intervene at every turn, why?"

Taylan drops the fried rice container and closes the space between him and I, getting nose to nose with me. Xander shifts, ready to step between us if he has to.

"What are you going to do if those records come back saying she did lose her memory and you were wrong all these years, huh?" The fucker doesn't give me a chance to answer. "How are you going to be able to live with the guilt knowing you thought the worst of the person you were supposed to love most in this world and left her alone to be used and manipulated by her father? I mean, if they come back and show she is faking it, why not just sell her off to Gio? Get rid of her once and for all." Without thinking my hand wraps around his throat and I drive him back until he smacks into the fridge with a grunt. Xander grabs at me but I shake him off. I open my mouth but no words come out. Tay shakes his head and shoves me off him. Stumbling back a step, I catch myself on the edge of the counter. "Decide now what your fucking choice is before you find out the truth. If it says what I think it does and one day she does remember everything, this will be the moment she remembers most. She'll remember you blaming her and doubting her because you chose to hold onto your hatred."

"My sister is fucking dead," I say in an even tone, making his eyes soften.

"I know, but Lake isn't. You need to understand that Wave may not have been our blood but we share in the pain of your loss, Knox. She wasn't just some girl to Xander and me, she was the sister we never had. Losing her and now... River, I don't think I could cope with losing Lake as well."

"Boss, we got a problem." The three of us turn to see Floyd standing in the doorway looking pissed.

"What is it?" Xander asks. Floyd chews on his lips for a second before looking at me.

"You're all over the news and it seems Gio is the one leading the manhunt for his friend's kidnapped daughter with Percy *and* Karl at his side." The three of us rush into the living room and change the channel to the news. We're immediately greeted by the sight of Giovani Dario's hideous mug. Percy stands behind him with a distraught look on his face but it's the sight of Karl that angers me most. That motherfucker is supposed to be neutral and not choose sides in another families war, yet there he stands beside my enemies.

"We ask that the man who kidnapped Mr. Deveraux's daughter do the right thing and let her go. Lakeland has a medical condition and needs to be tended to daily by a nurse. She has been without her medication for days, without those she will be suffering." I spy the woman herself shifting forward on the couch. The camera shifts from Gio and goes back to the news woman.

"Police are searching for this man pictured in the image above." The screen shifts to show a picture of me from three years ago. "The man is believed to be Knox Bronson—"

"Son of a whore," Xander grits out. I stare at the

screen, not hearing a word this bitch is saying. The guys begin discussing what we do next but there isn't anything we can do. I own a shitload of properties and businesses under my name, they are legit but I'm worried the more they dig into my past they will find the skeletons I have buried which could cause a shitload of trouble for me. The sound of my phone ringing pulls me from my thoughts. Pulling it from my pocket I see it's Ian—the leader of the English.

Answering the call I bring it to my ear. "What?" I snarl.

"You may run Canada, boy, but I have friends there that are telling me you have a lot of heat on you right now." I mouth to Xander and Taylan that it's Ian before I place the call on speaker for them to hear.

"Seems your partner is in on this shit. You know what that means, right?"

"Now, you listen to me, Knox. I've pulled all my men back from any work with Karl and the Irish. I will stand clear of this shit." Suspicion curls inside me.

"Why?"

"I'm a businessman not a nark. Karl may be seen in the pictures but as far as the treaty goes, he hasn't broken the rules. He hasn't come forward and said a thing to the news, you can't go after him without breaching the treaty yourself."

"Why the fuck do you care? You and Karl have been gunning for me since I cut off my ports to you and refused to allow you to ship women and children." Lakeland's face is a mask of outrage and disgust at hearing that.

"I don't want a war. You may be separate countries, but

the moment you go to war with me and Karl over this misunderstanding, I have no doubt The Murdoch's will aid you."

I scoff. "Bishop doesn't owe me shit—"

"He may not owe you personally but he will fight alongside you. By ending the two of us he would have ended the skin trade and we all know that is his ultimate goal here. I want no part of a war, Karl is on his own here. We have a meeting shortly with the heads, don't bring your shit to the table, boy. If you do, they will see you as weak. I have nothing against you, Knox, you seem like a level headed kid. Don't make me regret pulling my men back from Karl who has been a friend for decades." He ends the call, leaving me standing here, mulling over his words—the fucker is cryptic as hell.

"Karl's on his own," Tay says drawing my attention to him.

I nod before looking at Lakeland as I speak. "We need to pack up and move, they know my name now so they will raid all the properties. We head to Jersey City to meet up with Knight, and then go to the meeting and gauge Karl's intentions from there before we go after Gio." I can't kill Karl without risking the other families coming after me. This treaty is something that has benefited us all and I won't be the one to break it. If I do, I'll have the Greeks, Russians, English, Irish and the entirety of the US on my ass.

"We need a plan," Xander says.

"We need to move within the hour," Floyd tacks on.

"I'll get the guys packing now, we need to get to the private airstrip before they block the roads," Taylan adds.

"Get the pilots ready to fly within three hours," I respond.

"I'm not leaving without seeing my sister." The four of us all turn to Lake as she climbs to her feet and stares directly at me. "Take me to her and I'll willingly go with you, deny me and I will fight and scream at the top of my lungs to anyone who will listen and tell them who I truly am."

"You would go back to your father, you know that, right?" Tay gently says.

"I won't go back to him but I will not leave without seeing River. You told me you know what it's like to lose a sibling, would you go without being able to say goodbye to your sister?" Scrubbing a hand down my face in agitation, I shake my head reluctantly. She stares at me waiting for my response. I weigh up all our options and the prospect of being caught but all of that is outweighed by the fact she is right, if roles were reversed I wouldn't go anywhere without seeing my sister. I would give anything in this fucking world to see my twin one more time. With my mind made up, I turn to Floyd.

"I want this house scrubbed and everyone at the airstrip within the hour. Call Patrick and tell him to clear out my house and set my mom up somewhere else until the heat dies down." Floyd nods and races off to do as I instructed. Turning to the guys next I say, "Get your shit, you two ride with me." Xander nods and stalks off while Taylan shoots me a smile and nods proudly.

"Good choice, brother, good fucking choice." Ignoring him I focus on Lake.

"You listen to everything I say, you disobey me once and you—"

"Take me to her and I'll do everything you say." Reluctantly I nod and turn to go get my shit. "Knox?" Pausing, I peer at her over my shoulder and watch as she nibbles her bottom lip.

"Yeah?"

"Thank you," she mutters. My brows raise and I roll my lips over my teeth to keep from smiling, she looks pained at having to say those words.

Twenty minutes later we pull up out front of the funeral home. I clasp Lake's hand in mine, telling myself I'm only holding it because I don't want her to run. Jerry meets us at the front and leads us through the building, the closer we get to the morgue in the back the tighter her grip gets. I say nothing knowing exactly how she is feeling, it's been six years since Wave left me but I remember it like it was yesterday, the feeling and the trepidation of what comes next in life without them.

The instant we pass through the swinging doors, a chill washes over me from the cold temperature in here. Jerry moves toward the middle of the room where a body lies covered by a white sheet. Lakeland pries her hand free of mine and hesitantly moves toward Jerry who stands silently waiting. Xan and Tay come to stand on either side of me, giving her space and time with her sister before we say our final goodbyes. As she reaches the edge of the metal table she grips the edge and drops her chin to her chest. Tay nudges me with his shoulder earning a glare.

"Go to her," he whispers.

I shake my head. "No."

"Pussy," he snarls before rushing forward and placing a hand on her back in support. "Whenever you are ready, Lay, give us a nod and Jerry will uncover her for you." A soft whimper escapes her at Tay's words and suddenly I hate my best friend for being able to know what to say and being man enough to let go of his hate. Unlike him, I can't let go until I know for sure.

"Okay," she whispers and nods her head. Jerry steps forward and peels the white sheet back, exposing only River's face. "Oh God," she cries out just as her legs give out. Tay is quick to wrap an arm around her waist and hold her up as she screams. I can feel her pain through the anguished screams. Fuck, my legs carry me across the room without consent. Suddenly Taylan isn't the one holding her but I am. I bury her face in my chest and hold her as she breaks down.

I turn and peer down at Riverland Deveraux, one of the most badass women I have ever met in my life. She took no shit from anyone and whenever she was told she couldn't do something the stubborn bitch would do everything in her power to prove you wrong. No matter how hard it was or how long it took, she would always prove you wrong. I shoot Taylan a pleading look to help me. Lakeland continues to claw at my sides and arms as I hold her, she hasn't stopped screaming and I'm beginning to worry she will black out soon.

"You are nothing but a weak ass pussy," he says. My eyes widen at the fucking dickhead. Lakeland suddenly pulls free of my hold and spins around to face Taylan as he stares down at her sister.

"What?" Lake snarls. Tay smirks and turns his sad eyes to her.

"That is the first thing your sister said to me when we met." I frown trying to recall the memory.

"What the fuck are you smiling at, asshole?" I turn to Xander who saunters forward with a sad smile on his face.

"Huh?" Lake says. Xan stands opposite us, forcing Jerry to move as he looks to Lakeland.

"That is the first thing she said to me." Lay smiles and wipes the tears from her cheeks before turning to face me. The three of them eye me expectantly, rolling my own eyes and groaning I add.

"You look like the type to overcompensate for having a little dick." A burst of laughter comes from Lake before she quickly covers her mouth to silence it. I narrow my eyes at the little shit. "I'm sure you can attest to the fact my cock is anything but little," I growl. Her eyes widen a fraction before she tears her gaze from me to look at Taylan.

"How did you even know my sister?" Tay chuckles and within a split second Xan and I both join in shaking our heads. Our laughter grows as each of us gets lost in the first time we met the spitfire that is Riverland.

"We all went to school together and one day Knox pissed off the wrong group of guys–"

She cuts Xan off. "Wait, you went to school with us?" Xander snorts and shakes his head.

"No. We were dirt poor so there is no way we could afford your private school tuition." A frown mars her face, I can see she is trying to put the puzzle pieces together in her own head. "Your sister was walking home and spotted the group Knox had pissed off picking on Waverly." At the mention of my sister's name she flinches and grinds her teeth in pain. Xan looks at me and I nod for him to continue wanting to see what happens if we keep talking about the past. "Instead of being a rich snob like we thought all those private school pricks were, she stopped and ended up beating the three of them, even breaking one of their noses before we could get there."

"When we got there after they ran off, she tried to have a go at us until Wave stopped her. She was willing to fight for a poor girl she had never met. We had never met a rich kid that wasn't an asshole so we were shocked until she opened her mouth and tore the three of us down with just her words," Tay adds on, smiling.

I clear my throat, drawing her attention to me as I speak. "She started hanging around us and we found out we really liked her."

"How old was she?"

"Sixteen."

Her lips purse. "I would have been thirteen."

I nod. "She had told us all about you and you must

remember her bringing you around to hang out with us?" I push, Xander and Taylan both watch her closely for any sign of recognition but all I see in her eyes is confusion and frustration.

"I..." She clamps her mouth closed and takes a deep breath. "I don't know any of you," she mutters bitterly.

"That's okay. How about we share stories of her later when we're on the road. I don't mean to be a dick but we're running out of time, Lay," Tay says with a smile. I'm starting to hate how he fucking looks and talks to her, even worse I hate that she fucking responds to him.

Chapter Sixteen

Lakeland

Leaning over the table I place a kiss to her cold forehead and hold there for a second with my eyes closed, committing this moment to my memory. Without anyone needing to say it, I know this will be the last time I will ever get to see my sister, this is the last memory I will have of her for the rest of my life. Pulling back and putting a couple inches of space between us, I rub the top of her head, her hair is dull and doesn't hold the shine it used to, her lips have a purplish tinge to them. Her skin is pale but it's the sight of the bruises that mar her beautiful face and collarbone that anger me the most.

I lift my gaze to Jerry and ask, "What was her cause of death?" He flicks his gaze to Knox. I growl drawing his attention back to me. "She is my sister, not his, now answer my damn question."

"Do it," comes from Knox.

Jerry nods. "Blunt force trauma to the head. She suffered many blows to the cranium which led to her death." I bite down on my lips to keep from sobbing. Rubbing the top of her head, I place another kiss to her cheek before whispering in her ear.

"Whatever I have to do, wherever I have to go, no matter how far or how long it takes, I swear to you I will find who did this to you, Riv. Thank you for always being my hero and saving me, even when I didn't know I needed saving. I love you, big sister," I choke out past the lump in my throat. Without waiting for the others, I pull away from my sister and march out of the room. I latch onto the anger inside me for my sister, my hero, when our mom died she took me under her wing and protected me. How our own father could allow this to happen to his own flesh and blood is something I will have to ask him before I send his ass back to hell.

I climb into the backseat of the car and wait for Knox and the others. I'm alone for a minute before I see the three of them stalking toward me but my attention is on Xander. A stabbing in the back of my head has me hissing.

I'll make sure he knows what you did tonight, you took the love of my life from me.

I gasp at the sound of Xander's voice inside my head. I cry out when the pain in my head explodes, then I feel hands on me but my vision is gone. I have a few seconds before I pass out. The pain inside me stalls when I feel lips on mine, I'm unable to lift my arms or even see who the fuck is kissing me. I feel a hand fist in my hair angling my head while another arm wraps around my waist and draws me in closer. It takes a minute before my vision slowly starts to clear, blinking a couple of times to focus.

My eyes widen at the sight of green eyes staring back at me. Knox doesn't stop kissing me, even when the car jolts forward. He shifts so I'm in his lap. Only then does he slowly draw back never taking his eyes off me, our breaths are rapid as we try to suck in air but confusion wars inside me.

"How did you stop me from passing out?" I whisper.

"What happened?" he counters. I nibble on my lip, debating if I should tell him or not but then I remember that he still doesn't believe me about not knowing him or his friends, that all me telling him would do is cause more doubt.

"I... I was overwhelmed." His gaze searches mine.

"You're lying."

"If you have the power to tell when I lie then you should know I'm telling you the truth about not knowing who the hell you or your friends are and I can tell you for certain I never harmed your sister." At the mention of his sister all the softness in his features disappears just as he tosses me off his lap and I land on the other side with a grunt.

"Not another fucking word out of you," he clips out. Crossing my arms over my chest, I slouch back in my seat and stare out the window. If he thinks not talking to them is a punishment, he is fucking mistaken! The drive to the air strip passes by in a blur, I'm too lost in my own thoughts. I refuse to be a pawn for Knox to use against my father, if I'm going to survive long enough to have a chance at living my own life, I need to make a break for it when we get to the

US. Once we make it to the airstrip, Knox drags me out of the car and pushes my head down not allowing me to look around. On board he shoves me into a seat and fastens the belt across my lap while I glare daggers at the manhandling bastard.

"I can do it!" I snap when he keeps fumbling with the buckle.

"Shut the fuck up and sit your ass there. Don't fucking move." We're stuck in a glare off for a minute before his name is shouted from the front of the plane, forcing him to pull away and storm off in the other direction.

Fuck him!

I unfasten the belt and hop over to the next seat by the window and fasten the belt, then cross my arms over my chest and close my eyes. The sooner we land the sooner I can put a plan into motion and get the hell away from him and his heavy handedness. I don't care how breathtaking he is to look at, his asshole attitude makes him ugly. He's a pompous ass who thinks his word is above God himself. Seriously, who the fuck died and made him king. I cringe at the thought, that was low of me to think that considering I know he lost his sister. I feel bad for him I do but the fact remains that this whole situation is his fucking fault. If he hadn't come after us, River would still be alive, Colson wouldn't have been shot. I don't even know where Colson is or if he's okay, he probably thinks we abandoned him.

"I warned you," I hear him snarl but refuse to open my eyes until he yanks my arm. Snapping my eyes open a second too late, I see him handcuff me to him. I tug my arm hoping to get free but the bastard just smirks as he claims the seat beside me.

"Uncuff me right now!" I snap, not caring who hears.

"You disobeyed me. I warned you, Lakeland."

"I'm not a fucking child," I shout, his upper lip twitches as if he wants to snarl at me.

"No, you're just a pain in my fucking ass. Now shut the fuck up before you really piss me off."

I scoff but before I can answer, Taylan claims the seat opposite me and says. "Just because he's good for your hole doesn't mean he's good for your soul." I balk at him as Knox growls at his best friend.

"Nothing about him is good for me," I grit out through clenched teeth. Knox scoffs so I add, "He's just trying to compensate for his little dick." Knox's head snaps toward me so fast I swear I heard his neck crack. Taylan bursts out into hysterics across from us while I spy Xander sitting across from us shaking with silent laughter.

"She just used her sister's words against you," Taylan wheezes out through fits of laughter. Knox snakes his uncuffed hand out and grips the back of my neck in a bruising hold, drawing me as close to him as my seatbelt will allow.

"The next time you open that mouth of yours and utter a single fucking word, I'll be shoving my *big* cock in it to teach you a lesson." My face contorts in disgust.

"Fuck–" I only manage to get that word out before he's unclasping my belt and dragging me to my feet. I fight the fucker and plant my feet trying to stop him but he yanks on the wrist that is cuffed to him causing pain to shoot up my arm.

"Mr. Bronson we are about to take off," someone calls from behind us. I try not to look at the seats filled with his men who clearly know what he is trying to do to me, fuckers won't even help me!

"Get the fucking plane in the air," Knox calls back as we reach the back of the plane where he shoves open a door. I dig my heels in, refusing to go willingly. He steps inside and tugs on the fucking cuff again, yanking me forward and slamming the door closed behind us. It's then I notice we are in a bedroom. I try to move as far from him as I can, well as much as the fucking cuffs will allow me. "On your knees, now." His eyes are dark and filled with unconcealed loathing as he glares down at me.

"No." My reply only fuels his temper. He grips the tops of my shoulders and forces me down. I grunt when my knees make contact with the carpeted floor. I keep my mouth closed refusing to allow this to happen. Tears prick the backs of my eyes as he begins to unfasten his jeans.

"You're going to learn that I call the fucking shots around here." He pulls his cock free and it revolts me to see he's already hard. As if to shame me further, he taps the fucking thing against my lips. I snap at the fucking thing, trying to take a bite out of it but he jerks it away. He fists his hand in my hair and tugs on the strands to the point I cry out in pain, tears immediately springing to my eyes. Crouching down, he gets in my face, I keep my mouth shut. "You bite my cock or I feel your teeth at all, I'm going to cut you and use your blood as lubricant for your ass." My eyes widen in indignation bringing a smile to his face. "Hmm," He purrs as he licks a trail from the base of my neck to the shell of my ear. "I miss your ass, Lay. You came so hard every time I buried my cock deep in that ass." He sucks my lobe into his mouth, drawing a gasp from me.

"You're sick," I grit out. He releases my lobe only to bury his tongue inside my ear. I try to move away but he holds me in place with the grip on my hair.

"Please bite my cock just so I can bury it deep in your ass, I want every fucker out there hearing you scream my name as I fuck your tight ass raw." A shiver travels down my spine and I try to play it off as revolution, but the cocky smirk on his hideous face tells me he knows his words have hit their desired mark. "You're wet for me, aren't you?" I turn my face to the side, refusing to look at him. He yanks my hair, pulling another cry from me as I'm forced to face him. "If you weren't such a defiant pain in my fucking ass I would help you out with that ache between your thighs." As if his words have a direct line to my greedy pussy the bitch flutters, my treacherous pussy just fucking fluttered for him! "Hmm, I bet you have a pulse between your legs right now," he taunts as he rises.

Gripping his cock, he strokes himself twice groaning, pre-cum coating the head of his cock and I loathe to admit my mouth waters to taste him. Disgust rolls through me, I'm fucking sick. He manhandles me, degrades me, abuses me and here I am drenched and no doubt about to soak through the jeans I'm wearing.

"Open," he demands as he rubs the tip of his cock along my lips, coating them with his pre-cum. Without consent my tongue darts out and licks the tip of his cock, drawing a strangled hiss from him. "Open your mouth, Lay, you want this just as much as I do." Powerless to stop this from happening I open my mouth, preferring to suck his cock rather than having him destroy my ass. He slides inside my mouth groaning, hitting the back of my throat, causing me to gag but he doesn't pull back, forcing me to breathe through my nose. I feel the plane gaining speed and try to stabilize myself so I don't tip sideways. "Give me your hands." I dart my gaze to his, he nods toward his hands just as a moan slips free when I swallow around him.

I interlock my fingers with his, His hold on mine is tight as he widens his stance to balance better as the plane begins to take off. He draws almost all the way out before thrusting in again. I gag and sputter but he doesn't ease his thrusts as he continues to fuck my face. Spit drips down my chin, tears leaking from the corners of my eyes.

"Fuck yes, baby, take it like a good girl." Out of nowhere with no warning pain explodes inside my head.

You're my good girl aren't you, baby? Take my cock like a good girl.

Knox's voice booms inside my head, those words play on a loop until my vision is hazy and I know I'm about to pass out with his cock still in my mouth.

Chapter Seventeen

Knox

I hiss when I feel her teeth scrape the underside of my cock. The hazy look in her eyes has me cursing before I rip my cock out of her mouth just as her hold on me loosens. Releasing her hands, I catch her just as she passes out.

What the fuck?

Worry churns inside me at the sight of her passed out in my arms but my balls are aching now with the need to come worse than ever before. I wonder if she would care if I finished myself off in her mouth? I shake away the thought quickly, scolding myself, I'll have to take care of myself clearly. This whole passing out thing is getting fucking old real fucking quick. I lift her and shuffle over to the side of the bed, not able to take large steps thanks to my fucking pants around my ankles. I place her down and snag the key from the pocket of my jeans and uncuff myself. I look down at my cock, the fucker is hard as rock and clearly not getting any action anytime soon. I tuck him back in my boxers and fasten my jeans before I lean over and cuff her other wrist.

"Knox," she mumbles in her sleep. I turn my head to find her eyes open but I can see her eyes are still unfocused and the pain she feels is etched into her features. "I think I did know you," she says barely above a whisper before her eyes close and her head drops to the side. Dropping down onto the edge of the bed, I clasp my head between my hands, this whole thing is fucked up. I remember that night as clearly as if it was yesterday.

Six years ago...

Taylan, River and I all sit around my living room waiting for Xander to get back with the food and for my girl to finally get her ass here. I roll my eyes, we're all idiots for thinking those two would get here on time, my sister never arrives anywhere on time. Even with this fucking storm raging outside, Wave refused to stay in for the night. She says our birthday is something to celebrate and we are not sitting at home being boring assholes, her words not mine.

"You kids sure you want to go out in this?" Mom asks as she enters the living room.

"I'd rather stay here and make Alexander notice I have boobs now but hey." Tay and I both scrunch our faces at River in disgust, which makes her laugh. "I was joking, you idiots,

calm down." That girl is just as bad as my sister. I'm so fucking grateful Wave hasn't tried to date yet, I don't think I would ever be okay with my sister dating a guy, no one is good enough for her.

"Knox and I noticed you had titties ages ago," Taylan snarks. I glare at the fucker.

"I didn't notice shit, plus it isn't her titties I want to be looking at or trying to motor boat." Mom fake gags and leaves, practically rushing from the room. She loves River and Lake and is always telling me to be respectful and mindful of Lake's feelings and never overwhelm her with my feelings.

"You're fucking disgusting, that's my little sister you're talking about," Riverland scolds. I waggle my brows at her and smirk. Taylan starts to laugh as she launches across the sofa and begins punching me, leaving me no choice but to laugh at her antics. "Say mercy and it will all stop!"

"Mercy, Mercy!" I shout through my laughter. She pushes off me smiling, River is the fourth and final piece Tay, Xan and I didn't know we were missing. The girl keeps us grounded and more times than I care to admit she has fronted me some cash to help Mom pay the bills, raising four teenagers isn't cheap and even though me and the guys work it barely covers all our expenses. Mom told me our deadbeat uncle has helped her a few times but I refuse to take anything from that piece of shit. He called last year saying that our sperm donor wanted to meet me. I told him to suck my dick and hung up. After what that cunt wanted to do to my sister I will never have anything to do with him, he only wants me because I have a cock.

The three of us hang out and watch TV while we wait for the girls and Xander. I keep checking my phone and begin to worry that I haven't heard from Lake. I've tried to call her five times and it just rings out, I have even called Wave twice with no answer. Tay has been blowing up Xander's phone for the past hour but he isn't answering either. I jump to my feet ready to go in search of the girls and Xan not giving a fuck that Lake's dad hates me. In Percy's eyes I'm no good for his daughter. He's tried to force her to break up with me and has forbidden her from seeing me, which is why she has no choice but to sneak out and see me.

"Let's go find them." River and Tay follow me out the front door, rain pelts down and lightning streaks the sky but it isn't the sound of the thunder or the rain that has me freezing on the doorstep, it's the sight of blue and red flashing lights. Xander walks toward us with his head down, soaking wet, four officers following after him. My heart races inside my chest as dread begins to take hold of me. If Xander was in trouble it would only be two cops and he would be smirking. When he lifts his head and I see his red puffy eyes, he looks broken and I just know something bad happened. I race down the stairs and ignore the officers as I grip his shoulders and shake him. He chokes out a sob.

"What happened?" I feel Tay and River at my back. Two of the officers continue past us to go to my mom. He opens his mouth only for another gut wrenching sob to tear out of him. "Fucking answer me!" I roar.

He shakes his head. "I tried to save her, I jumped in after her but I couldn't find her." He drops to his knees sobbing and ripping at his hair. River kneels beside him, trying to comfort him but I can't. I can feel it in the pit of my gut that something terrible has happened, call me crazy but I feel this immense pain in my chest like my heart has been ripped out.

"Son?" I look to the officer on my left, his eyes filled with pity. The sound of my mom's screams from behind confirm everything I'm feeling but I need to hear the words, I need someone to make it real, to confirm my greatest fear.

"Tell me," I snap.

"There was an accident, a car went over the bridge with one of the passengers trapped inside—" His mouth continues to move but I hear nothing over the sound of my blood pumping in my ears. When he reaches out and places a hand on my shoulder it pulls me back and I blink a couple times, trying to focus. "We are doing everything we can but we can't send out a recovery team until the storm passes."

"A recovery team is for when someone is dead," I snarl, yanking free of his hold. He nods sadly.

"I'm sorry, son, there is no chance anyone could have survived that fall—"

Cutting him off I ask, "You said one of the passengers?"

"Yes, one was trapped in the car and the driver is being rushed to hospital now."

"That bitch killed her!" Xander snarls. I look down at my best friend to find him staring at me with hatred in his gaze.

"Who?" I demand.

"Lakeland fucking killed Waverly, that bitch left her in the car to go over the bridge." I stagger backward, shaking my head denying what he is saying. Lake would never do that, she loved Waverly, they are best friends and closer than her and River are. She would never hurt my sister.

"We have reason to believe the driver was heavily intoxicated—" I snap my gaze back to the officer.

"Do you know that for a fucking fact?" I roar.

"Paramedics are running a tox screen but the smell of alcohol was hard to miss when loading her into the ambulance."

I want to deny it all, Lake would never do that. She's responsible and would never risk herself or Wave. She would have called me to come get them if she was drinking. They're wrong, she would never do this.

"I have to go, I need to go to my sister. I'll call you from the hospital," I hear River say as she rushes off to her car but I can't move. Mom continues to scream behind me. My chest feels like it's caving in, my heart is beating but I don't understand how it could possibly continue to beat if what these fuckers say is true. The girl I wanted to ask to marry me and runaway from here, where we didn't have to worry about her father trying to break us up, she couldn't have done this.

"I saw Lakeland, Knox. She was there. She did this. Wave is dead and it's all her fucking fault!" Xander screams. His words slam into me, my legs give out. I feel numb as I stare at Xander breaking before me. Waverly's gone, my baby sister is gone.

She's gone.

Lake killed her.

My girlfriend killed my sister.

The sound of ringing pulls me from my thoughts. I look

around in confusion, I don't remember moving into the house or sitting on the sofa. The sound of ringing cuts out only for it to start up again. I realize it's my phone. I pull it from my pocket, looking around to see Xander sitting in the corner with his face buried in his hand., Taylan is sitting in the tiny kitchen with my mom as she sobs. I answer the call.

"Hello?" My voice sounds hollow and devoid of emotion.

"Knox." The sound of River's voice has me sitting up straighter, I need her to tell me that Lake is innocent. I can't lose them both, it would fucking destroy me. I can't even comprehend the fact that Waverly is not going to walk through the front door any minute now and shout at me to get off my lazy ass.

"Tell me."

"Understand that we come from two different worlds. I would give mine up in a heartbeat to live in yours."

"What the fuck does that mean?" I snap, my patience is non-existent at this point.

"It means I need you to remember that because one day I will make this right."

"You aren't fucking making sense!"

"Lakeland won't ever know the truth, he won't allow her to. Lake was drunk and lost control, Knox, I'm sorry."

Chapter Eighteen

Lakeland

I bolt upright and dart my gaze around the room, when I spot Knox standing against the far wall with his arms crossed over his chest everything comes back to me. I passed out while he was shoving his dick down my throat! But it's the memory of him calling me a *good girl* that sparked the black out—no, it wasn't that. It was the sound of his voice in my head, I think it was definitely a memory.

"Lakeland was drunk and lost control, Knox." I reel back at his words, his gaze is hard and unyielding as he stares down his nose at me. "That's what your sister told me, then I found out years later you thought it was me or my guys who ran you off the road." I remain silent, unsure what to say, plus the look on his face scares me. He looks like a caged animal ready to strike at a moment's notice. "Here's the thing, Lakeland. Six years ago—the night of your accident," he snarls the word like it burnt his tongue. "I was just a poor teenage dirtbag, living at home with his mother, sister and two best friends. I didn't have two fucking pennies to rub together, no men, no car of my own. Xander, Taylan and I all shared a car because none of us could afford our own."

Cocking my head to the side, I study him trying to decipher what he is saying. "I don't understand," I finally say after a long pause. He kicks off the wall and places his hands on the end of the bed, leaning in close. I refuse to shift away and give him the satisfaction that he intimidates me.

"Six years ago I hadn't even taken over the Da Luca family, the Re Della Strada wasn't formed until months later." I see the truth in his eyes and even hear it in his words. "I was nowhere near that bridge, nor was Taylan or Xander. I was at home waiting for *you*." My jaw unhinges. I try to recall a single memory of him but the harder I try to remember the more the pain starts to throb in the base of my skull.

"You were telling the truth when you said I was your girlfriend?" He sucks in a shuddering breath before nodding. "If you thought I was drunk and I thought you ran me off the road because of who my father is then, what is the truth? What happened to me six years ago, Knox?" I hear the plea in my own voice but I don't care, I need to know what happened the night of the accident. "Why would my father lie to me?" I say aloud, not expecting him to answer me.

"To use you against me."

"Why would he think you gave a shit about me?" A shadow falls over his features as he pushes off the bed and steps back.

"At that point in time, you had me eating out of the palm of your hands. Percy knew that. He wanted me gone so he could use you to form an alliance with... with someone that could have helped make him a very wealthy man. I believe something happened that night between you and your father and you angered him enough for him to come after you." A knock sounds at the door, halting our conversation. "Yeah?" The door opens to reveal Xander.

"We need to move, we've been sitting here for nearly two hours," he says. I scurry off the bed to peer out the tiny window to see we aren't in the air but on the ground. I spin toward Knox.

"We've been on the ground for two hours?" He nods while still eyeing me with distrust. "Why are we still on the plane?"

"Casanova didn't want to wake you," Xander sneers before stalking out of the room.

"Come here." I go to him without complaint, I don't fight him when he lifts my handcuffs. I don't even argue when he undoes one cuff only to secure it around his own wrist. I follow closely behind him as he leads the way. I appreciate the fact he slows his own strides so I can keep up. We slip into the back seat of a waiting car with surprising ease. Taylan rides shotgun beside Xander and neither says a word as Xander plants his foot down and follows after the other cars in front of us. I look out the back window to see more cars behind us. I feel like the president with this much security. Given who Knox is and his line of work, I understand the need for extra protection. After a few minutes, he growls and reaches for me, pulling me into the center seat. I shoot him a questioning look, so he lifts the wrist that is cuffed to mine.

"Oh." Is my only response. I've never been outside of Canada so I drink in the sight of this stunning country. I don't even think as I lean over Knox and press my face against the glass to see large skyscrapers in the distance, it looks like a huge city. I snap out of it when I feel him shift beneath me. I scurry to move but he surprises me when he grabs my waist and deposits me on his lap. I peer at him over my shoulder only for him to lift our cuffed hands again. I raise a brow not calling him on his bullshit.

Time passes by quickly before we arrive at our destination—it's a large, swanky-looking hotel. "Tay, toss me your jacket," Knox says. Taylan tosses it over his shoulder effectively smacking me in the face with it. I scowl at the back of his head as Knox pushes the door open and helps me out before following after me. He drapes the jacket over the handcuffs. I snort out a laugh that earns me a glare from the man himself but my laughter dies the moment he interlocks our fingers. I remain silent at his side as he checks us in, then leads me to an elevator, we're only on the second story which is good. If I plan to escape then the closer to the ground I am the better for me.

Taylan and Xander both take the rooms on either side of the room I assume I'm sharing with Knox. The moment we step inside the room, I turn to face him ready to argue my point about needing to have our own rooms but he covers my mouth with his other hand.

"I'm not in the mood for your shit. I'm tired and I have a meeting first thing in the morning. I want to shower and then sleep. Don't make this hard because I'm still suffering from blue balls. Fight me and I promise you neither of us will be sleeping until I'm fucking that pretty little mouth of yours and coming down your throat." I gulp audibly and nod my head. He drops his hand and leads me toward the bathroom. "Jackson will have clothes waiting for us when we finish. I'm going to uncuff us, then you're going to get your ass in the shower."

"Okay." He kicks the door closed and makes quick work of uncuffing us. I decide to play along and make him think I'm being compliant. I strip off and step into the shower, making sure to shift over enough that he fits. The moment he steps in, he eyes me warily but I just smile and go about washing myself, feeling his gaze on me the entire time. Once I'm finished, I step out and snag one of the towels, drying myself, then turn to him to find his gaze laser focused on me. "Can I go change or do I have to wait for you?"

His eyes narrow suspiciously. "You know I have men blocking every exit, right?"

I nod. "I guessed as much, can I change now?"

"Whatever you're planning, don't," he warns.

"I'm not planning anything, I just want to change and sleep. You said if I listen and obey you won't be mean to me."

He frowns. "I never said that shit but whatever, go change," he says as he turns the shower off and steps out. I can't help it, my eyes drop to his cock and I bite my lips to keep the groan from slipping free. His body is a work of fucking art. "Keep looking at it like that and you'll get reacquainted with how it feels inside you real fast." I squeal and quickly dash out of there with his husky laughter following me. I find clothes laid out perfectly on the bed and purse my lips at the sight of the silky night dress. If he thinks I'm wearing that thing he has another thing coming. I snatch the blue shirt from his pile and drop my towel, pulling the shirt over my hair. I may not like the night dress but I am grateful to see a hairbrush, perfume, some hair pins and deodorant. I pin my hair up and spray myself quickly only to still at the sound of him sniffing the air behind me. I turn to face him.

He quirks a brow at the sight of me in his shirt. I place my hands on my hips. "I am not wearing that thing whatever his name brought in here. I also noticed you got underwear but I didn't!" The bastard just purses his lips and shrugs. He brushes past me, dropping his towel to the floor, my eyes immediately drink in the sight of... Jesus Christ, even his ass is tattooed! I slowly inch forward trying to get a better look at the ink. Just as I get close enough, he turns around and I'm greeted with the sight of his dick. "Fuck," I snap as I reel back, my cheeks flame as I turn away from him huffing.

"Get in the bed, Lakeland. I'm tired." I peer over my shoulder to see him standing there in a pair of sweats that hang low on his waist, emphasizing that glorious V.

"Can you at least put a shirt on?"

"You're wearing my fucking shirt. Now shut the hell up and get your ass in the bed before I drag you over here."

"Asshole." I snicker as I stomp over to the far side of the bed, then rip the covers back still muttering under my breath about how much of a dick he is only for the words to die in my throat at the sight of a gold letter opener sitting right there on the bedside table. I remain calm to not alert him to the weapon sitting within reach and quickly climb under the covers leaving an ocean of room between us. Seeing him naked and getting that close to his dick has set my blood pumping and my libido into overdrive. I need to stay as far away from him as I can. The moment he slips under the covers, he eliminates the space between us. I try to push him away but the distinct sound of a cuff clicking shut has me halting. I lift the cover and gawk at the sight of my wrist once again cuffed to him. "Are you freaking serious?" I snarl.

Ignoring me he reaches over to his side and flicks the lights off, then keeps shifting until he is comfortable, which in turn forces me to my side so I am plastered against his back thanks to the fucking handcuffs! Absolutely livid and outraged by the fact he has once again cuffed me to him I bite him.

"Fuck," he roars, then moves so freakishly fast it's like a blur. Suddenly he's nestled between my legs, pinning me to the mattress with a hand around my throat. "I told you not to fuck with me, I warned you what would happen." Panic flares to life inside me, I need to get the upper hand here or he is going to shove his cock down my throat and I refuse to allow him that privilege. In a bold move I reach down and cup his cock. His eyes widen as a hiss escapes him. Before he can protest, I lift my cuffed hand to grip the back of his neck and pull him down so I can capture his lips in a kiss. I try to remind myself that I am doing this to gain the upper hand, throw him off his game so he will be less vigilant, giving me a chance to escape, except the second his tongue invades my mouth and the taste of him fills me, all thought of escape flees.

Knox Bronson is a dangerous addiction I can't afford.

Chapter Nineteen

Knox

She strokes me through my sweats. I can't help thrusting into her hand, loving the way she tightens her hold on my cock. I devour her mouth, showing her without words that I own her, she may think she is the one in control here but we both know I am the one who calls the shots. Releasing her throat, I trail my hand down her side, loving the way she shivers under my touch. I grip her shirt and yank it up, breaking the kiss only to growl when the fucking thing gets stuck on the cuffs.

"That will teach you for being a caveman." She giggles, earning a scowl from me. Rather than answer her, I suck one of her nipples into my mouth. Her back arches off the bed as she cries out. She has always been so responsive to her nipples being played with, sucking on them gets her so fucking wet. "Knox." The way she moans my name has me thrusting into her hand harder. Fuck, I need to be buried inside her, my balls are aching and there is no fucking way I am coming in my sweats. Releasing her nipple with a wet pop I stare down at her.

"I need to be inside you." Her eyes search mine for a second before she gives me a jerky nod.

"I... Can I try something?" My brows draw in. She gently pushes against my chest until I'm on my back and she is straddling me. She tries to position her hands accordingly but the cuffs keep getting in the way. She growls. Reaching up, she tears a pin from her hair and lifts her cuffed wrist, stabbing the pin into the lock. I watch in wide-eyed fascination as she picks the fucking thing! The moment her wrist is free, she smiles wide down at me. It takes a second for that smile to disappear and a frown to mar her beautiful face. "I don't know how I just did that," she whispers, seeming genuinely horrified that she knows how to pick a lock. A proud smile scratches across my face as I lean forward and cup her cheeks, placing a chaste kiss to her lips.

"I taught you how to pick locks." She reels back, the horrified look on her face is almost comical. "Forget the lock and continue doing whatever it was you were about to try," I say, dropping back and tucking both my arms behind my head. Lake shakes her head to clear it and smirks as she shifts down my legs tugging my sweats down with her. She tosses them to the ground before kissing along my legs as she makes her way back to me. I'm man enough to admit that I tremble beneath her touch. The moment she straddles my lap, she leans down and licks and nibbles my skin, making me groan.

"Hmm," she purrs against my ear as she grips my wrists

and then a move I didn't fucking expect but should have she cuffs my other wrist. I yank my arms forward only to find I am cuffed to the fucking headboard!

"Lakeland–" She silences me by kissing me until I relax into the mattress, grinding against my aching cock. Without breaking our kiss, she reaches between our bodies and lines me up with her entrance before leaning back, resting her hands on my hips as she slowly sinks down onto my cock.

"Fuck, you're so tight," I grit out, a sheen of sweat coating my forehead. This is the most blissful torture I have ever experienced.

"Oh shit, I feel so full," she breathes out as she swallows the last inch of me inside her tight wet cunt. "Fuck, Knox, you feel so good inside me." Her eyes are dazed and filled with lust. I yank against my restraints, needing to touch her.

"Uncuff me now." She shakes her head and shoots me a sexy smirk as she lifts up until only the tip of my cock is inside her before slamming down, drawing a groan from me. "Now, I need to touch you."

She continues to bounce up and down on my dick trying to find her rhythm as she answers, "No, you get what I give you. Now shut up so I can fuck you." I want to argue but I'm robbed of words when she shifts and starts rotating her hips so I feel all of her at a different, more delicious angle.

"Fuck, Lakeland, stop! I'm going to fucking come!" I grit out. She throws her head back moaning.

"Oh, fuck, don't come. You feel so fucking good." I'm three seconds away from exploding inside her if she doesn't stop.

"Sit on my fucking face now or you won't be coming on my cock." She freezes, looking down at me. "You want to come, sit on my face so I can eat your pussy or else you won't be coming anytime soon."

Cocking her head to the side and pursing her lips she studies me for a moment. "Promise not to bite it?" I growl at her, earning a giggle. Her cheeks are tinged red as she shifts forward. I want to weep at the loss of her tight warm heat covering my cock but the thought of tasting her on my tongue after so fucking long has my mouth salivating. "Are... are you sure?" Her shyness would be cute if my cock wasn't rock-hard and my balls were full as fuck from being denied my release earlier.

"You're my prisoner and yet I am the one cuffed to the fucking bed!" She scrunches her face at the bite in my tone. "Put that pussy on my fucking face now. I'm about lose my shit and you won't like what happens next." She huffs but does as she is told and settles her knees on either side of my head. Fuck, her pussy is practically weeping. I don't wait for her to put that pussy on these sideburns, I push up and swipe my tongue through her slick folds. She screams out and falls forward, gripping the headboard as she drops that cunt onto my waiting tongue.

"Holy fuck!" she screams out as I push my tongue inside her moaning at the taste. All I can taste and smell is her, it's fucking intoxicating. It takes her a minute before she grows bold enough to begin grinding against my tongue, her hands drop into my hair, threading her fingers through the strands, tugging my head up as she fucks my face chasing her orgasm.

"Oh shit, yes, like that, please don't stop." Her head is thrown back as her free hand pinches her nipple between her fingers. "Knox!" she screams as her orgasm rips through her. She shudders and tries to shift but I suck her clit into my mouth drawing another scream from her as tremors wrack her tiny body.

"Get back here!" I snarl when she finally moves. Nibbling her bottom lip, she shakes her head while straddling my lap. The moment she grips my cock, I groan. This time there is no hesitation as she slams that glorious wet cunt down onto me. With the need to come overriding my senses, I thrust up inside her, meeting her each time she drops down onto me. "Fuck, Lakeland, I'm about to come," I growl.

"Oh fuck, keep fucking me like that, Knox." I force myself not to fucking come, but when I feel her pussy clamp down on my cock, I know I won't be able to hold off much longer.

"Pinch your clit, I'm about to come," I grit out. She does as she's told and then, as if the stars finally fucking aligned for the first time, we both come at the same time. I'm powerless to keep her name from tearing out of me as I come deep inside that perfect little cunt, marking her from the inside out as mine. She flops against me panting and trembling. I smirk, loving that I am the cause of her exhaustion and sated state.

"I think you're right." She pants.

"About what?" I breathe out.

"You may just be my God after that performance." Laughter bursts out of me, I had not been expecting her to say that. She lifts her head and rests her chin atop her hands on my chest as she looks at me smiling. "I like the sound of your laugh."

Looking at her with her hair wild and her eyes glassy from her orgasm brings a smile to my face. Fuck, I wish shit wasn't so fucked up. This was us, nothing else in the world mattered to us as long as we had each other. She was the air I needed to survive, she was my choice but one fucking night changed everything. That night changed me. I lost my rose colored glasses and didn't see the world as some fancy fucking love story with a happy ending anymore. The sun stopped shining for me, my days were filled with shadows and darkness as I fought my way to the top to seek retribution for the life stolen from me.

"I stopped laughing six years ago when you fucked my life up." The relaxed look on her face disappears and her eyes harden as she sits up, cringing when she remembers my cock is still buried inside her. "Uncuff me now."

"Fuck you, asshole," she sneers as she climbs off me. I yank against the restraints.

"Un-fucking-cuff me now!" I roar as she snatches the shirt off the ground, then snags the sweats I was just wearing and pulls them on, rolling them at the waist so they fit her. When she darts her gaze around the room and spots the window next to the bed my anger soars. "You try to fucking escape and I'll make you wish you were fucking dead." She throws the curtains open and pushes the window up. My eyes widen in horror, we're on the second fucking floor! I continue to tug on the cuffs. When the crack of the wood sounds out, she spins around to face me with wide eyes. We both stare at each other as I use all my strength to break the fucking headboard as she lunges for the side table. The second the wood gives, I roll toward her and push to my knees ready to launch at her, until I feel a sharp pain in my side.

"Oh shit," she mutters with a horrified look on her face. We both look down to see a fucking letter opener lodge into my side. "I'm sorry," she rushes to say before shoving against my chest. I lose balance and drop back onto the bed with a painful groan, just in time to see her jump out the fucking window!

"Lakeland, no!" I scream. The pain in my side is forgotten as I rush to my feet and peer out the window expecting to find her bloodied and broken on the pavement below. However, what I don't fucking expect is to see a swimming pool below us and the bitch swimming to the edge, unbroken and not bloody. When she pulls herself out of the water she looks up to me and waves, the fucking bitch just waves at me.

"Nice to meet you, Knox Bronson," she shouts before running. Fuck! Spinning around ready to go after her only to feel the fucking bite of the letter opener in my side.

"Fuck." Shifting around the bed, I grab the keys from the side table and uncuff myself before making my way into the bathroom. I tug on the discarded pair of jeans from earlier, then grab my phone I left on the counter and dial Xander.

He answers on the third ring. "This better be good, dick," he grumbles.

"Get Tay and come to my room now," I bite out.

"Why?"

I grip my phone so tight I fear I may crack it. "Because Lakeland just fucking stabbed me, then jumped out the window!" I snap before ending the call, only to dial Hendrick and telling him to get Floyd and the others to go after the little bitch. They have orders to not harm her but they are to bring her back by any means necessary.

Chapter Twenty

Knox

"Wait, so she fucked you, stabbed you then she jumped out the window?" I glare at Taylan as the doctor finishes stitching me up. I have no fucking idea where Tay found the doctor but the guy doesn't seem nervous or panicked in the slightest, which leads me to believe he does this type of shit often.

"Yes," I grit out.

He whistles between his teeth. "Wow, she really does hate you."

"Fuck off, Taylan," Xander snarls at our friend. "What's the plan now?" he asks, looking at me.

"I have no choice but to wait and meet Knight before we go after her."

Xan nods. "Okay, we have about an hour before the meet. Floyd and Hendrick have split the men but none of them have been able to locate her." The doctor finishes and dresses the wound before gathering his things and exiting quietly. Xan and I both shoot Taylan a questioning look.

"What? I know a guy who knew a guy who gave me the number to a local doc who does this shit on the side for a sum of money." Rather than asking more questions I just nod and accept his bullshit ass answer.

"What are the chances of anyone here knowing who she is?" I ask.

Xander and Tay take a minute to think before Xan answers, "Anyone in our world would know about her, they would be keeping tabs on you." Fuck, I stab a hand through my hair and nod, I thought as much. When my phone rings, I tune out of Taylan and Xander's conversation and answer when I see Floyd's name on the screen.

"What's the update?"

He sighs. "We had to fall back."

I sit forward in my seat. "Why?"

"She's in New York city. We didn't want to start a war with the Murdoch's by crossing into their turf."

"Mother fucker!" I snap. "Get your asses back here," I order before ending the call.

"What happened?" Tay asks as I climb to my feet and yank my shirt on.

"She's in New York. I need to call Bishop and ask to enter to get her."

"Well, isn't it a good thing I smoothed things over with the Don?" Xander and I both glare at the cocky fucker. I send both of them away to pack their shit so we can leave after the meeting with Knight, and so I can be alone as I call

Bishop. If he denies me then I'm fucked or I have to start a war with the American mafia to get her ass back.

He answers on the fourth ring. "Knox?"

"Bishop, I need to ask—"

"To enter my city to track down your girl?" I reel back astonished that he even knew about this.

"How did you know?"

"I knew the moment you landed here with thirty-seven of your men, your two underbosses and the daughter of Percy Deveraux, who I am also informed is in business with your uncle and Karl." Surprised doesn't even begin to explain how I am feeling right now, he knows things he shouldn't and I'm not fucking sure how.

"How–"

"My brother is the best at what he does but one thing you didn't factor in was that his wife is twice the hacker he is. So, of course whenever someone from another family calls to ask for Knight's services, his wife gets protective and digs deeper making sure we have blackmail material if we need it and it turns out you, Knox Bronson, have a shit load of skeletons in your closet." Grinding my teeth I try to force myself to calm down. I'm fucking raging at the fact they were able to find all this shit out about me without even having to try hard.

"What do you plan to do with that information you have about me and my family?"

He stays silent for a moment which just sets my nerves on edge. "Give me your word you won't touch Karl no matter his involvement in whatever is happening between you, your uncle and Percy." Clenching my fist at my side I curse. "If he is involved, you will get your chance to take him down, but not until I find an adequate replacement for him, one that doesn't deal in the trade of women and children."

That is something I can support. "How long would that take?"

He chuckles but there is no humor to it. "As long as it takes. This treaty is new and still has kinks in it. Prove to me that you can be someone I can count on."

"How do I do that?"

"My family has suffered a great... loss recently." That stumps me, I've heard nothing about it through my sources. "Knight will not be meeting you today. Luka will be the one to deliver the information you need. You are not to contact my brother again. If you need information, you come to me."

"With all due respect, why would I do that?"

"Because he just lost his fucking son and because I told you to." My jaw unhinges at that information. "My nephew believes his girl escaped into Canada–"

"Grant me entry to your city and your nephew, son and niece may enter my territory but only the three of them."

"You have my word, you have forty-eight hours to get in and out of my city."

"Thank you."

"Thank me by agreeing to push the meeting with the heads of the families back until my family can deal with this tragedy."

"You have my full support, I understand your nephew's loss."

"One more thing?"

"Name it."

"Knight and Koby will go after everyone involved in the death of their son, my nephew will seek vengeance for his brother as well."

"Your brother, sister in law and nephew have every right to claim the lives of any fucker who aided the death of their loved one. Your family has my full support on the matter."

"Good, as a show of my gratitude, I included a few extra things in the report you requested from Knight." He ends the call without another word. I stand here silently for a moment, replaying what the fuck just happened and then it hits me, I think I just made an alliance with Bishop and by default the *Memento Mori*, that shit could come in handy. I'm actually looking forward to this meeting now. Karl may have immunity but Percy and Gio don't.

Stepping out of the elevator with my boys, I come to a halt at the sight of my men surrounding someone. The three of us share a look before I push my way through my guys to see a man standing there unbothered by the show of force. He lifts his gaze to meet mine and a smirk tilts the corner of his mouth.

"Knox Bronson, I presume?" he says.

"I guess you're Luka," I say, stepping into the man-made circle. He reaches into his jacket but my men all shift and draw their guns forcing him to freeze with his hand inside his coat.

"Calm the fuck down, dipshits, any of you fire a single fucking shot and you will start a war you can't win," he snarls.

"I don't think the Murdoch's care that much about a lackey." Tay snickers, earning a sneer from Luka.

"Considering Rook Murdoch is my brother in law and fucking hates seeing my sister cry, he would willingly wage a war against you all just to put a smile back on her face." I did not see that coming. "Bishop may be the Don but he isn't the only ruthless one in the family." He pulls a manila envelope from his jacket and tosses it to me. "You have forty-seven hours, Knox. When your time is up, look for my face because I will be the one chasing you out of our city."

"Thanks," I mutter. He turns to leave but stops and looks back over his shoulder.

"Since you are doing Knight and Chaos a solid, I'll do you one. The cab that took your girl away dropped her at Central Park. I'd hurry since the cabbie called the cops on her for doing a runner and not paying." I nod my thanks as he strolls out of here without a care in the world.

"Let's move," I snap. We all usher out of the hotel and climb into the waiting cars. We have about a thirty minute drive to reach Central Park, so I spend that time texting each of my men where to go so we have the park surrounded. She isn't fucking getting away from me this time. Once I finished directing them, I turn back to the envelope, debating if I should open it or not. If I do, the contents could distract me. If I don't, it will eat at me.

"I vote we chain her fucking ass up," Xander snarls, pulling me from my thoughts.

"We get her then we head home," I say.

"Wait, like home as in home *home*?" Taylan asks. I peer out the window as I answer.

"Yeah, I'm done fucking around. We get her, head home and move in on Gio. I'm tired of waiting for Christiano to lead us to his brother. We storm through his borders and take out any son of a bitch that is loyal to the Dario family."

"Are you going to give his men a chance to surrender and join us?" Xander says.

"Why the fuck would I do that?" I snarl.

"Because you are the rightful heir to the Da Luca family, they may not know who you are because you're under your mother's last name but if you tell them who you really are, I think a lot of Gio's men will jump ship and follow the true heir to Canada." I mull over Xander's words. I know they hold merit but if I come out of the shadows and admit to the world who I truly am, that means I would never be Knox Bronson again.

Stepping out of the car, I look around and take in the crowds of people strolling through the park, like it's just another ordinary day in their lives. I see them smile and take photos. I spot a family wrangling their three kids to try to capture the moment in a picture but the children refuse to stand still and just want to go off and play. I bet that family has thousands of photos, unlike mine. I never met my father until the night I killed him. My mother never had any photos or wanted to share any details about him with us, she claimed we were safer not having anything to do with him.

"Let's go," I bark as I make my way into the circus that is Central Park. Xander and Taylan flank me as we scour the area for one little girl who has started a fucking war. If Percy hadn't promised her to Gio I would have stayed out of her life like I said I would. Agreeing to that deal with River was the only thing that kept her safe from me. I guess it turns out even with me staying away she was never truly safe. Her father has lied to her and manipulated her for years. She has no idea how much danger she is truly in.

"Knox." I grind to a halt and turn to where Xander is pointing. My brows raise in surprise.

"This seems way too fucking easy," I grit out as I make my way toward the park bench where Lakeland sits under the shade of a tree. Me and the guys are on high alert. Either this is a trap or she really is fucking stupid. She should be hiding or at the very least running and not sitting in plain sight. I motion for Xander and Taylan to stand back and keep watch as I approach Lake, keeping my eyes peeled and remaining on high alert for anything out of the ordinary or anyone acting sketchy. At the sound of my approach, she doesn't look up or even make a move when I sit down beside her. She looks like a homeless person sitting here in my clothes with her hair in a tangled mess. I see the stains of her tears marking her cheeks.

"You were right," she says barely above a whisper. Narrowing my eyes, I debate if I should indulge her with an answer or drag her ass out of here. The decision is made for me when she continues, "I stopped by a local Pharmacy to see if they stocked the medication I have been taking for years."

I take in the way her shoulders are hunched and she keeps picking at the cuticles on her fingers. Intrigued by what she is saying, I reach out, grip her chin and force her gaze to mine. "What the fuck does that have to do with you thinking I am right about something?" My tone is hard and unyielding but she doesn't flinch, it's the sight of shame in her eyes that has unease crawling up my spine.

"The pharmacist had no idea what I was talking about. The labels on my medication said the names were Xanoral and Linoium. I could never pronounce the names correctly and thought that was the issue but when she handed me a pad and pen and I wrote them down, she still looked at me like I was nutcase. I explained to her what the pills looked like and how often I took them. She called a friend who said they had never heard of them either. It took the better part of an hour for four of us to figure out that the medication I was on wasn't legal." The bitterness that laces each of her words has me searching her eyes for the reason why.

"What did you find out?" I push. She inhales sharply as her eyes begin to harden when she looks up at me.

"My father was drugging me." This news has my brows raising and my teeth clenching. I knew he was a sick fuck after what he allowed to happen to River but this is sadistic.

"How?"

"The names, Xanoral is Xanax and Doral mixed

together. Linoium is Librium, Klonopin and Valium mixed together. Percy had someone mixing these fucking medications. I took those fucking pills every day for the last six years!" She's getting hysterical now.

"What does mixing them together mean?"

Her eyes spark with anger. "Mixing them together and taking them daily makes them act as a memory suppressant." I recoil, dropping my hold on her chin as I stare down at her.

"What?" The amount of anger that laces that one word has her tensing and drawing back slightly. She darts her tongue out to moisten her lips in a nervous gesture.

"I think my sister was right. Percy was drugging me to keep me from remembering that night." I heard her words, I heard her speak them myself, but it's not sinking in. My mind won't process what I very plainly just heard her say. If she lost her memories then that means she really can't remember who I am or what happened that night. The fact her own father continued to drug her means that something bigger is at play here, something I am not seeing and in my world, that shit can cost you your life if you aren't vigilant and a step ahead of your enemies. Feeling suddenly exposed, I grip her arm and pull her to her feet as I drag her back to the car with Xander and Taylan following after us.

Chapter Twenty-One

Lakeland

I don't protest or even struggle when Knox shoves me into the car or even when we arrive at the airstrip and he drags me onto the plane. No one has uttered a single word. Worry gnaws at me at the sudden change in Knox. I expected him to be furious when he found me—I knew he would, I didn't bother to run after discovering what my father had been doing to me for years. Call me crazy but I would rather be stuck with Knox's overbearing ass then be forced to go back to my father, until he is behind bars or dead I can't risk being on my own. I sit in my seat silently and gaze out the window of the plane. Chatter from Knox's men sounds out as we take off. Once we are level in the air, Knox unfastens my seatbelt and leads me to the back of the plane. Unlike last time he doesn't need to drag me, this time he walks with my hand clasped in his.

Once we enter the small room where he forced me to my

knees, I gnaw on my lip wondering if he will do that again. He releases my hand and moves toward the tiny bathroom nestled into the back of the room and flicks the light on before looking back to me.

"There is shampoo and soap in there. I had Mary leave a toothbrush out for you as well." A strange sense of loathing washes over me and I frown, trying to decipher what this feeling is but words spew out of my mouth before I can stop them.

"Who the fuck is Mary?" My eyes widen but I quickly school my features when I realize the feeling coursing through me is jealousy! Knox's face starts to piss me off when I see him trying not to laugh. I growl at the bastard and shoulder past him into the bathroom and slam the flimsy door closed.

"Mary set out some clothes for you on the bed," he calls out.

"I'm not wearing that whore's clothes," I mutter bitterly to myself as I begin to undress.

"I heard that." My nostrils flare at the sound of laughter in his voice.

"Dick," I call back as I step into the shower that is so small I have to shuffle around to reach for the soap. As uncomfortable as the shower is due to its size, I enjoy the feeling of the hot water and allow it to wash away some of my stress. I work hard to keep my mind off my sister and the guilt I feel for leaving her alone in that place before fleeing with Knox.

Stepping out of the shower, my jaw unhinges, the clothes

I discarded are no longer on the floor and two white towels sit on the small counter. Fucking Knox! I wrap my hair in a towel before securing the other around my body and brushing my teeth. Mary may be a whore but I am grateful for the supplies she got me. I rinse my mouth out before taking a long look in the round mirror. My eyes seem to have a bit of life back in them and the handprints around my neck are barely visible now, which I am grateful for. Deciding that I can't hide out in here forever, I steel my spine and exit the bathroom to find Knox sitting on the edge of the bed with his phone clasped in his hand. I spot the clothes beside him and scowl at the pile.

"They're brand new," he assures me.

I turn my scornful gaze to the annoyingly handsome asshole. "Did your little whore enjoy picking out the bra and panty set as well?" He flicks his eyes to me and the lustful look I see in them has me clamping my mouth closed as my pulse begins to thrum to life inside me. Warmth spreads through my body as he slowly rakes his gaze over every exposed inch of skin, I feel gooseflesh begin to spread over me.

"Hmmm, jealousy looks good on you, Lay." I huff out my annoyance refusing to give him the satisfaction of answering as I step around and begin to pull the panties on under my towel. I admit they are fucking stunning. Purple lace with a low-cut front that just covers my pussy. Turning my back to Knox I drop the towel as I slip the bralette on, the cups so low they only cover my nipples, sometimes having big tits is a fucking curse because you can never find a decent fitting bra. I reach out to clasp the back but gasp when Knox knocks my hands away.

"What are you doing?" I breathe out. When his knuckles brush along my back, I shiver, my breathing accelerates and I close my eyes as I try to calm myself. He finally secures the clasp. I wait for him to retreat only he doesn't, he grips my waist possessively and leans down so his lips brush against the shell of my ear, sending tingles through my body and has my core clenching with need.

"Mary picked out the clothes but make no mistake, Lakeland, I am the only one who gets to pick what touches that perfect little cunt." My eyes pop open and I gasp when he reaches around and cups my pussy. He wraps his arm around me, anchoring me to his front as he applies enough pressure to my clit that has me arching into his touch. Darting his tongue out, he licks the shell of my ear, unwilling to fight this pull toward him any longer I tilt my head to the side and offer him my neck. He growls his approval as he skims his lips along my sensitive skin and sucks it into his mouth.

"Hmmm." The feeling of him sucking on my neck and the pressure against my clit has me needy and feigning for his touch. The ache he has roused to life between my thighs is agonizing. "Knox." I moan his name as he releases my neck, I know there is going to be a hickey there but I can't bring myself to care. I would rather him brand me this way then choke me again just so he could see his mark on my skin.

"What do you need, kitten?" he purrs, sending a wave of arousal through me.

"I... I... want..." I clamp my mouth closed feeling suddenly unsure. He says he knows me but I can't say the same back, only my body seems to reject the notion that I have no idea who he is. My mind screams that this is wrong but my body is overriding my senses and telling me without words that Knox is familiar and will keep me safe.

"You want me to touch you, then you're gonna have to say the words, Lay." His husky tone has another shiver shooting down my spine. He slides a finger along the lace covering my pussy, teasing me. His other hand reaches up and cups my breast through the lace. Suddenly he spins us to the side and I balk at the sight of a mirror I didn't know was hanging there. It's a floor-length one. I drink in the sight of Knox's hands on me and the possessive look in his eyes. It's that look that bolsters my confidence to tell him what I *need*.

"I want you to make me come." A smirk tugs at the corners of his mouth but I'm not done. "This time, I want you to be gentle," I whisper, his eyes spark.

"I promise to be gentle if you promise not to rip my stitches open?" My eyes widen, for a split second I forgot all about stabbing him. Suddenly being this vulnerable in his arms has fear slowly rising inside me.

"Knox, I didn't—" The words die on my tongue when he pushes my panties to the side and slides a finger through my slick folds, pulling a sharp cry from me.

"You make another sound and I stop." My jaw unhinges as I gape at him in the mirror. "You take that as your punishment for stabbing me and jumping out a fucking window *or...*" I brace myself for the other option knowing it will be a dreadful one. "I can bend you over that bed," I gasp as he begins to circle my clit while he speaks, "peel these cock-teasing panties down your legs," a moan tumbles from my lips as he pushes a single finger inside my greedy little cunt, "part those perky fucking cheeks of yours and eat your ass—"

"Oh fuck," I moan as he curves his finger inside me, hitting that sweet spot.

"Before I sink my cock into it." I shake my head trying to form words but I can't concentrate thanks to him fingering my pussy so fucking good that I can already feel my orgasm building. He pinches my nipple through my bra and I bite down on my lip to remain silent. "You love it when I fuck your ass, you told me you come so hard that you almost black out each time. You want me to remind you what that feels like, baby?" My mouth parts on a silent gasp as he slips another finger inside me, I meet his gaze in the mirror. The hunger I see in his eyes has me debating if I should make a sound just so I can pretend I broke the rules and force him to carry out his threat, rather than admitting to the fact I want to know what it feels like to have his thick cock slamming into my ass while I bite down on the pillows on the bed to keep my screams from reaching the ears of his men.

A shudder rolls through as I feel my orgasm cresting ready to tear through me only for Knox to pull his fingers free. I watch with rapt fascination as he brings those fingers that were just inside me to his mouth. He holds my lustful stare as he sucks them clean, moaning at the taste of me. He pulls his fingers free before pushing them inside me again. I moan, unable to remain silent. He smirks knowingly before pulling them free again but this time, he brings them to my lips.

"Open up, kitten." The husky tone of his voice has need pulsing in my core, obeying him without complaint and completely surrendering to his demands knowing without an ounce of doubt that Knox won't hurt me. It's so strange to not know someone only to trust them completely because of a feeling in the pit of your gut. He slips his fingers inside my mouth. Wrapping my lips around them, I moan as the taste of my own arousal. He draws his fingers almost all the way out before pushing them back in, his eyes darken when I swirl my tongue around them. "Fuck, time for your punishment." Rather than feeling terror at the thought of him punishing me I feel buzzed, slightly drunk off the lust thrumming through me. He turns us in a swift movement and pushes me until I'm sitting on the edge of the bed.

I watch with rapt interest as he grabs the black stockings beside the white cashmere knitted dress and kneels before me, slipping them on. I start to think he has changed his mind and plans to leave me on edge as my punishment, until he slips the black heels I didn't see earlier onto my feet, he grabs my hand and pulls me to my feet. I stare up at him in anticipation, he cups my face and leans down capturing my lips. I open for him without a fight and allow myself to get lost in the taste of him and the feeling of his hard, muscled body pressing against mine. He thrusts his hips softly and I gasp into his mouth at the feeling of his hard cock. He breaks the kiss and peers down at me with a sinful look in his eyes that has me shivering. Grabbing my hand, he leads me around to the other side of the bed and pushes me forward, my feet remaining planted on the ground with my ass in the air.

"Look ahead." I lift my gaze and gasp, he wants me to watch him in the mirror as he fucks me. His hands run along my spine teasingly. When he reaches my ass he groans and bites his bottom lip as he grips my cheeks. "Fuck, I love this ass. I've always loved fucking your ass while you wear heels, Lay, it gets me so fucking hard seeing you like this again." His words have another rush of heat pulsing through me, I can feel my pussy dripping. I'm proven right when I clench my thighs to relieve the ache pulsing inside me to find my inner thighs slick with my own need. "You ready for your punishment?" I meet his gaze in the mirror and nod. His eyes narrow and before I ask what's wrong, he lands a swift slap to my ass. I jolt forward and gasp.

"Knox—" He lands another smack to my other cheek. "What the fuck—" I'm cut off again as he lands another two smacks to each cheek—I'm horrified at the fact I'm enjoying it! When my shocked gaze collides with his, a cocky smirk is present on his handsome face.

"*Yes, Sir,* that is what you say. Am I clear?"

Heat like I have never felt before radiates through me as desire overshadows every other thought in my mind.

"Yes, Sir." My voice is breathy to my own ears and the smile that tugs at the corner of his mouth is all I need to see to know he's pleased with me. He loves the fact I am so turned on and pulsing with need for *him*.

"Good girl." A dull ache begins at the base of my skull hearing those two words, making a frown crease my face. Knox must notice because suddenly the towel wrapped around my hair is yanked off and tossed to the side before his fingers tangle in the strands and he gives it a tug. Unlike the times before, he doesn't do this to hurt me, he does this to distract me and keep me focused. "Repeat to me what your punishment is going to be?"

I try to recall what he said earlier but the moment he glides his finger down the crease of my ass to my pussy my thoughts turn to mush as I moan. That was clearly the wrong thing because he releases my hair and slaps my ass, jolting me out of my lustful haze.

"You want to be on your knees?" he growls.

I swallow audibly and shake my head. "No, Sir." His eyes spark with pride at my words.

"Start relaying the terms of your punishment or I stop stroking this dripping cunt and leave you on edge as you meet my mother." His words don't register as he pushes my panties to the side and slips a finger inside my greedy pussy.

"Y-you're going to bend—fuck!" I cry out as he hits that G-spot and before he can stop I quickly push on. "You're going to bend me over the bed, pull my panties down, eat my ass then push that glorious cock inside it inch by fucking inch until I come so hard I nearly pass out, Sir." The second I finish speaking he withdraws his finger from inside me. I whimper at the loss but he silences me with another slap to my ass, only this time I moan.

"You're my dirty little girl, aren't you, Lay?" he purrs as he drops to his knees behind me, gripping my panties and pulling them down my legs. The appreciative hum that comes from him at the sight of my wet pussy has me feeling emboldened. I've felt so unattractive since the accident because of the scars that cover my body, but somehow Knox makes me feel like they aren't even there, they don't deter him from seeing me beneath them. He tosses my panties onto the bed beside me. "You're panties are fucking ruined," he growls. "Put them in your mouth." I open my mouth to protest but he continues before I have the chance. "That's the punishment for your greedy cunt ruining the gift I chose for you." His dirty words send a bolt of need to my core. Reaching over, I gather my soaked panties and shove them in my mouth. I moan at the taste of my own need. Knox shifts to the side so he can see me in the mirror. "Fuck, Lakeland, you're perfect."

My eyes widen at his praise but I don't get a chance to ponder his words before he's gripping my cheeks and parting them. I moan around the panties as he licks from my clit to my forbidden hole. I want to shift away and do what any self-respecting woman would do and forbid him from poking his tongue there but... I can't. The feeling of his tongue lapping at me has wanton moans falling from my lips. When he pushes his tongue inside my ass, I cry out and jerk forward. All that gets me is another two slaps to my ass before he's tugging me back onto his waiting tongue. Jesus Christ, never in a million years could I imagine having your ass eaten would feel this fucking good. Without me realizing it, I've reached back and gripped his hair holding him in place as I push back against his tongue needing him deeper inside me.

He tears free of my hold and I growl at the loss. He climbs to his feet behind me, smirking. "Don't fucking move." I stay exactly where I am and watch as he moves to the other side of the bed and pulls the drawer on the bed-side table open. My eyes snap wide at the sight of a purple vibrator in his hand. He says nothing as he makes his way back to me. I watch him through the mirror as he lays the vibrator beside me on the bed, then yanks his shirt over his head, exposing all those glorious tattoos that cover him. He pops the button on his jeans and reaches for the zipper but when he meets my gaze in the mirror he tuts me and shakes his head. "Nah, baby, you don't get the pleasure of seeing my cock. After what you did last time we fucked, you only get what I allow." A shocking ripple of anger shoots through me at him denying me the pleasure of seeing his cock. Stepping behind me he kicks my legs further apart, distracting me from my anger.

He grabs the vibrator and runs it through my folds teasing me, I moan and buck my hips trying to gain friction but he doesn't allow it. "Ahhhh," I shout out around the panties in my mouth in anger. The bastard chuckles, knowing exactly what he is doing to me.

"I'm going to put this in your pussy, then I'm going to sink my cock into this perfect ass. You don't come until I say you can." I nearly choke on the fucking panties as I gape at him through the mirror. "You come without permission and you'll be on your knees for the next two weeks." I can see the horror in my own features. "Isn't it funny, you hated me for turning your body against you and now look, you're acting like a spoiled toddler who is about to lose their favorite toy." I want to scream and shout at the heavy-handed fucker, but all protests die when he pushes the vibrator inside my pussy. I cry out. The panties do nothing at all to quiet my scream. When he finally pushes it all the way inside, I know without a doubt that he loves the fact all those men on the other side of that door can hear me scream, he wants them to know exactly what he is doing to me.

My stomach knots with nerves when he rids himself of his jeans. He rubs the globes of my ass, trying to soothe me, it helps a little but not much.

"Relax, baby," he coos. I try to take a deep breath but it's only possible to breathe through my nose. "I'm going to switch the vibrator on, it will distract you from me sliding inside this perfect ripe ass."

Chapter Twenty-Two

Knox

I turn the vibrator on and immediately she begins to tremble and moan. I use that distraction and push her cheeks apart and spit on her asshole. I feel her eyes on me the entire time I swirl my spit around her hole before spitting in my own hand and rubbing it along my cock.

"Hmmm," she moans. I shoot her a glare of warning not to come. Her features tighten as I push the head of my cock against her hole. She tries to tense but the vibrator does its job and distracts her. I didn't plan to fuck her but the sight of her in those panties changed my mind. I push inside her slowly making sure to pause to give her time to adjust. My grip on her hips tighten when she jolts forward as I push further inside. I grit my teeth and continue to ease inside her, it's so fucking tight. Fuck, I can't go slow. I slam the rest of the way inside her. She screams out around the panties in her mouth and I hate that I see tears in her eyes.

I remain still giving her a chance to adjust. She tries to say something but I can't make out what it is so I yank the panties out.

"What?" I grit out through clenched teeth.

"I feel so full," she moans, my eyes blaze with approval.

"Hold on, baby." She fists the blankets in her hands as I draw almost all the way out of her before slamming back inside, the ear piercing scream that rips out of her is so loud I know everyone would have heard. The possessive fucker inside me wants to do it again just so no one can mistake that she is screaming because I'm fucking her so good. So, I do it again loving how she takes my cock. After the fourth thrust, she begins to push back against me, needing me to fuck her harder. "I thought you wanted gentle?" I taunt. She shoots me a scathing look in the mirror.

"You gonna punish me and fuck me like you mean it or you gonna be gentle and reward me?" Her smart mouth has me growling, my hold on her turning punishing for a second before I reach around her and click the button on the vibrator, turning it to full speed. She cries out and slams her eyes closed trying to ward off her impending orgasm. "Oh shit, please, Knox—"

"You fucking come and you will regret it," I snarl as I grip her waist and slam into her like a ruthless bastard. I ignore her pleas as I get lost in the feeling of finally claiming her ass again after so many years. When she reaches down to pull the vibrator out, I smack her hand away. "Take it like a good fucking girl, baby, you get to come when I fill this ass up, not before." She bites down on her bottom lip and slams her eyes closed. Her features are pained as she tries to fight against her need to come.

"Fuck, it's too much, Knox. I can't take it," she cries out. I feel my balls tightening, I'm so close. Gripping the back of her neck I pull her to me, shifting my hold so my hand is wrapped around her throat, forcing her to watch as I pound into her. I reach around and pinch her clit between my fingers. "Come." She throws her head back against my shoulder as she screams out her release, tremors tearing through her tiny body. I bite down on her neck to silence myself as I thrust inside her one last time. I come so fucking hard I almost see stars. I hold her against me as she continues to jolt and whimper, then release her clit and ease the vibrator from inside her. A whoosh of air escapes her the moment she is free of it. I gently push her forward as I slowly ease out of her. She flops on the bed clearly exhausted but I'm not about to let her sleep. She needs to shower and get cleaned up, I can't take her back to my mom with my cum dripping out of her ass.

"Up, you need to shower and to get changed before we land."

"Go away," she mumbles sleepily.

"Get your ass up before I fuck it again and you get to meet my mom with a double cream pie dripping out of you." Her eyes snap open and she bolts upright, standing before me with a shocked look on her face.

"Your mom?" she squeaks.

"Shower, now," I say as I push her toward the bathroom and close the door behind her. That fucking shower is too small to fit me in it so I quickly dress while I wait for Lake. I smirk at the sight of her panties on the bed. Mary got her a sweater dress thing so she will be meeting my mom without panties, that thought has a laugh bubbling out of me. Lakeland is going to be pissed.

Lakeland still refuses to meet my gaze. Since the moment she stepped out of the shower and changed, realizing only then that her panties were ruined, she has been silently fuming. When I grabbed her hand and dragged her out of the room back to our seats, she was red faced and refused to look at anyone or even speak to Taylan when he tried to tease her about what happened in that room. As soon as the plane landed, she leapt to her feet and shoved me away when I tried to grab her and stormed off the plane like an angry pint-sized fairy.

I can feel the anger wafting off her as she sits with her arms crossed over her chest in the passenger seat. Xander was pissed to find her riding shotgun when we got off the plane. Taylan, the bastard shoved us both out of the way so he could drive. I keep sneaking glances at her before switching back to glaring at Taylan in the rearview mirror.

"Doesn't it feel good to be home?" Taylan singsongs, the cheery lilt to his voice grates on my nerves, he's only doing this to fuck with me. Any other time I would brush it off and just deal with his bullshit, but him using Lakeland to get at me is starting to get real fucking old real fast. I watch as Lake's jaw locks before she turns and focuses her glare out the window. I want to laugh but I refrain, it's not my fault her pussy was so fucking wet she ruined her panties.

"Shut up, Taylan, and drive," Xan says sharply.

"Calm down, dick, unlike you grumpy fuckers I'm actually glad to finally be home and being able to sleep in my own bed." Now that he mentions it, sleeping in my own bed would be fucking amazing. "Plus, I can't wait for Mom to see Lake. It's been years since—"

"Shut the fuck up, Taylan." My voice booms throughout the car. He wisely shuts his fucking trap and continues to drive. I'm already on edge after hearing from Patrick and Cohen that my house was raided. We've had to fly back under the fucking cover of nightfall so we don't get seen by the local cops or worse the fucking CSIS. The drive home is spent with me texting orders to each of my head guys to meet me first thing in the morning so we can form a plan. I pulled Mase off of tailing Christiano and told him to be back at my house in the morning. It's not just taking out Percy and Gio that has me in a mood, it's the manila envelope I have stashed inside my jacket pocket that is driving me insane.

Open it.

Don't do it.

It's the only way to know for sure.

Those fucking thoughts have been taunting me for hours, the only time they weren't was when I was buried balls deep inside Lakeland's ass. That's it, once we get home I just need to fuck her again until I pass out or make a fucking decision! I finally manage to get out of my own head when we pull up to the front of the house. Stepping out of the car, I look around checking to make sure the men are actively patrolling the grounds. I may have men stationed around my borders and keeping their eyes peeled for any sign of Dario soldiers and Percy, but I also need men stationed around my house so I know my mother will always be safe, especially after what happened to Sophie and Laura. Xander doesn't wait for us as he makes his way inside. Taylan steps up beside me.

"She won't get out of the car," he mutters before following Xan. Scrubbing a hand down my face in annoyance, I move around the car and pull her door open. She sits there with her arms and legs crossed, glaring out the windshield. I lean against the door and wait. It takes her two minutes before she begins to squirm under the pressure of my gaze and another minute before she finally huffs and turns to me.

"Not gonna drag me inside by my hair and force me to my knees so I can meet your mother?" Pushing off the door I get right in her face. She presses further into her seat to try to get away from me but I just move in closer.

"You're angry because you learned your daddy is a manipulative cunt and I get it. I also get you're all shy and shit because I had my cock buried in your ass hours ago." Her jaw unhinges but I push on. "I also get you're mad because Mary wasn't some young blonde slut who rides my dick on nights I get lonely." Her eyes spit fire but I ignore her jealous bullshit. I told her who Mary was before we landed—

she is my fifty-seven-year-old personal shopper. "But what I won't allow or even let slide is you disrespecting my mother." My tone is ice fucking cold. "You may be telling the truth about not remembering shit about me or your life, but that woman in that fucking house remembers *you!*"

She searches my eyes for any sign of deceit. "I knew her?" she whispers, confusion and annoyance at the fact she can't recall shit is plastered all over her features.

A tired sigh escapes me as I reach across and unclip her seatbelt before gripping her legs and turning her to the side so I can nestle my way in between them. Shockingly, she doesn't fight me.

"Yes. You both spent a lot of time together. You grew to love her and enjoyed spending time with her because it reminded you of your time with your own mother." Tears spring to her eyes but she doesn't allow them to fall. "I'm a heartless cunt, I know." She snorts, earning a scowl from me. "My mother is the opposite and believe it or not, Lakeland, that woman has been fighting for you for years. The reports told us you were drunk that night—" She reels back, shaking her head.

"I can't stand the taste of alcohol," she defends.

"I don't have time to go down memory lane with you. Now you can either hold my hand as I reintroduce you to my mother or I can throw you over my shoulder so she can see your pussy first before seeing your face." Her cheeks burn a bright shade of red. She tries to shove me back but I push her arms down as I grip the back of her neck and pull her to me, slanting my lips over hers. She moans into my mouth and shuffles forward, wrapping her legs around me. Fuck, as much I would love to fuck her right here, right now, I won't allow any of my men to see her like that. I am the only one who gets to see her face as she comes, that is the promise she made me years ago and I refuse to allow her to break it even if she doesn't remember.

Chapter Twenty-Three

Lakeland

Knox keeps my hand clasped in his as he leads me inside the mansion, it's stunning. Marble floors, high ceilings with wooden beams displayed, a grand staircase in the foyer, and paintings of landscapes adorn the walls.

"In here," a woman calls out. Knox sighs before leading me toward the sound of voices. As we enter, I notice it's a large kitchen. It's huge! Stone countertops, stainless steel appliances but it's the sight of the plants littered throughout the space that has me gasping and tearing my hand from Knox's as I spin around taking in the greenery. I love plants. I always have but Dad never allowed me to have any inside our home. He said it looked tacky and distasteful. "Lake." I spin around at the sound of my name and come face to face with a gorgeous woman. She wears a blush-pink silk blouse and black, boot leg slacks, her brown hair is loose around her shoulders but it's the warm smile on her face that holds me captive as I flick my eyes to hers and gasp—hazel colored eyes!

Those eyes have pain exploding in the back of my head, I stumble backward and groan in pain as I clutch my head.

"Knox is just salty I got Mom's eye color and his resembles the color of a dying tree." She laughs when I shove her shoulder.

"Your brother's eye color is stunning, Wave. Don't be mean." Her hazel eyes spark with disgust.

"I think I threw up in my mouth."

Gasping, I bolt upright and try to catch my breath as panic threads through my veins, that was a memory!

"Are you okay?" I shriek in fright and jerk backward. I look around to find I'm in a bedroom and currently sitting on a bed while Knox stands at the edge peering down at me.

"Your eyes are the color of a dying tree." All traces of worry from a second ago vanish as his features harden. I don't want him to be angry. I can't take it, so I ignore the resounding pain in my head and push to my knees, shuffling closer to the edge. He stands there stiff and without an ounce of emotion present on his face as I reach out and wrap my arms around his neck in a bold move, hoping he won't push me away. "I... I think I had a flashback," I say quietly. I hope it was because if that is what these strange flashback things are, then that means I'm slowly starting to remember.

"My sister always said that about my eye color. How did you... know?" His tone is firm. I bite the corner of my mouth trying to think of the right words to explain it. He reaches up and uses his thumb to pry my lip loose, his simple touch has a fire swirling in my belly.

"I think I had a memory or flashback or whatever you want to call it of me and your... sister." I can see him struggling with his emotions. He wants to scream at me and blame me for her loss but another part of him, the part that claims to have known and loved me years ago, won't allow him to push me away. "She was teasing you about your eye color and I told her your eyes are stunning." He quirks a brow. I feel heat creep into my cheeks. "She gagged and then I woke up." Silence stretches, I try to keep my mind from drifting and thinking he will hurt me. But, given how we met and the way he handled me, I fear he may fall back into those habits. I see now, mentioning anything from the past especially, anything to do with his sister is a very sore subject. Suddenly his hands grip my waist and without warning he leans down and ghosts his lips over mine. This moment feels... strange. Our eyes are locked, our breath is mingling but it is the raw emotion I see in his gaze that has me stilling with bated breath to see what he does next.

"I don't want to think, when I do it doesn't end well for you." Sucking in a sharp breath I nod grazing his lips with my own. "I'm going to fuck you until I can't think anymore." He doesn't wait for a reply or permission, he seals his lips to mine taking what he desires from me without asking, he doesn't need to because he and I both know I will give in. It's strange to not know him from Adam and yet my body responds to him like a dog obeying its master. He uses his weight to force me back flat onto the bed as he nestles himself between my legs without breaking the kiss. My fingers slide through the strands of his hair. I gasp into his mouth when he grinds against me.

He grips the hem of my dress and pulls it up, exposing my bare pussy before reaching between us and making quick work of freeing his cock from the confines of his jeans. Unlike on the plane, there is no build up, no teasing or fore-play, just carnal need. He lines his cock up with my entrance. Breaking the kiss for the first time, he cups my cheeks as he eases inside me inch by delicious inch, watching me the entire time as if he is documenting every sound and shift in my features to his memory. This moment feels so inti-mate. I feel tears pricking the backs of my eyes as he stares down at me with such an intense look of longing in his green eyes.

"I want everything from you, Lakeland," he growls as he draws out of me until only the tip remains inside before slamming back inside, drawing a sharp cry from me as my back arches off the bed. He latches onto the exposed skin on my neck, sucking the flesh into his mouth, marking me as his again. Gripping his hair, I hold him there as I lock my legs around his waist so I can take him deeper.

"Give me all of you, Knox," I rasp out, pulling back and bracing his hands on either side of my head as he stares down at me.

"You have no idea what you are asking for."

Gripping the front of his shirt in my hands, I pull him to me until there is just a sliver of space between us. "You want me to give you everything, then I need you to do the same.

Help me remember *your* Lakeland." His mouth parts in a silent gasp as his eyes fill with pain before he quickly masks it and silences me with a kiss. Any argument I may have had evaporates as he continues to move inside me. Suddenly this doesn't just feel like sex or him fucking me to prove that he can do this... it's more. He's showing me without words that I meant something to him—still do. Unlike every other orgasm he has given me, this one doesn't tear me apart, this one crests slowly and washes over me like a warm embrace. I'm a panting mess beneath him and slowly blink my eyes open to find him still gazing down at me. There is something empowering about looking him in the eyes as he comes with my name on his lips.

"You've always had me," he murmurs as he pulls out of me. I expect him to leave after that declaration and even prepare myself for his exit, then he drops down beside me and wraps me in his arms, pulling me close. Neither of us utters a word as we slowly come down from our highs. I can feel him slowly leaking out of me and coating my inner thighs with his cum.

"Knox, I need to clean up." Rather than letting me go, he just chuckles and pushes me onto my back and bends his elbow, resting his chin in his hand as his other one skates down my body leaving gooseflesh in its wake. As he reaches my pussy, I stiffen. "What are you doing?" I breathe out as he runs a finger through my folds and pushes that finger inside me and draws it out, bringing it to my lips.

"Suck it." Heat blooms inside my belly as a dark depraved beast awakens inside me. Never would I have ever thought I would beg to have my ass eaten or fucked but I did, now the thought of tasting both our cum has me opening my mouth and sucking his fingers clean while moaning. Without being prompted to, I reach between my legs and circle my clit, moaning around his finger. His brows bunch for a second until he flicks his gaze down and sees what I'm doing. Heat blooms in his eyes as he tears his finger free and leaps off the bed. "Turn around, head over the edge of the bed, now." The gravelly tone of his voice has excitement thrumming through me. "Lose the fucking dress," he also growls. I do as he says and reach for my bra but he shakes his head. "That stays, you're going to be punished for touching what doesn't belong to you."

My jaw unhinges. "Seriously?" I squeak.

His eyes darken as he strikes out and grips the back of my head, tangling his fingers through my hair, dragging me forward and positioning me how he wants me. My neck balances on the edge of the bed. Releasing his hold on me, he undresses but my eyes are glued to his cock that is still glistening with both our releases. He peers down at me while gripping his cock. I dart my tongue out, needing to taste him.

"Open your legs and show me that cunt." I eagerly obey him and can't even find it within myself to be ashamed of how fucking wet I am. His stance widens as he steps forward, forcing me back, his balls resting on my chin. "Open your mouth and suck them." Opening my mouth I tease him and dart my tongue out tasting him. He jerks forward and growls. "Sneaky bitch," he snarls. I cry out when he smacks my pussy.

"Knox!" I scold but he delivers another two smacks. I shiver and fight the urge to clench my thighs together for some friction.

"Suck them!" Doing as he demanded, I reach out and grip the globes of his toned ass and force him lower as I suck his balls gently. "Fuck, swirl your tongue," he snaps. I obey without complaint, loving the taste of him as the salty taste of his cum covers them. Moaning at the taste, I suck him harder, loving the strangled groan that comes from him. Just as I start to enjoy myself, he shifts and crouches down beside my head, then grips my throat as he leans in close. "I'm strong because I have been weak. I'm fearless because I've been afraid. I am wise because I have been foolish. I won't make the same mistake twice." I try to sit up but his grip on my throat keeps me in place, my head spinning slightly from this angle.

"I don't understand," I say honestly.

"I was weak six years ago, then I became strong. I was afraid of losing anyone else I loved, I'm not now because I'm strong enough to protect them. I'm wiser and smarter now because I will never be foolish again. Don't make me break those vows."

"I would never," I say still slightly confused.

"You make me weak because I need you. You bring fear to life because I won't survive losing you again. You make me foolish because I can't seem to stay away from you when I know I should until I know the truth." His raw honesty stumps me for a moment until I gather my thoughts.

"Women love what they hear and men love what they

see, that's why women wear makeup and men lie. I don't wear makeup, Knox. I'm not hiding anything... willingly and I believe you aren't lying to me. We aren't like everyone else. Don't let the fear of striking out keep you from playing the game. Believe me when I tell you that I am in this with you, I want to know the truth as much as you do." He releases his hold on me and stands. I can see in his eyes he is going to leave so I do the only thing I can, I scramble off the bed and drop to my knees before him.

"Lakeland—" Before he can finish pushing me away, I grip his length as I wrap my lips around the head of his cock, making sure to keep my eyes locked on his as I swallow as much of him as I can. His mouth opens and a groan slips free. I bob up and down on his cock, stroking the base with my hand. "You fool me again, Lake, and I will slit your fucking throat myself and bathe in your blood," he warns before his hand delves into my hair. Holding me in place, he begins to thrust his hips, forcing me to drop my hand back to my side. "Play with that greedy cunt while you choke on my cock."

I almost weep in gratitude. Pushing my knees apart, I plunge two fingers inside my drenched pussy, moaning. He groans as the vibrations travel up his cock. I finger fuck my greedy little cunt in rhythm with his thrusts. He may be the one setting the pace but in this moment, I am the one with all the power. I hold the key to bring him to the greatest of highs. Spit trails down my chin as I gag around him but the sight just seems to spur him on. I love the unhinged look in his eyes and the way his lip is pulled back in a snarl—he looks like a fucking nightmare, *my* nightmare come true.

"Fuck, baby, I'm gonna come." I quicken my pace as I ride my fingers. He throws his head back and groans so loud it reminds me of a grizzly bear. I feel his cum slide down the back of my throat and savor the taste of him just as my own orgasm begins to crest. Knox pulls his cock free and drops to his knees in front of me, he grips my hand and yanks it free as I whimper. He replaces my fingers with his own and my eyes roll back as he grips my throat, forcing my head back so he claims my lips in a kiss of ownership.

""Knox... God," I cry out, breaking the kiss.

"Who's your fucking God, Lay?" he snarls.

His eyes darken and I know if I don't answer correctly he'll pull his fingers free and leave me here on edge. Being bold, I reach out and grip the hair on the back of his head, pulling him in closer. "You are." His eyes blaze with approval. "Now make me come on your fingers so I can ride your cock." A sexy smirk tugs at his lips. Pressing the pad of his thumb flat against my clit, I cry out as the orgasm rips through me without warning. I scream his name as I ride this fucking high like there is no tomorrow. We may have a fucked-up history that only one of us can remember but that doesn't diminish the chemistry or sexual tension that is constantly present when we are near each other. Knox Bronson is the ring around my Saturn and I can't find it within myself to be pissed about that.

Chapter Twenty-Four

Knox

I've created a monster... Again.

Don't get me wrong, I'm not complaining about Lake being a freak in the sheets, she was never one to be shy about voicing what she wanted. She was never fucking tame when it concerned sex, always wanting to fight for dominance until I would force her to submit and show her that giving me control didn't make her weak, it just meant she trusted me to care for her and give her the ecstasy she craved, that only my cock could deliver.

It's been years since I have woken and felt utterly fucking wrecked in the best possible way. Looking to the space beside me, where she has her face buried in the pillows and the blanket bunched around her waist, I bite my lip, debating if I should sink into her and wake her with another orgasm. I shift ready to do just that until my phone begins to vibrate on the nightstand beside me. Fighting back the urge to groan, I reach for the fucking thing to see Xander's name blaring on the screen. I hit answer and bring it to my ear as I make my way to my bathroom and close the door quietly behind me.

"Yeah?" I bite out.

"Mase is here, you were supposed to be down here first thing to brief the fucking guys." The anger in his tone brushes me the wrong fucking way.

"You got something you want to say to me?" I snarl.

"Yeah. Pull your head out of that bitch's pussy long enough to realize she's playing you." The motherfucker ends the call before I can say anything else. It takes me showering, changing and staring at Lake's naked back for five minutes to calm down enough to go downstairs and not murder my best friend. Stealing a final glance at her, I put my poker face in place and clear my head of all thoughts of her, until I grab my jacket off the back of the chair in the corner and the manila envelope drops to the floor.

Knox Bronson.

My name on the front taunts me as I stare down at it, reading what's inside could change everything and rid me of all this anger I feel toward Lake, or it could solidify her future by holding the documents I have already read years ago which would guarantee her death by my hands.

"Hey," she says sleepily. I turn around and take a long hard look at the girl that believed in me when no one else did. She didn't see me as the poor kid from the wrong side of the tracks, she just saw me and always said I was worthy and would make something of myself. The longer I take to answer, the happy look in her eyes slowly fades. Reaching down, I snag the envelope and make my way over to her and drop down onto the edge of the bed. She gathers the blankets and draws them up to shield her nakedness from me. I say nothing and allow her to act like I didn't fuck her seven ways to hell all night long.

"I met you when you were thirteen," I say as I look down at the fucking stupid envelope in my hands. "By the time you were fourteen I had a crush on you when I had no fucking right to. You were River's little sister but that wasn't the reason I stayed away."

"Why did you then?" she asks quietly.

A sad smile makes its way to my face. "Because you were my sister's best friend and Wave made it crystal fucking clear you were off limits to all us degenerates." A quiet laugh leaves her, earning a scowl from me which she ignores. "At fifteen you made it known you felt the same way about me but my sister threatened to cut my balls off if I touched you, she said I had to wait until you were sixteen."

"You waited, didn't you?" I slowly turn to meet her gaze to find no malice or disgust in her eyes, just pure innocence.

"I counted down those 365 days, hating each day when time moved slowly. On your sixteenth birthday I told River she had to deal with me loving you because I was done waiting and watching you from a distance." Her eyes are wide and filled with unshed tears. "I went to my sister to tell her I was claiming you and it didn't matter what she said, I was prepared to fight her if it came down to it." Sadness laces each of my words.

"What happened?" she asks barely above a whisper, her grip on the blanket is so tight her knuckles begin to turn white.

"I didn't get a chance to utter a single word, she told me she was proud of me for proving that I was worthy of you by waiting out the year for you to turn sixteen." I toss the envelope onto her lap and stand turning my back to her. I can't look at her, it's too fucking hard. "The contents inside are the truth about what happened six years ago, do with it what you want." I make my way to the door, needing to get the fuck out of here and clear my head but the sound of her voice has me freezing with my hand on the door knob.

"I thought this is what you wanted? You said you had to know the truth, and now you have it you don't want it?" She's confused and I get it. My own head is fucked up. I keep my back to her as I answer.

"After last night, I think I made it clear it doesn't matter what you do to me because I'll always come back to you. I should have been more careful about who I trusted but salt and sugar look the same just like how you look like *my* Lake but you don't have my Lake's memories or heart." I laugh but there is no humor to it. "You may not have her heart or mind but my own fucking heart doesn't seem to care, so do what you want with the information inside there. If you plan to take me down just do me a favor and spare my mom, Taylan and Xander." I slip out the door and close it behind me. I give myself a solid minute to get my shit straight before I make my way downstairs to get my men sorted into position.

"That doesn't work!" Cohen snaps at Floyd.

"Then what the fuck do you suggest because no one can find Gio's brother, no one even knows what the fucker looks like," Stu shouts. I scrub a hand down my face and slouch back in my chair. We have been at this for fucking hours. All my captains are here and so are Xander and Taylan, the latter trying to help but Xander has just been sitting there glaring at me and I'm about to pound the fuckers face in soon.

"Mase, you were tracking him, what does he look like?" Patrick asks. Mase opens his mouth, then snaps it closed twice before he finally manages to speak.

"I actually didn't see his face." Chaos erupts, they all begin shouting and blaming each other for us not being able to find Gio and Percy but I can't deal with this shit any longer.

"Shut the fuck up!" I roar. The bickering instantly stops at my outburst, all bowing their heads and claiming their seats. I reach into my desk drawer and pull out the folder on the Dario and Da Luca family, it's time I told the truth. I find the picture of Christiano and slap it on the edge of my desk so they can all see.

"He looks familiar," Patrick mutters and scrunches his face as he tries to recall why he thinks he looks familiar.

"I've heard whispers about some of the men thinking I was scared and that's why I didn't take Gio out years ago."

They each exchange a loaded look while Taylan and Xan stare at me in surprise. I haven't told anyone the truth about how I came to be the Don of the Re Della Strada formally known as the Da Luca family.

"We'll take care of it," Mase vows but I raise my hand stopping him. I should have come clean years ago but I was too jaded and angry. Taylan's words were what spurred my decision to give her the documents. If she has really lost her memories and my sister's death wasn't her fault I need her to know I choose her! She needs to know I will always fucking choose her without thought because make no mistake, Lakeland Deveraux is my person.

"Some of you worked for Roberto Da Luca." It wasn't meant as a snide remark but Stu and Cohen both drop their gazes. I gave each man a choice to follow me and prove they could be trusted or fall to their knees and eat a bullet. "Some of you think he chose me to lead before he was murdered. Some think I murdered him in cold blood while others assume I was chosen by the people as the new head of the family." I search through the file of the Da Luca family and pull the two papers I need out and place them on the edge of my desk. Stu grabs them and reads over each one before darting his shocked gaze at me before passing them to the others who each have the same look on their faces.

"Holy shit," Patrick mutters as he hands Tay the papers, who doesn't bother to glance at them before tossing them back onto my desk.

"As you can see from both mine and Waverly's birth certificates, Roberto Da Luca was our father and I did kill that motherfucker in cold blood and stole his empire out from underneath him before his body was even cold. Giovani only lives because he is Roberto's half-brother and my...Uncle. The night I shot Roberto in the back, Gio was there. We came to an agreement that he could take up in Quebec and live out his days there in peace so long as he never tried to rise against me."

"Did working with Percy break that deal?" Cohen asks. Blowing out a loud exhale, I continue on.

"I took Roberto out because he wouldn't have helped me take out the Deveraux family for killing my sister." All their eyes are wide, knowing there is a Deveraux under this very roof. "Well, that and learning my mother ran from him because he wanted my sister to turn tricks when she came of age." Disgust is present on every one of their faces. "Lakeland was promised to Roberto when she was seventeen, that deal was struck because Percy, the dirty cunt, found out Roberto was my father and wanted to punish Lakeland for falling for a street rat and that union would have made him a shit load of money, of course, I ruined that deal. For years we lived peacefully until Gio broke his end of the deal by agreeing to marry *my* girl—"

"Your girl?" Xander sneers. Pushing to my feet, I lay my hands flat on my desk as I bend forward, holding his gaze so he can see in my own eyes that if he continues to come after Lakeland that he and I will come to fucking blows.

"Yeah, my fucking girl. You got a problem with that?" His nostrils flare a second before he stands and mimics my stance, leaning in close to me.

"You forgot *your* girl is the one that killed *your* sister." I snap my arm out and grip his throat. Before he can fight back, I start pounding his face in with my other hand. I manage three solid punches before Taylan and the rest of the guys pull us apart. Xander and I continue to shout at each other, promising to kill each other.

"What the fuck is going on in here?" We both snap our mouths closed and turn toward the doorway where my mother stands, looking fucking livid but it's the sight of Lake standing beside her that captures my attention. My gaze drops to her hands and my breath lodges at the sight of the papers in her hand. I look back at her face and tense at the sight of the dried tear stains on her cheeks.

She may know the truth but I can see it in her eyes that she still doesn't remember who I am.

Chapter Twenty-Five

Lakeland

I stare at the closed door as his words continue to play over and over in my mind. I heard the truth as he spoke them. I could see it in his eyes how much he meant everything he said. It's so strange to hear how much he cares for me and loves me, while I know virtually nothing about him. The envelope in my lap draws my attention and I nibble on my lip, trying to decide what to do with it. I am dying to know what is inside it but I'm also scared to find out the truth.

"Ahhh," I groan as I toss the covers back and head into the bathroom to shower, giving myself some time to calm down and think clearly. After showering, I wrap a towel around my body and cringe at the sight of all the hickeys across the tops of my tits and collarbone. I turn my head to see two large ones on either side of my neck—those are going to be a bitch to try to hide. Resigned to the fact Knox is a possessive asshole and will continue to do what he wants, I pull the ensuite door open and enter the room only to slam to a halt at the sight of the woman with the pain-filled eyes sitting on the chair near the door.

She smiles warmly and some of the tension eases from me until I see her eyes land on the numerous love bites that mar my body from her son. I cringe. She tries not to smile at my clear embarrassment. "Knox asked me to bring you some clothes," she says, motioning toward the bed. I nod on auto pilot and snag them from the bed, then rush back into the bathroom to change. I roll my eyes at the sight of the red lingerie, knowing that it was all Knox. The jeans hug my curves perfectly. I pull the sweater style top over my head and groan, it's an off the shoulder top, leaving all the marks exposed. I pile my hair in a messy bun atop my head before steeling my spine and reentering the bedroom, only to cringe in shame at the sight of her making the bed.

"I can do that," I rush to say. She smiles and waves me off.

"It appears you have something that needs your attention." I frown, then she points to the manila envelope resting on the bedside table. The air whooshes out of me.

"I don't think I want to know what's inside there."

"The Da Luca family—now known as the Re Della Strada—rules are, all must tell the truth at all times, never be intimate with any family member, spouse or child of the family, never do any illicit drugs, never steal from the family and to never verbally, physically or emotionally hurt another member of the family." I scrunch my face in confusion. "I won't lie to you, I know you and my son have a past but I also know you are unaware of that past." Sadness laces her words.

"I'm sorry," I mutter. She pales before rushing around the bed to stand before me, grabbing my hands and holds them in hers.

"Lake, you have nothing to be sorry for, my dear. It hurts me to know that you don't remember how much you are loved." Unwarranted tears fill my eyes at her kind words. "Even if you don't recall who we are, we know exactly who you are and believe me, sweet girl, you are our family and we protect our own." My lip begins to tremble, it's been so long since I've been spoken to so lovingly.

"Thank you," I choke out. She smiles lovingly then wraps me in a hug that is filled with so much love. I slowly lift my arms and cling to her, breathing in her scent. She reminds me of my mom.

"I don't want to push you but you need to know the truth before my son goes to war against your father," she says as she draws back, resting her hands atop my shoulders.

"I know why—"

"You don't, sweet girl, there is so much Knox wouldn't have told you. He was so angry when he left to find you. I know my son is bossy—" I snort and mutter a quick sorry, she grins. "He blamed the wrong person for the pain he suffered years ago. Read those documents and put both your minds at rest. I hope knowing the truth will bring your souls back together because you and Knox, you two are meant to be." She steps back and smiles but I grab her hand halting her exit.

"W-will you stay with me while I... read them?" She smiles sadly and cups my cheek as she nods.

Sitting on the edge of the bed with Knox's mom by my side, I suddenly realize I don't know her name and feel slightly awkward asking her now, so I tear open the envelope and pull out the documents. There is a lot more in here than I originally thought but the sight of my name at the top catches my eye.

"That's your... hospital records." I nod my head, unable to form words. It takes me a minute to get my breathing under control and my mind right to finally start reading the written report from one of the doctors that treated me six years ago.

I have treated the patient for three weeks and clear signs of dissociative amnesia are present due to the trauma of the accident...

The papers slip from my hands, *amnesia*. It's written right there, clear as day for anyone to read but yet, in the past six years, no one has thought to fucking tell me that I am missing a huge part of my life that Knox was clearly a part of!

"It is my medical opinion that continued therapy would be in the best interest of the patient." I look to the side to see Knox's mother has gathered the papers and continues to read them for me. I'm grateful because I can't do it myself. "The doctor continues on to say that your father refused his medical opinion and said therapy is not an option for you as the events of that day are best left forgotten."

I clench my fists on my lap. "Who the hell gave him the right to make that decision on my behalf?" The anguish in my tone is clear, he robbed me of memories, *my* fucking memories!

"At the time you were seventeen so as your legal guardian he had the right to make all these calls on your behalf. I'm so sorry, sweet girl." I don't realize I have started crying until she swipes a tear from my cheek, her own eyes are filled with heartache for me.

"I don't understand, why would my father not want me to remember?" I whisper. She cups my cheek and smiles sadly.

"Your father never approved of you being with my son." At her revelation my mouth parts on a gasp. "He always thought Knox wasn't good enough and he tried to do every-thing in his power to make sure that you believed that." I shake my head denying what she says.

"I'm not shallow."

"I know that and so does my son. You never saw him as anything less than the boy who stole your heart. You always looked at him with stars in your eyes. The first time you called him and told him your father was sending you away, Knox lost his mind and drove to your house where he stole you away and brought you back to our house, promising he would never let you go. It was then I knew that my son had finally found someone for himself. He spent most of his life worrying about me and his sister and also trying to help Xan and Tay, but he never did anything for himself until the day you stumbled into our lives. You gave my son hope." Unable to deal with the information overload about Knox, I grab a paper from her hand and read the contents.

"Oh my God." Knox's mom tries to shift to get a better look at the paper but I quickly fold it and shove it into my pocket as I fight back tears. "I need to see Knox." Whatever she sees on my face and hears in my voice has her nodding and handing me the papers as she leads me from the room without protest. I numbly follow after her, trying to keep my tears at bay, I need to look Knox in the eyes as I ask him if he knew about this.

"What the fuck is going on here?" I shake my head and snap out of it as I look around the room and tense at the sight of men holding Knox and Xander apart. I look to Knox to find his gaze already on me. "I won't ask again," his mom snaps, breaking us out of it. He tears his gaze from mine but I can't seem to do the same. It's as if I'm seeing him in a whole new light, I realize now that all his anger toward me the first time he saw me was because he thought I left him, that I hurt him willingly. I may not have memories of our past together but now that I know for sure and have the proof that what he and my sister said is true, I will fight with everything I have to get them back.

"Knox is on his period and being extra sensitive," Xander snarls. Knox fights against the men holding him as he tries to get to Xander.

"Keep running your mouth, asshole, and I'll shut the

fucking thing for you." The venom that laces Knox's tone has me standing straighter.

"Enough." His mom scolds them as she shoots each of them a disapproving look that only a mother can muster. "You need to stop fighting and figure out what you are going to do next. You don't have the luxury of time now, thanks to Percy and Gio putting you to the media."

"I told you she was fucking trouble—" Xander roars but Knox cuts him off.

"You don't get a fucking say with anything to do with her, she is not up for discussion with any of you!" His protectiveness over me is astounding, I've never had someone fight for me like this before it's... strange and I'm loathe to admit that's it a fucking turn on.

"You're so blinded by her pussy you've forgotten about what really matters!" The hatred in how Xander speaks about me is clear and has me shrinking back a step. "You have been too distracted by her to notice Gio and Percy have slipped through our fingers, we can't even find Gio's fucking brother because you're—"

"What brother?" Knox's mom cuts in and asks. Knox and all the other men turn to her with confused looks on their faces.

"Christiano," Taylan says.

"Who?"

"Clara, are you trying to tell us you don't know about Gio's brother?" Clara, that's her name! It's such a beautiful name and fits her perfectly.

"Stu, the only brother Giovani Dario had is dead." At

her revelation, all the men in the room share loaded looks before they release their holds on Xander and Knox who creep in closer with Taylan.

"Mom, Gio has another brother?" I don't know if Knox meant to voice it as a question but that's the way it came out. Clara turns back and the remorseful look on her face stumps me.

"The papers you hold, my sweet girl, explain everything." I reel back feeling like a dog in a show ring with all the men's eyes on me.

"What?" I squeak.

"Those papers are about her, Mom," Knox says but Clara shakes her head.

"No, Son, there is some information in there that is for *you*." Knox and I stare at each other. I see untrust and worry in his gaze as my own emotions begin to spiral, did she see it before I could tuck it away in my pocket?

"What is she talking about, Lakeland?" The cold tone which he uses to address me has worry coiling inside me as I prepare myself for him to resort back to the old habits of hurting me.

"I don't know," I whisper. The space between us is eaten up in three strides as he gets right in my face. I back up, only for him to follow until I am pressed flat against the wall with his arms caging me in on either side of my head. A whimper escapes me.

"Don't fucking lie to me." His quietly spoken words have the same effect as if he had shouted them.

"I didn't know," I choke out. His face contorts into a mask of fury.

"Knox, she doesn't—"

"Stay out of this, Mom," he growls without taking his eyes off me. He grabs the back of my neck in a punishing hold and forces me to my tiptoes. "Tell me what the fuck she is talking about."

"Roberto is alive."

"I was pregnant," Clara and I both say at the same time.

Chapter Twenty-Six

Knox

Three words.

Three-fucking-words.

That's all it takes for me to drop my hold on her, snatch the papers out of her grasp and ignore everyone in the fucking room as I escape. I hear Xan and Tay shouting for me to come back but I don't listen, I want to get in my car and get as fucking far away from here as I can but I can't. Not with all the fucking pigs on the lookout for me. I head for my bedroom, slamming the door closed behind me. I pace the length of my room until I can calm myself enough—well, enough that I don't shred the papers in my hands. I rest my back against the far wall and slide down until my ass meets the hardwood floor. Ignoring the sounds of shouting from outside my room, I sift through the papers. The top ones are all Lakeland's medical records. I exhale sharply at the sight of the word *amnesia*.

She was telling the truth!

I comb through the rest of her records seeing that the doctors strongly urged for her to see a therapist to help with gaining her memories back but there are no records here of her ever seeing one. Her discharge papers state Percy signed her out against doctors recommendations that she needed to remain in the hospital. He used her amnesia against her but why? What the fuck did her father get out of keeping her away from me? The next one is a report on medication for Lake. None of the medication listed is what she said Percy had been giving her for years. I scan over the next couple of reports to find a receipt from a pharmacy for a script under her father's name for all five of the medications she mentioned to me at Central Park. The fucker was drugging her to keep her memories suppressed.

I place those papers to the side and will myself to remain calm as I see Roberto's on the next set of papers, I scan over the report and still at the last paragraph that is addressed to me.

Knox,

You owe me nothing, you owe no one a thing except for your mother and sister.

There is a key attached to the back of this letter, find the safety deposit box and everything you need to take over will be there. It's in your hometown, your mother will know which bank.

You hate me and I understand that, I wanted your hate, I wanted you as far away from me as possible. You owe it to yourself to know the truth. That girl was nothing but a pawn in a battle of men wanting more money.
Find the truth.

I turn the page over trying to see who it's from but it's stapled together with the medical records that show Roberto didn't fucking die. I thought I managed to shoot him in the back of the head but by the looks of these reports, I grazed the side of his neck with the bullet. If this shit is true, why the fuck did he pretend to stay dead all this time? I stand and grab the manila envelope from the bed and turn it upside down, a single gold key falls to the bed. I stare at the fucking thing like it's going to attack me. Grinding my teeth, I snatch the key and shove it in my pocket, then scan through the rest of the documents Knight gathered for me. Anger courses through me at the still shot image of Percy, Karl and Giovani. There is a fourth person with them but their face is obscured by a mask. It's not the fact that I can't see that has my blood boiling, it's the fact that I can tell from the body shape that it's a woman who has a leash clasped to a collar around her neck. Karl holds the leash in his fat stubby hands.

I flick to the next photo to see it's a picture of a man's back as he stands next to a white Honda. I flick to the next image which gives me a side-on view of his face and every-thing inside me stills, my heart rate slows at the sight of my father's face. Too lost in the sight of Roberto Da Luca's face, I don't hear the door open.

"Knox?" Tearing my gaze from the picture I turn to see Lakeland and my mom standing in the doorway with Tay and Xan behind them. Lakeland nibbles on her bottom lip for a second before pulling a piece of folded paper from her back pocket and crossing the room to hand it to me. I stare at it for a second before finally standing and taking it from her. The moment I read over the contents it slips through my fingers. As I stare down at her, tears cloud her eyes. "I lost our baby," she chokes out. Without thinking, I toss the other papers to the bed and wrap my arms around her and bury my face in her hair as she cries for the loss of the child we will never know.

"You were pregnant the night of the accident?" Xan says. I flick my gaze to him to see a horrified look on his face. Tay reaches out and places a hand on his shoulder but he shakes it off before storming out of the room. I don't have it in me to deal with his pity party right now, I've got too much on my mind and can barely process everything I have just learned.

"I'm so sorry." Lake hiccups. Pushing her back, I bend down and grip her face between my hands as I swipe away her tears with my thumbs. The shattered look in her eyes spears me.

"You did nothing wrong—"

She shakes her head as she reaches up to grip my forearms. "I killed our baby and I can't even fucking remember it! I don't even remember you! I deserve everything my father did to me, what kind of mother forgets about their fucking child—" I stop her hysterical rambling.

"None of this is your fault. I read everything, Lay. Your father did this to us. Giovani, Roberto, Percy and Karl are going to fucking pay for what they took from us." I vow.

"Knox, we can't kill Karl," Taylan says. I cut a glance to him.

"You think I'm going to let that fucker live?"

"You can't kill him without proof. We need solid evidence that he had something to do with what happened to Wave, River and Lake... without it we start a war we can't win."

"I'm not waiting–"

"You won't have to." He cuts in, then says, "I got a message from King, the meeting with the heads of the families is set for two days' time. We go to the meeting, get a read on Karl and if he does anything, we go to the others and tell them." I mull over his words for a second before turning back to Lakeland. Her eyes are filled with fire and pride swells inside me at that look.

"You ready for what comes next?" I ask her, this is the only chance she is going to get to say if she wants in on the war that is to come.

"I want them all to pay for what they took from us."

Unable to contain my smile at her reply, I nod and look back at Tay. "Get Xander and the men ready to fly to

Switzerland, we meet with the heads and then we go to war against my father and uncle."

We all sit around the table. The fucking thing is round so no one is able to be seated at the head of the table, giving us the illusion that we are all equals here. There are no weapons allowed in this gothic style church that serves as our meeting ground, only the leaders and their seconds are allowed in here. I ignored that rule when I dragged Lake inside. I felt Karl's beady eyes on us the whole time but ignored the cunt. I know Xander is on edge and if Karl makes one wrong move, Xan is going for his jugular.

Ian, the leader of the English sits while his four seconds stand behind him, Andreas and three of his men sit while four others stand behind them representing the Russian's, the Irish cunt sits with four of his men seated on either side of him and three stand at attention behind him. Costa, the leader of the Greeks sits while his two men stand behind him. Bishop and his four brothers plus his brother-in-law sit with his man Luka standing behind them but it's the sight of Royal, Chaos and Chanel with a man standing behind her that holds my attention. They are all young, around my age, but the fact a woman sits at this table as a leader is fucking awe inspiring. Karl, Ian and Costa will be hating it.

Switzerland puts all of us on equal ground, this is the one country no one runs. It's not through lack of trying, anyone who has tried to take over this country has been pushed out by all of the families currently claiming a seat at this table. I must stare at Chanel too long because her father and the man standing behind grunt and growl in my direction. I raise my hands and smile.

"I meant no disrespect, Murelo. I'm just honored to be alive to see a woman claim a seat at our table for the first time as a leader." Chanel smirks and winks at me, I can't help but grin at the badass.

"Now you've seen it you can look elsewhere," the guy standing behind her sneers. It's obvious in the way that he stands directly behind her and how he grips the back of her seat that they are together. The fact he is able to stand behind his woman and not feel inferior is a fucking testament to him.

"You allow your men to speak out of turn?" Karl the dirty fucking mutt asks.

Royal shakes his head. "He isn't *my* man, he's *hers* and if you try to silence him you will learn why we call her Sin."

"Noted, young Murdoch," Karl answers but it appears Royal doesn't approve of being called out as young.

"We're here and kept our word to introduce all the families to the *Memento Mori*, is there anything else?" Bishop says directing all our attention back to him.

"Yes," Ian answers. "The war between you and the Albanians has caused setbacks for us. Our shipments have stopped and with them out we no longer have a supplier." Well sucks to fucking be them, dumbasses should never have gotten into business with the Albanians, they have too many enemies.

"Your shipments will continue." All eyes turn to Royal. "Constance will now be running the arms shipments under our guidance. The price for the firearms will remain the same but the contract you had with Halil will be changing."

"You do not dictate the terms, boy, the Albanians weren't yours to take out–"

Chaos cuts Ian off. "Yes, the fuck they were. Those cunts took the life of my brother, they're fucking lucky we stopped at killing just them and didn't go after their fucking families!"

"And the feds that were killed, that brought a lot of heat on your family," Andreas adds.

"My son had nothing to do with that," Knight snaps. "I will not apologize—my wife and I took the lives of the survivors from that day. You want to argue over heat from the feds and the loss of Halil, come at me. I'm right fucking here and ready to go to war with any of you if you so much as show me an ounce of disrespect over avenging my fucking son!" Everyone in the room lowers their heads in a show of respect for the loss Knight Murdoch suffered, no one should have to lose a child.

"No one will take action against your family, you were within your rights to avenge the death of your son, Knight," I say with conviction, daring any of these other fucks to argue against me. Before the Murdoch's arrived we all agreed that no one would take action against the family.

"I say you should have taken the families out," Costa

adds. The Greeks do things differently to the rest of us, they keep everything to do with their family hidden and never disclose any information to outsiders. They are a wildcard in this little peace treaty we have going on.

"If you are here to argue or try to come after my family for the backlash over the death of my cousin, then I am telling you now, you will have the entirety of the *Memento Mori* and the Murdoch mafia coming after each of you," Chanel's tone is cold and void of all emotion, earning smirks from all the men around the table. I spy Karl grinning at her like she is a prize and clench my fists under the table.

"I just said, no one will come for any of you. We voted earlier about that, Knight was within his rights to do what he did. Any of us here would have done the same thing." I pull my gaze from Sin to look at Knight for a second before settling on Chaos knowing that he is the one that needs to be tamed. I can feel the bloodlust clinging to him and I know exactly how it fucking feels to need the blood of the cunt that took your sibling from you to coat your hands. "You have my condolences; my twin sister was murdered six years ago and she is the reason I currently sit where I am. The bloodlust will pass over time, but the hunger for revenge will never stop. Well, for me it hasn't stopped. It may be different for you but just know, the Canadians will never seek repercussions against you for avenging the loss of your brother. If you ever need to cross my border to find a fucker involved in his slaying, you need only ask."

He nods his thanks. "Appreciate it."

"As new members to this table there are rules to be followed," Andreas says.

Royal scoffs. "Coming from the guy who only has his seat at this table because my aunt gave it to him?" The Russians begin to spew insults at Royal in their native tongue.

"Zakroy svoy chertov rot, poka ya ne zakryl yego dlya tebya!" (*Close your fucking mouth before I close it for you!*) Gage roars, silencing the Russians.

"Your nephew disrespects us, we will not stand for that," Andreas claps back, glaring at Gage.

"And I will not stand for your men hurling insults at my family, pull them the fuck in line now. Do not forget who you are speaking to, Andreas. My wife may not be present but remember who the fuck she is and it is by her mercy you have Russia. Push me again and see what happens." Fuck me, Gage Murdoch just spanked Andreas' ass in front of all of us without a single fuck given.

"Enough! I did not come here for petty squabbles between families," Ian snaps. Since the moment we arrived here and he saw me, Ian hasn't spoken a single word to Karl which leads me to believe he has severed ties with the fucker.

"I move to petition the *Memento Mori* as a head family in the US alongside the Murdochs. All in favor?" Bishop declares.

"Before we vote," Costa cuts in. "What guarantee do we have that they will not disturb the peace we have built? It has taken generations for us to get to this point where we are able to meet. I will not vote *yes* just because they are your kin."

"They will be under our guidance and we will vouch for them," King says, speaking for the first time.

"That is not enough, they are young and seek power," Costa says, earning glares from the Memento Mori. "Rumors have reached us that they operate without your consent and they have a man who is on the FBI's most wanted list in this room with us." Costa brings a valid argument to the table, none of us can afford that type of heat right now, especially not me as I'm preparing to go to war and have CSIS on my ass.

"Those charges were overturned," Chanel snaps.

"Forgive me, but that means nothing to me. I want assurances, Bishop."

"What assurances, Costa?" Bishop's tone is hard and unyielding.

"I want the peace to remain amongst our families. If they are coming for the Albanians and from what I hear, they also possess Columbia through a union of your son and his wife to be, what is to stop them from trying to wage war against us? Can you stop that and personally guarantee me that if I was to offend your son he wouldn't retaliate?"

"A school," Chaos announces drawing all our attention to him.

"What?" Karl says in disbelief.

"We can guarantee peace through a school," he says.

"How?" I push.

Chaos looks around the room as he speaks. "We open a school here on neutral territory, where all future heirs attend. It will be a school for kids like ours. If we can raise our children in a setting like that, then peace will be achievable for all future generations."

"A school?" Andreas says in wonder.

"Yes. Hatred and bias is taught. No child is born with hatred in their heart, they learn it from us." He has a valid point and after learning about the loss of my own kid two days ago, I want to ensure that the day I decide to have a child that they are protected.

"Who would run this school?" I ask.

"We would all be able to vet any potential staff members, as this wouldn't be a normal school, it would be a school that teaches our children how to run our empires—fighting, shooting, self-defense—we would be raising our children in a unified setting," Chaos answers without missing a beat.

"We do not operate like you, my children are raised and taught–"

Chaos cuts Costa off. "We make the school a maximum of four years, from the ages of sixteen to nineteen so if they should so choose, they can still attend college but this is mandatory. This way none of us are there to influence them and they are able to mingle and meet others, brokering their own form of peace without us interfering."

"You will send your children to this school?" Ian asks.

"Yes," he says with zero hesitation.

"I don't have children so therefore my vote is null and void for this," Andreas announces.

"Who covers the cost for the school?" Karl asks Chaos, the sound of his voice grates on my fucking nerves. Before Chaos can answer, Rook cuts in and takes over.

"We all do. I have two young daughters as you know, if this school is a way for me to protect my daughters, then I say we all fucking fund it." The next hour is spent going over the terms of the school and trying to decide if this is a good idea or not. Karl and Ian agree, which surprises me but given the fact none of their children will attend the school as they are older, it makes sense. Andreas has agreed to go with the majority given the fact he isn't planning on having children and the fact he bats for the other team. Costa tried to vote against the school but lost to the majority. The construction on the school will begin immediately. They will board at the school for four years and need to integrate with other kids from different families. We have also agreed to open the school to politician's kids, princes and princesses and so on, as long as they understand how the school is run, they may attend.

"Now, all in favor in offering the *Memento Mori* a seat at this table with the notion of peace in the works?" We all agree to allow them to share in the heads of the families on a trial as long as the school works out.

"Don't fuck this up, kids. See you for the opening," Karl snickers as he and the others head out. I call out to Chaos before he can follow after his family.

"Yeah?"

"Your uncle asked for permission for you to cross my border," I say.

"He did, but turns out, she isn't there."

"Really?" I say surprised.

He narrows his eyes. "The fuck does that mean?" I smile

and shake my head before shooting a glance over my shoulder at Lake who looks fucking furious. I get it, she is pissed that I didn't call Karl out but Taylan was right, without proof I can't touch the cunt.

"It means, I know what it's like to be led on a woman hunt, only for them to outsmart us."

"Oh, this bitch thinks she is smart but she isn't that good. I'll get her ass back and show her what the fuck happens when she runs from me."

"If you manage to keep her ass by your side, send me instructions on how you did it. I think I may need it." Lake must sense my gaze on her, she pops her head up and shoots me a glare. Chaos snorts. "Looks like you just need to cuff her ass to your side."

Now I scoff. "I tried that. She picked the lock and then stabbed me before jumping out of my second-story window and running."

"Yeah, good luck with that one," he says with laughter in his tone.

"Thanks, I'm gonna need it." We shake hands and say goodbye, then I turn back to my boys and Lake. The three of them stand there with murderous looks on their faces and I get it, now with this shit out of the way, it's time to go to fucking war.

"Let's move, we got a lot to prepare for," I say.

"What about him?" Lake grits out, sighing I scrub a hand down my face.

"Unless he gets involved or we have concrete proof he has been aiding the others, we can't touch him, Lay. I'm sorry." Her nostrils flare in anger and her tiny hands clench into fists at her sides.

"I want Percy dead. If that bastard helped him in any way, I will kill him and not give a single fuck about the repercussions, do you understand?" My cock twitches in my pants and I bite down on my lip to keep from smirking. She looks fucking sexy barking orders at me. I'm so fucking her ass on the plane as punishment for making me hard in front of my boys.

Chapter Twenty-Seven

Lakeland

"Knox, I can't," I beg but the overbearing asshole just growls and smacks my ass twice, before fisting my hair and yanking me back so my back is flush against his chest.

"You take that fucking dick like a good girl and I'll make you come." A whimper escapes me as he draws almost all the way out of my ass before slamming back inside, drawing a strangled moan from me. The moment we stepped foot on the plane, he dragged me straight to the bedroom and ripped my clothes off. I didn't even get a chance to protest before his face was buried in my pussy then my ass.

"It's too much, I can't," I whine. I'm boneless and on the verge of passing out from the amount of orgasms he has given me, he is relentless and each time I feel him swelling inside me with the need to come, he pulls out and eats me until I come on his tongue or fingers.

"You're not in control here. Shut the fuck up and give me what I want, Lakeland, or I'll be fucking that cunt while you're passed out." His crass words send a shiver down my spine and my pussy clamps down on air. He shifts his hold from my hair to my throat, turning my face to him. I reach up and wrap my arm around the back of his neck, pulling his face to mine and kissing him. He swallows my moans and I relish in the groans tumbling from him. His hunger for me only seems to grow the more he takes me. He uses his free hand to circle my clit.

I break the kiss moaning. "Oh fuck, yes, like that, Knox." He buries his face in the crook of my neck, licking my salty skin. We're both covered in sweat and it only seems to add to the sexual tension in the air.

"Hold on, baby, I want you to come with me."

"Yes, I want you to come in my ass." He growls his approval and rests his forehead against mine. We hold each other's gazes as we come with the other's name on our lips. This moment, right here, gazing into his eyes as we reach the greatest climax together feels surreal. Our breaths intermingle. I shudder with aftershocks but that doesn't deter from the loving look in his eyes. Releasing my throat he cups my cheek gently and leans in to place a soft kiss against my lips.

"I'll make this right, Lay. I'll fix it all," he whispers against my lips. My heart beats faster hearing his declaration.

"You can't fix me," I say quietly. I can hear the bitterness in my own voice at not being able to remember.

"Nothing about you needs to be fixed, if you don't

remember the past then we'll deal with that. We can just make new memories and I can tell you stories about us from back then. Losing your memories doesn't mean you have to lose *us*." Tears spring to my eyes at his heartfelt words.

"I can see why I fell in love with you. I just hate that I don't remember how." A raspy chuckle leaves him as he slowly eases out of me.

"It started with you loving my cock in your ass." I shove the arrogant dick away only for his laughter to fill the small room. I march into the bathroom, keeping my back to him so he can't see me smiling.

The entire way back to Knox's house, Xander hasn't uttered a word, even when we left the bedroom on the plane to join him and Tay he refused to look at us and kept his gaze focused out the small window. I've caught both Knox and Taylan shooting him skeptical looks but neither of them have said a thing to their friend. Something feels off, I can't pinpoint what it is but I just have this feeling in the pit of my gut that it has something to do with why Xander is off.

Knox wouldn't allow his friends to head to bed once we got back to his house. He ordered them to follow him to his office. I thought that was my cue to head to his bedroom but he surprised me when he grabbed my hand and dragged me after him. I feel out of place sitting on Knox's lap in front of his best friends and the guys from the other day that were in here when Clara and I heard shouting. Knox's arms tighten around me as if he can sense my anxiety growing. I stifle a yawn from breaking free and relax back into him. I look around the room and manage to catch Xander staring at me with a guilt ridden look before he turns away from me.

"I want men on the ground and ready to roll at a moment's notice. I want more information on this safety deposit box," Knox orders.

"The bank is legit, so is the safety deposit box. It's even under your name," Patrick tells Knox, who stiffens beneath me a second before he leans forward and rests his chin on my shoulder making me feel really awkward. All his men are in here seeing him being all... sweet and judging from the looks on each of their faces this is out of character for him. Well everyone except for Taylan, who looks fucking thrilled at the sight.

"We head to Winnipeg first thing in the morning," Knox says.

"How are we going to do that when you are wanted for kidnapping?" Floyd steps forward and asks. I can see from the strain on his face that he didn't like questioning his boss. Before Knox can answer I cut in and answer for him.

"The moment we get to Winnipeg, I meet with the media to keep the attention on me and then Knox can come forward saying I am with him willingly. I'll tell them about my father drugging me and shift the blame onto him in the hopes that it will make it harder for him to move around freely." Every set of eyes in the room are on me. Knox grips my chin and turns me to face him, searching my eyes for a second before he frowns.

"Are you sure about this?" he asks quietly.

"Knox, her doing this means the CSIS will get off our asses." He ignores Taylan as he waits for me to answer.

"Yes," I answer. His lips thin, clearly he isn't happy about this but he isn't going to argue with me about it now. We spend the next twenty minutes forming a plan of action. We are leaving first thing in the morning to head back to Winnipeg. A knot of dread has formed in my stomach as I follow Knox into the kitchen once all the preparations have been completed for the morning. I come to a stop at the sight of Clara sitting on one of the stools, sipping a cup of tea and reading over a stack of papers in front of her.

"You're up late," Knox says to her as he mills about the kitchen grabbing plates and other things, so I climb up on the stool next to his mother. She smiles lovingly at me before turning back to her son who is cracking eggs in a bowl.

"Couldn't sleep. What's your excuse?" I bite my lip to keep from smiling. He may be the boss but clearly his mother still rules over him. He keeps his gaze on his task of making omelets by the looks of the ingredients as he answers his mother.

"Just got off a plane and had to prep my men and now I have to feed my girl." Hearing him call me his girl has warmth spreading throughout my body. "So she has the strength to go another three rounds on my dick." I choke on my own spit. Knox shoots me a wink as his mom smiles and shakes her head. I feel heat in my cheeks and shoot Knox a death glare.

"There are just some things a mother shouldn't know, Knox, and that is one of them." The asshole just laughs as his mother gathers her things and climbs to her feet. She places a kiss to the top of my head and heads out, only to stop and peer back at her son. "I'll be with you tomorrow." Knox opens his mouth to no doubt protest but she pushes on. "You and your men do whatever it is that you have to do and I will mind Lakeland for you." Knox and I both stare at her as she leaves the room with her head held high. I watch in amazement as the men she passes bow their heads in respect.

"That woman will be the fucking death of me," Knox growls as Taylan saunters into the room and claims Clara's vacated seat. I wait to see if Xander will follow after him but I don't even catch a glimpse of him.

"Dude, Mom is a badass and if she catches you talking shit about her, she will whoop your ass in front of everyone." Knox mumbles something beneath his breath as he returns to his task while Taylan faces me with a wicked smirk on his face. "So, how does it feel to be the queen of this empire?" I reel back and shake my head.

"Cut it out, dickhead," Knox scolds but Taylan ignores him.

"I mean, given the fact my brother over there made it pretty public that you're not some fling in that meeting, it has to feel pretty good." I narrow my eyes at the little shit, I know what Taylan is doing. He's trying to get a rise out of me in the hopes I'll deny what he says, it's a test. I feel Knox's heated stare on me waiting to see how I will react so I play with them both. Leaning forward I place my hands on the tops of Taylan's thighs. I see Knox's jaw lock and his eyes spark with darkness as I lean in close to Tay leaving a sliver of space between our faces. I give him credit, Taylan's mask of indifference lasts a solid four seconds, but falls the moment I lick my lips and now a lustful look enters his eyes.

"But what if I don't want to be just his?" Before Taylan can respond, Knox has thrown the bowl of eggs against the wall and stalks around the counter, shoving Taylan off his seat. He grabs my waist and lifts me until my ass is balancing on the edge of the counter. He pushes his way between my legs, grabs my throat and gets right in my face.

"You trying to get me to fucking kill my best friend?" I don't use words, I reach and wrap my arms around his neck and ghost my lips over his as I answer, feeling Taylan's gaze on me the whole time. A stabbing pain begins at the base of my skull and I scrunch my left eye to try to alleviate the pain but it does nothing. Knox sees the strain on my face and cups my cheeks trying to soothe me but it doesn't do anything when a pain so blinding slams into the back of my head, I scream out.

"That's it, baby, you take his cock so fucking well." I tear my gaze from Knox and look up into the startling blues of his best friend.

I snap my eyes open and gasp. Knox is right in my face so I shove him away. He stumbles but rights himself. I dart my gaze between Taylan and Knox in shock, shame, confusion and a whole other range of emotions swirl inside me. I spot Mase and two other men and pin them with a glare.

"Get out," I snap, the two men behind Mase do as I say but the bastard looks to Knox who gives him a curt nod before he leaves the kitchen. I push off the counter and place my hands on my hips, the pain in my head has reduced to a dull thud. I ignore all of that as I stare at these two assholes who are looking at me like I'm a car wreck waiting to happen —no pun intended.

"Kitten—"

"Shut your fucking trap, Taylan," I snarl. Wisely he clamps his mouth closed and raises his hands as if surrendering.

"You have two fucking seconds to explain to me what the fuck that was!" Knox shouts. I don't even react to his angry tone as I swing my glare from Taylan to him, his eyes spit fire but fuck him.

"Oh, you want me to explain what that was?" I taunt as his jaw works side to side. "How about, I didn't know what the fuck that was until a memory of him fucking me came out of nowhere!" I scream. Both of them flinch and recoil but I'm not done. "How many of your friends have fucked me at your request? Did your men line up and take turns or jump at the opportunity to fuck a seventeen year old?" My chest is rising and falling in quick pants as I try to reign in my temper but the longer we all stand here in awkward silence, I begin to realize I'm not really angry, I'm ashamed. I can't believe that I would allow someone else to touch me while Knox watched. Bile rushes up my throat but I swallow it back down.

"It isn't what—"

Taylan cuts Knox off before he can continue. "What was the memory?" This is the first time Taylan has used such a firm tone with me and it's kind of shocking.

"It was just a flash," I mutter bitterly.

"Explain it to me, Lay," Taylan pleads. All the air whooshes out of me and my shoulders slowly deflate.

"Knox was..." I dart my gaze away, unable to look at them as I speak. "Knox told me I take your cock well and when I looked away from him I saw your face. That was it, I didn't see anything else." Shame washes over me, I wish that flashback was just a trick but I know what I saw was real. Taylan and I have slept together and Knox allowed it. Taylan steps forward. Knox grabs at him but he bats his hands away as he comes to stand in front of me. He places his hands on my shoulders and I cringe as the memory of him thrusting inside me replays in my mind.

"Lay, what you saw wasn't something depraved or dirty." I swing my gaze back to him and scoff. "Without you remembering everything this is going to be hard to believe but, can you just try to keep an open mind?" The plea in his voice is the only reason I nod. "You and I have only slept together three times—" I jerk out of his hold.

"Three times?" I screech. Knox moves forward but Taylan shoots him a look that has him stopping in his tracks.

"Yes," he says, drawing my attention back to him. "All

three times Knox has been present, you won't believe me but this was what *you* wanted." I gasp.

"I wouldn't... No—"

Knox cuts off my rambling. "Knowing what you know about me now, do you really think I would let anyone touch you if it wasn't what you wanted?" I balk at him.

"You are seriously kidding, right? You were a fucking asshole to me when we met—"

"No, I wasn't. I was a dick to you this time because I thought you had killed my sister and ran off to help your daddy. I would never allow anyone to hurt you, Lakeland. Did I allow anyone to touch you aside from me?" I ponder his words for a second and begrudgingly shake my head.

"Lake, the three times we were together it was consensual, you wanted it." I open my mouth to argue but Taylan pushes on. "Don't get me wrong, I was a willing participant. You wanted to embrace a... kink if you will and Knox being the jealous, possessive asshole he is, wouldn't allow anyone to touch you until you asked me."

My jaw unhinges and my eyes widen. "I asked you?" He gives me a tight lip smile and nods.

"Yeah, Lay, you came to me. Knox only agreed because he knew I would never hurt you or do anything you didn't like. You both trusted me to care for you and not treat the gift you gave willingly like some cheap fuck." I scrunch my face in disgust. "I would never hurt you, Lay. Have I not shown you that? Have I not shown you that I am a friend not only to Knox but to you as well?" I can't argue because he is right. Taylan has shown me nothing but kindness and I am grateful to him for that because his kindness was one of the only things that kept me fighting for my freedom from Knox.

"I wanted this?" I repeat, looking at each of them.

"Yeah baby, this was something I wasn't okay with at the start. I'll never be okay with sharing you but after you explained things to me, I understood." Knox's words settle me and make me feel like what I did wasn't something to be embarrassed about.

"What if I wanted to do it again?"

Chapter Twenty-Eight

Knox

I stare at her like she is out of her fucking mind. Tay stands beside me, rubbing the back of his neck, looking all kinds of fucking awkward. Taylan sleeping with Lake was something I was okay with before but it isn't something I can stomach now. Was it fucking hot to watch my best friend make my girl come? Fuck yes, it was, and I enjoyed myself but the last time ended in us in a threesome and that was fucking euphoric, then two nights later I lost my sister and Lakeland. Thinking about her and Taylan together brings me back to that night and I won't do it, I can't.

I meet her gaze as I speak. "If that is something you want, what you really want then I can't give it to you." Her mouth parts slightly. "Before that was something I was okay with but now, no. I won't allow anyone to touch what is mine and make no fucking mistake, kitten, you are mine."

"Well that's good because I was fucking with you." I gape at the dirty little minx. Tay laughs and claps.

"What?" I snarl annoyed as fuck.

She shrugs. "Don't get me wrong, Taylan is hot–" I growl. "But I'm not interested in whatever that was."

"Babe, you'll get sick of his mediocre cock soon enough and be begging to have mine just so you can feel what it's like to be fucked by a real man." I smack Taylan over the back of the head, Lay and him laugh and within a couple of seconds I join them as I wrap my arms around my girl and hold her close. Tay smiles and nods, telling me without words that he will never bring this topic up again or ever accept an offer to repeat history should she ever ask. "Right, well since we have decided that Knox has sharing issues and ruined what should have been our midnight snack, I'll see you both in the morning."

"Night," I say as Lay pulls out of my hold and closes the space between her Taylan. When he looks down at her I can see the love he feels toward her in his eyes but it's the love of a... Brother? It feels weird thinking that after we just talked about them fucking.

"I may not remember it but out of everyone, I'm glad it was Tay because I know without a shadow of doubt you have taken care of me and treated me with respect." Tay gives her a tight lipped smile, then she shocks the fuck out of both of us when she wraps her arms around his waist and hugs him. Two seconds, that's all it took for him to melt into her.

"I would never hurt you, Lay. I got your back, always," he

says as he releases her and places a kiss to her cheek before walking out. That right there is one of the many reasons why I fucking love him and Xander, they are my brothers and always have my back. I don't know what the fuck is eating at Xander but I plan to find out whatever the fuck it is in the morning.

"So..." Lake says as she makes her way over to me, stopping a couple inches away. "I guess without my meds, I'm slowly starting to get my memories back." I nod and try with all my might to snuff out that spark of hope inside me.

"With or without those memories, you will always be *my* Lakeland." Her eyes soften at my words. "You may not recall our past but I do. I'll spend every day reminding you of the reasons why you fell in love with me the first time. Until the time you do remember, I will love you enough for the both of us." She covers her mouth with her hand as tears fill her eyes.

"You love me?" she mutters. I roll my eyes.

"I have said it in so many different ways, was me not killing you not enough of a clue?" She shakes her head. "How about the fact I risked being caught by the CSIS so you could say goodbye to your sister?" She shakes her head again. "How about the fact I gave you the documents from Knight?" Before she can shake her head again I push on. "How about I just tell you now that I love you and tell you that you were my first love, my first girlfriend, my first heartbreak. Lakeland Deveraux, you own me, mind, body and soul. You have owned every part of me since you were thirteen and I plan to make you fall in love with me again just so

I can own every inch of you willingly because we both know I own you now, but I want you to give me everything you have freely."

"I feel like you already own every part of me and I don't need my memories to tell me that I am already falling for you. Just give me time to work all of this out in my head because I can't say those three words back to you right now." I smirk and close the space between us placing a kiss to her forehead.

"You could never say it before either and just so we are crystal fucking clear, that was the first time I have ever told you I loved you. I've never told anyone I loved them since I was six." She gasps. I walk out of the room leaving her to mull over what she just learned.

I'm not fucking happy about my mom coming with us, she should be at home safe and tucked away but no, she had to be here and I do kind of owe her for organizing all the funerals of my fallen men. Lakeland has been withdrawn since we arrived in Winnipeg. I've noticed she has been having pain and tries to hide it but I see through her mask. I had wanted to stay in Calgary but I knew it would be too hard for Lake to stay in the house her sister was murdered in so I relented. Driving through the main town in Winnipeg is surreal and nostalgic, I haven't been back here since we fled after I took over the Da Luca family. This place holds too many memories for me, all those memories include one person, my favorite person in the whole fucking world aside from Lake.

We pass by the local park where Wave, Taylan, Xander and I used to hang out after school. We spent so much time there hanging out just so we wouldn't have to go home, going home meant we had to see the sadness in our moms eyes and see her worrying about how she was going to put food on the table for four kids. Those times were fucking hard and there were some nights we had gone hungry. It wasn't the hunger pains that upset me, it was having to hear my mom cry and berate herself for failing us.

I don't own a house here in Winnipeg, I never will. This place is not somewhere I ever want to come back to. If I had the power I would shut the fucking place down and make sure no one ever came here. Pulling up to the cabin style homes we rented, I look out the window and debate if I should have Xander turn the car around and get the fuck out of here.

"We do this, then we get the fuck out of here, deal?" Taylan's softly spoken words ease some of the tension inside me.

"Yeah," Xan answers.

"Let's move," I say as I climb out of the car with my mom following after me. Before I can take a step, she reaches out and grabs my arm, drawing my attention down to her. Her eyes are filled with misery and I know if I wasn't wearing sunglasses she would see the same look mirrored on my own.

"I want to go there." I yank my arm free of her hold and step back.

"You can't be serious?" I seethe quietly. She sighs sadly and nods her head as she wraps her arms around herself like she is trying to keep the pieces of herself together.

"I need to do this, Knox. I need the closure—"

"There is no moving past what happened," I say in an angry, cold tone that has her recoiling slightly.

"You don't get it. Losing your sister destroyed you but losing my daughter fucking obliterated me. I have been half a person for six years because my baby left. No parent should ever have to bury their own child!" she shouts. I can feel Lakeland and the guys staring at us but I ignore them. "All I have are memories, those mean nothing to me because they are from the past. I will never get a fleeting moment with my daughter because she is gone. You think Lakeland is unlucky because she doesn't have her memories." I open my mouth to argue but she pushes on. "Let me tell you something, Son. She is the fucking lucky one because she doesn't have to be haunted by the past, she doesn't have to wake each day knowing that her daughter died."

I stand here and stare after my mom as she follows Mase to the cabin we will be staying in. I know most of my men heard what was just said but I don't care. Hearing the pain in her voice fucking kills me. For years I thought I was the only one suffering and drowning in the loss of my sister but I was fucking wrong.

"I'll take her." I turn to the side to see Xander standing there with a hard look on his face.

I shake my head. "No. If she needs to go back then I will be the one to take her. She can't let go," I whisper.

"How the fuck could she?" I face my best friend and scowl at the fucker.

"Got something to say?" I snarl. Xander slowly turns to face me and the angry glint in his eyes gives me pause.

"She buried an empty fucking box. They didn't even find the car until weeks later. Your mother didn't get the chance to dress her baby girl, kiss her cheek or hold her one last time before they closed the lid. She buried a wooden box filled with the things Waverly loved most because no body was ever recovered. Think on that for a second before you go off on me. You sought out your vengeance and claimed your birthright so you would have the power and means to avenge your sister, your mother didn't get that chance. You parade the woman who killed her daughter around her like it doesn't fucking hurt to know she—" He points toward Lakeland as he continues to shout at me, "is still breathing while my girl—while your sister isn't. Pull your fucking head out of your ass, Knox." He shoulders me as he storms past, heading toward our cabin. I stand here mulling over his words and start to wonder if he's right, is having Lake around my mom destroying her without me knowing? Am I really that fucking selfish that I didn't know I was hurting my own mom.

"He didn't mean it. Just give him a chance to cool off before you two fight it out," Tay says before clapping me on the shoulder and going after our best friend.

"Knox—" I raise my hand stopping Lake from continuing, I can't look at her or even speak to her right now, it's too fucking much.

"Go inside, I'll be back later," I clip out as I climb back in the car and plant my foot on the gas, needing to get the fuck away from here.

Chapter Twenty-Nine

Lakeland

I watch him drive away and see several of his men scrambling to get back in their cars and chase after their boss. Guilt churns inside me, after everything I have learned these past few weeks how could I have never thought about my presence being hard for any of them? I'm so angry with myself—no, I'm fucking angry that this horrible thing happened and I can't even recall a single fucking detail about it! I look back to the cabin Clara and the others entered and sigh, I can't go in there. They all hate me and I truly can't find it within myself to be mad at them for it, I deserve their hate.

I decide to give them some time alone and not have to deal with seeing my face and take a walk through the woods that surround these campground style cabins. I see men milling about keeping watch so I know I'll be safe. I follow the worn path and realize after a few moments that this is a trail. I wrap my arms around me to ward off the chill in the air. As I walk, I try to force myself to remember anything from the past about Knox. Each time I try my head begins to pound, the stabbing pain in the base of my skull has my bottom lip trembling as I try to fight off the pain.

I don't realize how far I have walked until the trees give way to a clearing and I spot a moss covered picnic table that has clearly been there for years. Feeling mentally and emotionally exhausted, I decide to take a seat and pray no one finds me. At least out here there is no one around to judge me as I finally allow my tears to fall. I bring my knees to my chest and wrap my arms around them and weep. I don't even know why the hell I am crying, I'm so confused and angry and I hate not being able to remember. Before finding out about losing my memories I was okay being alone in my father's house. I didn't know any difference until meeting Knox. Now, all I want is to just remember what the hell happened to me and why my father wanted me incapable of remembering anything about Knox or about that night.

A gust of wind sends a chill through me and I shiver. Not wanting to get sick at such a tense time, I stand ready to head back and hide in one of the cars but I freeze at the sight of a man standing at the edge of clearing. He wears a black jacket, gray slacks but it's the sight of his leather shoes that tells me he isn't one of Knox's men. His salt and pepper hair is windblown, his face is taught with tension, but it's his eyes that hold me captive, they are rich brown and hold so much guilt in them, that it has me tensing.

"I swore I would stay hidden, never let them know I was here and guard them from a distance but it seems, I can no longer keep that vow." I dart my gaze around, trying to find a quick escape but his eyes narrow as if he can sense my need to flee. "I'll chase you down."

"Why?" I ask, proud my voice doesn't quiver in fear. I know that this man isn't Karl or Gio, I saw their faces on the news.

"I know what happened to you, Lakeland." I suck in a sharp intake of breath.

"How do you know my name?" This time I can hear the hint of fear in my voice.

"I know a lot about you, I also know what it's like to be with the people you love but because of your past you are forced to stay away because you don't want to continue to hurt them." I cock my head to the side and study him, something about this man seems so familiar, is he someone from my past?

"How do you know me?"

"I will explain everything to you, I swear it but I need you to come with me." I reel back and shake my head.

"You come anywhere near me and I'll scream." I warn him as fear begins to work its way through my body.

"Knox left nearly an hour ago, half of his men followed him and the rest have no idea you have even left the grounds." I back up only to hit my lower back against the table. "I won't harm you, I just want to help him."

My eyes widen a fraction. "Help who?"

"My son." I gasp, my jaw is practically on the floor but

before I can utter a word or even scream the pain in my head returns with vengeance crippling me as I slam my eyes closed and cry out in pain.

"If you agree to marry me, I can get rid of Gio and stop him from going after my daughter. I need you to help me save my twins, I'm not the monster they think me to be, help me please, I beg you."

I come to with a groan and grip my head as the pain in my temples makes itself known. I slowly blink my eyes open, only to be hit with nausea. I swallow the bile that is threatening to surface and whimper. I must have blacked out again. I try to recall what caused it and when the memory of the man in the woods hits me, I gasp and bolt upright snapping my eyes open. I look around the dimly lit room and sigh in relief, I'm in a cabin. Knox's men must have found me and brought me back. Swinging my legs over the side of the bed, I stand only to have to grip the bedside table until my head stops spinning. I spot the glass and two white pills there and I smile, thinking about how Knox still cares even though he is hurting. I down them and decide I need to face the others and tell them what I learned.

I take a deep breath and steel my spine before opening the door and walking out only to frown. I don't hear anyone talking but then the scent of mouthwatering food hits my nose so I follow the smell into a tiny kitchen. I slam to a halt at the sight of the man from the woods plating up food on the counter. He flicks his gaze to me and smiles. I spin around and spot the door. I rush to it and try to yank it open but it's locked.

"Sit down and eat, let me explain and if my explanation doesn't appease you I will unlock that door and give you the keys to my car with directions on how to return to my son and his mother." I try to calm my breathing as I release the handle and slowly turn to face him. He grabs the two plates and walks over to a small four-seater table that is set out with candles and all. He takes his seat and motions with his hand for me to take the other. I debate ignoring his request for a second before he sighs and speaks again. "Please, let me explain." The pleading tone of his voice is the only reason I obey him.

I plop down unceremoniously into the seat opposite him, I want to toss the plate at his head but my stomach lets out an embarrassing grumble that has a smirk gracing his face. I glare at the pasta on my plate for a second, before deciding I will need my strength if I have to run so I dig in. I watch out of the corner of my eye as he fills my glass with red wine. I don't drink, never have since dad always told me medication and alcohol never mix well.

"You seem tense." I glare at the asshole.

"You best get right with the Lord and play with Jesus, not me!" I snap, his eyes widen for a second before he throws his head back and releases a throaty laugh that has me staring at him. He doesn't seem jaded or anything like the monster I had conjured him to be in my mind. He almost seems... sad.

He grabs his napkin and dabs the corners of his eyes, then takes a sip of his wine before clearing his throat.

"Excuse me, it has been a long time since I have laughed like that. You may have lost your memories but not your spunk."

Frowning, I ask, "How do you know about that?"

The amusement from a second ago vanishes from his features only for them to be filled with sorrow.

"Because I was there that night." I gasp and jerk back into my chair as I grip the edge of the wooden table.

"The night of the accident?" He takes a shuddering breath and nods.

"Yes."

"How? What happened? Tell me—" He raises his hand silencing my onslaught of questions.

"I wasn't in the car, Lakeland, I was with you before you took off with..." He swallows and clears his throat. "My daughter." I hear the pain in his voice, I can feel the agony radiating off of him like I do with Knox whenever he speaks about his sister. I search his eyes and frown, I see it in the depths of those brown eyes.

"You loved them?" I whisper.

He smiles sadly. "*Loved,* is past tense. I *love* them is what you mean to say."

I shake my head, feeling more confused than ever. "But, Knox shot you. He took over your family and wiped out the Da Luca name and rebirthed it as the Re Della Strada."

"Ah, yes. The *Street Kings*." I frown. "That is what Re Della Strada means. Knox renamed the family under a name he thought best described him. He deemed himself the king of the streets so it was only fitting he named the family what he thought would fit. Plus, I knew he would never take my last name, he still remains under his mother's, Bronson."

"How are you not angry with him, he shot you!" I screech.

Roberto sips his wine and shrugs. "Given what Knox was told about me from his mother I understand his reasons and I commend him for it because I would have done the same thing."

"This makes zero sense," I growl.

"Let me make it make sense." I pin him with a deadpan look, he smiles but continues. "As the head of the Da Luca family, I had a target painted on my back always. Clara was my world and I couldn't let her go. Loving her was putting her in danger but I didn't care, I needed her. Then the twins came. I was overjoyed. I had my son, my heir but I also had my little princess, my daddy's girl," he says wistfully.

"Why do I get the feeling you never hurt them?" He drops his gaze to his plate and shoves his pasta around.

"I did hurt them. I made Clara hate me."

"Why?"

"I tried to get her to leave but she wouldn't. She said we could overcome anything as long as we had each other but not this, we could never overcome this."

"If you agree to marry me, I can get rid of Gio and stop him from going after my daughter. I need you to help me save my twins. I'm not the monster they think me to be. Help me, please, I beg you. You said that to me the night of the acci-

dent, why? Did it have something to do with you pushing Clara away?"

He nods sadly and slowly lifts his gaze back to mine. "I made her hate me. I told her if she didn't leave I would kill her and put my own daughter out on the street to turn tricks." I gasp and cover my mouth with my hand as I stare at him in horror.

"You are one sick fuck," I sneer.

"I would never have done it."

"Then why the hell would you say that?" I snap suddenly feeling so freaking angry on Clara's behalf.

"Because my brother was trying to hurt my family so I would step down. I forced her to leave and take my children with her so they would be safe. Giovani and I have never seen eye to eye, we both had our parts to play in the crime world so no one would know we were divided. He wanted to hurt Clara and my children just to get to me and I couldn't allow that. I didn't give a fuck about titles or what being the don meant. If he had touched a single fucking hair on my daughter's head I would have killed him and allowed my men to exact their pound of flesh willingly for breaking the code."

"What the fuck happened, Roberto. None of this is making sense."

"In my world, you cannot kill another family member no matter what they have done. I couldn't kill my brother so I did the only thing I could, I chased her away and forced her to hate me... I needed her to. I knew as the children grew older and asked questions she would tell them I was a monster. I wanted that so they would never come looking for me. For a time, things settled between Gio and me, but I was still trying to find a way to get rid of him without costing me my life."

"Why?"

His features harden as he stares at me. "If a Da Luca Don disgraces his family then he is taken out but not just him, the men would have hunted Clara and the children down and eradicated my whole bloodline, it's our way."

"That is fucking barbaric!"

"It was the only way I knew until Knox took over—he changed everything."

"Why did he try to kill you?"

Roberto sighs. "I believe it's because he thought I wouldn't help him look for the people responsible for his sister's death. He didn't even give me a chance to explain, one second I was stunned at the sight of him being in front of me and then the next I heard Gio shouting for the men to take him out. I spun around to tell them not to touch him and that's when he shot me. I never had a chance to explain anything. He allowed Gio to live and to take some men with him as a show of good faith. Knox thought I was dead, turns out when he had his friends dump my body at the morgue, I wasn't dead and they managed to save me."

I stare at him in a whole new light, he gave up the love of his life and the chance of watching his children grow up because he was protecting them.

"But Gio helped Clara—" I clamp my mouth shut at the angry look he shoots me.

"No the fuck he didn't. She thinks it was him but it was me. I hated that she thought it was my brother but I couldn't correct her. I allowed everyone to think I was dead so I could protect Knox from the shadows. I knew after he thought he had killed me that he would take over but I also know my brother, there was no way he would allow my son to reign as the Don."

"What the hell did any of this have to do with me?" I ask, exasperated.

"Percy was working with me, he started as my real estate developer. I had enough dirt on him that I knew he could never go against me but what I didn't know was my brother was fronting the cash for Percy's side business. The real estate company became a front for his more lucrative business."

"Which is?"

"Your father has a tech company that designs apps... Those apps are used to buy women and children." I gasp, disgust rolling through me and bile threatens to spill from my mouth. "Giovani has always had a thing for... younger girls, preferably before they have reached puberty." I gag and cover my mouth, tears prick the backs of my eyes. "He and your father have made millions. The Irish and English still use your father's company. The Russians used to and so did the Americans, until Tony Murdoch fell and his son took over. Bishop has made it his life's mission to shut down the skin trade, but with how Gio and Percy operate the auctions now there is no stopping it. Karl is still protecting them because through your father's app he makes a shitload of money without having to get his hands dirty."

"I will ask again, why the fuck were you there with me that night?" I grit out through clenched teeth. Roberto meets my angry stare with a look of sadness that has me on edge.

"You led my brother and Percy to my son." Shock ripples through me.

"No—"

"You didn't do it intentionally, they never suspected Waverly was my daughter even though she hung out with you. They only put it together when they saw Knox on the cameras sneaking into your house. They had planned to sell you on the app in the hopes Knox would come to me for help. The only way I could think of to throw them off the scent was to demand your hand in marriage. Percy was outraged but he couldn't refuse the Don, they still thought I didn't know about their side business. They had planned to use my own children against me and force me to stand down so Canada could become the capital for the skin trade. I had only planned to marry you to protect my children."

I see the truth in his eyes and hear it in his words but something still isn't adding up. "What else happened that night?"

He scrubs a hand down his face and shakes his head as if disgusted. "I will spare you all the gory details but Percy agreed, you hated the idea and I asked to speak to you alone in the living room. You wouldn't listen to me at first, claiming you would kill me when I told you I was Knox's father but then I begged you to help me save my children and you agreed. The problem was, you then told me you were pregnant with my grandchild." Tears cloud my vision as he speaks about the baby I lost. "I didn't know Percy and Gio were listening. Percy lost his shit and struck you. I tried to get to you but Gio held me back. I fought my brother to get to you, I told Percy I didn't care that you were pregnant, that I would marry you now and take you with child but he already knew who the father of the child was and he and Gio could never allow another Da Luca heir to live."

Tears roll down my cheeks. "How did I end up in a car?" I choke out.

"Xander burst through the door." My blood turns to ice as the vision of him comes flashing through my mind, *I'll make sure he knows what you did tonight, you took the love of my life from me.* "I held Gio back while he got Percy off you, he told you to run and that Waverly was in the car waiting for you. One of Percy's guards managed to knock Xander out and then held me at gunpoint while Percy and Gio went after you. I wrestled with the guard giving Xander a chance to go after you girls in the hopes he could stop them but... it was too late."

"Xander was there," I breathe out in shock.

"Yes, he saved you."

"I... I think I was going to Knox, to tell him what had happened." I try harder to remember that night but I can't.

"The bridge where the accident took place is only a couple miles from where Knox lived, I believe you were trying to warn my son but Percy and Gio... stopped you."

"Percy told everyone I was drunk that night and fed me

pills to keep my memories of Knox hidden." Roberto's face darkens as his anger spikes.

"Your father is a cunt." I snort and quickly cover my mouth. "He wanted Knox to hate you. Gio and Percy both knew I was coming after them that night for what they did. Percy hid out in public places so I could never get to him. Gio went underground with the help of that Irish scum until the night Knox showed up, it was pure coincidence. They were both there to kill me but Knox being my son meant he had the stronger claim to the family. As long as you couldn't remember anything about that night, Percy knew no matter how much Knox hated you for what happened he would never go after you because he loved you, you were your father's shield."

"He wanted me to marry Gio," I mutter.

"Gio grew too greedy, he hated that the other heads of the families recognized Knox as the Canadian leader and chose him to sit at the head of the table. He knew marrying you would start a war with Knox. I'm sorry to tell you this, Lakeland, but you have just been a pawn in a very fatal game. None of this has been about you really, it's all been about my family and I am so sorry you were caught in the crossfire. I made a persona, Christiano, so that I could try to bring them down from the shadows so none of you kids would get hurt but I failed. You're all in this now and I don't think I can stop it."

Numb, that's how I feel right now after learning all of this. I need to remember. I need to know everything.

"I need you to take me back to that bridge, I need to go back to the beginning."

Chapter Thirty

Knox

I've been sitting in my car for the last forty minutes, staring at the safety deposit box in the passenger seat like it's going to grow a head and attack me. I should open it and find out what the fuck is inside of it but I... can't. I have the key in the palm of my hand, all I need to do is open the lock and that is it, but why can't I fucking move? When the back doors of my car open, I draw my gun and aim it only to sigh and shove it back in my waistband at the sight of Taylan and Xander climbing in.

"What are you two doing here?" I say dejectedly.

"We knew you would come here and we also knew you wouldn't be able to open it, so we came to tell you that you can and you should because I want to get the fuck out of this town and go kill some fuckers." Taylan's right, I need to stop being a pussy and man the fuck up.

"No matter how angry we get, no matter what happens,

swear on our lives right now that we will always talk shit out. We will never abandon each other or leave anyone behind." Taylan and I both stare at Xander, he looks worried and slightly pained.

"What the fuck?"

"You good?" Tay and I say at the same time. Xander sighs and nods.

"Just promise me you will always be there, no matter what. No matter how bad we fuck up we will always have each other's back." The pained expression on his face has me on edge.

"I swear."

"Always brother." Tay and I say, Xan releases a whoosh of air and nods, looking slightly relaxed. I reach for the box and insert the key. The moment the lock clicks open I get anxious. Flipping the lid back I find a letter, so I flick the interior light on and begin to read the fucking thing out loud.

Knoxville,

I had planned to leave all the proof you needed inside here but then your little traitor of a hacker managed to alert Gio that there was a safety deposit box under your name. I had no choice, I'm in town but so are Gio and Percy. Karl will not intervene but he will ally himself with them, he has offered his men at a price so that the families may never come after him. You need help. Make a call to your friends in Miami so they can stow his hand and pull his men back.

You hate me and I understand that but I also cannot let you die at the hands of my brother. Xander knows I'm innocent, ask your friend, he knows the truth about that night.

I drop the letter and turn back to Xander, my face is pinched in confusion. One look at me and my best friend's face morphs into one of guilt. "What the fuck happened that night?" I say in a tone deathly calm but filled with venom. Taylan looks between the both of us. I can read Xander and Taylan like the back of my hand, I know without a doubt that Xander is fucking hiding something from me and it's something fucking big! He darts his gaze between me and Taylan, looking pained. My heart begins to beat faster, knowing that whatever he is hiding is something so fucking huge it could destroy us, ruin us even.

The passenger door opens and Mase pops his head inside looking frantic. "Boss, we got two situations," he rasps out, the worry of what Xander is hiding falls to the back of my mind as I go into battle mode.

"What is it?" I bark.

"Your mom took a car and is heading to the bridge." Fuck, I pound my fist against the steering wheel honking the horn and scaring the woman crossing the street.

"Get in, we'll go get her," I snap but Mase hesitates.

"What?" I shout at him.

"Lakeland is gone, Knox." My blood turns to ice, my heart slows inside my chest. "We've been searching for her for hours—"

"Hours?" I snarl.

Mase frowns and looks at my boys in the back in confusion. "Yeah?" He voices it like a question.

"I haven't been gone that fucking long," I snarl.

"Knox, you've been gone for nearly four hours," Tay says from the back. I look at each of them to find them all nodding. I pull my phone from the center and balk at the fucking time!

"Where the fuck is she?" I roar.

"Calm down. Mase get in, we go get Mom first, then we go after Lakeland," Xander orders. I shoot him a dark look over my shoulder, he doesn't cower, just meets my stare head on.

"This shit isn't over, as soon as we get them back you're telling me everything." I start the car not waiting for his reply. I'll deal with him later and he will tell me every single thing he knows . The fact Roberto mentioned him in his letter has me conjuring all sorts of things in my head. If Xander is a rat and has been helping my father, I have no choice.

I will kill my best friend for betraying me.

I drive like a fucking lunatic as I race to get to my mom, the back roads around here aren't lit by street lamps. Growing up around here gives me an advantage, making it easier for me to navigate these roads.

"How the fuck did Lake get away?" Tay asks, breaking the tension filled silence. I grind my teeth, trying to tamper down my anger. My grip on the wheel tightens so I don't reach across and strangle the fuck out of Mase for allowing this shit to happen.

"I don't know, Stu called it in," Mase answers.

"Where the fuck were you?" I snarl, the anger in my tone can be heard but I don't give a fuck. It's his fucking job to make sure everything goes smoothly but it seems I put too much fucking faith in the idiot.

"Watching your back." I cut a glance to him and glare.

"What?"

Mase throws his hands in the air, clearly exasperated but if he doesn't watch himself, he will wind up under the fucking tires of this car if he doesn't rein that attitude in real fucking fast.

"When we saw you take off, half the guys split and some followed you while the others stayed behind. I called Taylan and Xander to come get you because you pulled a gun on me when I knocked on the window." I frown not recalling that shit but I also didn't realize I was gone for hours!

"Jesus, Knox. You need to get your head fucking right before we find Gio and Percy," Xander snaps. I ignore him because right now I want nothing more than to smash his fucking face in until he tells me what he's been hiding.

"Gio and Percy are already here, be fucking vigilant," I say before scrolling through my contact list and calling in a favor I never thought I would have to. I may hate that cunt but if what he says is true, I won't risk the lives of my family or my men, we've lost too many already.

"Yeah?" Chaos' annoyed voice fills the car stereo system.

"Chaos, it's Knox," I say.

I'm met with silence for a few seconds before he finally speaks again. "When I gave you my number I didn't think you would actually fucking call." I snort.

"I never thought I would either but here I am," I answer honestly.

"So you are, what do you need?" That's one thing I respect about him, he is a straight shooter and doesn't mince words.

"Karl, the head of the Irish, is offering his men for hire in a war I have with my family. I need the Memento Mori and the Murdoch's to back me if it results in a war." Again, there is silence before I hear voices in the background.

"Knox, you're on speaker."

"Okay..." I let my sentence trail off.

"Knox, it's Royal, I'm here with Chaos and Sin and few of our men, what do you need?" I explain to Royal the situation and that I need their help to either back me if I go to war against the Irish or help me stop Karl from sending his men to aid my enemy.

"We can't back you, without Blackwood academy open we are still on a trial basis," Royal says.

"But, we can put a stop to Karl aiding you. If he helps in

any way in a family matter, he breaks the treaty which means he would have the entirety of the families coming after him," Chanel adds, the woman is a fucking savage and already has my respect without even really knowing her.

"I need him out of the way so I can handle this situation and then find out why he is helping," I add.

"I'll make a call to my father and Andreas. Costa won't help, the Greeks never involve themselves unless they have to. Ian won't be a problem, he owes my dad a debt." I know there is going to be a cost for their help.

"What's this gonna cost me, Royal?" I say in a firm tone.

"Nothing," Chaos answers. "You were the first to agree to the school and from what Ian and Andreas told my dad, you were the one to demand that no family was to come after mine for what my mom and dad did." Gratefulness surges inside me.

"I hope you know I didn't do that shit for ulterior motives."

"It's because of that reason why we are helping. Get the vengeance you seek for your sister, Knox. I understand it and know what you are dealing with. If you need our help, then call." Chaos ends the call and suddenly I feel like I may have found a friend in him without meaning to. With Karl pushed out of the equation we have this shit in the bag. Gio may have turned Tristan against us and surprised me by being here in Winnipeg, but he won't win this fucking war. I'll kill him, Percy and then finally put my fucking deadbeat cunt of a father in the ground... but this time, I'll make sure he is really dead.

Chapter Thirty-One

Lakeland

Roberto and I haven't spoken a single word the entire car ride. When we reach the bridge and he parks the car off to the side, I begin to feel anxious. Have you ever had a feeling like something bad happened but you don't know what it is, you just feel it? That's what I'm feeling now as I open the door and climb out. We walk side by side along the bridge, the only lighting out here is from Roberto's headlights and the moon. The closer I get to the middle of the bridge, the pain in my head makes its presence known. We make it to the middle of the bridge when a flash of a memory plays out in my mind, I clutch my head and hunch over.

I gasp when I feel a hand on my back and jerk away from Roberto, tears gather in my eyes as I stare up at him. His eyes are filled with concern as he peers down at me. "Are you okay?"

"I know. All we need to do is get to my house and then we pack our shit and go."

"How do I say goodbye to him?" I choke out.

"You never have to. He won't let you go without a fight. He loves you so fucking much, Lakeland, that he even breathes in sync with you when you two are together. He is the person who will always choose you! Never doubt him, he will always find you and make sure you choose him, because without you, his soul would be shattered."

I shake my head. "I was driving, I told her what happened that night, she knew." I choke out as an overwhelming amount of guilt slams into me, robbing me of air. Roberto takes a step toward me but freezes at the sight of headlights at the other end of the bridge. Suddenly I'm hit with a sense of Deja Vu just before the pain in my head intensifies bringing me to my knees. I see Roberto shift so he is blocking me and has a gun in his hand. I can make out the figure of a person but I can see them clearly because of the headlights blocking their features. "Ahhh," I cry out.

"Hang on, Lakeland." I hear Roberto say as the figure finally comes close enough so we can see who it is. My jaw unhinges in shock at the sight of Clara Bronson standing there looking murderous, but her gaze is fixed on the father of her children who slowly lowers his gun. "Clara," he whispers.

"I'll fucking kill you, you will not hurt that sweet girl like you tried to hurt my baby!" she screams. I stare at her in horror as she pulls her own gun, tears flowing freely from her eyes as she points the gun at Roberto. I use every ounce of strength I have to push to my feet but I collapse, weakened from the pain in my head.

"Clara, please let me explain—"

"You are a fucking monster. I hate you, my children hate you!" Roberto flinches but doesn't try to defend himself. "You ruined us, you took everything from me. I loved you and you used me." He gasps and tries to step forward but she cocks the gun forcing him to freeze.

"I never used you," he says with such conviction that there is no way she can't hear the truth in his words. "I loved you, still fucking do." Clara shakes her head, denying him as she swipes her tears away with her free hand. "I love my children—"

"You don't get to speak about my kids! They are mine, you abandoned them, you wanted to hurt my little girl," she sobs out, I can feel the grief wafting her in waves.

"I never wanted to hurt them," Roberto whispers brokenly.

"Liar!" she screams.

"I swear it..." I tune out their argument as I force myself to my feet and stand shakily. I reach out and grip Roberto's arm to steady myself.

"Oh my God." I snap my gaze to Clara. She looks between me and Roberto but I don't understand the betrayal I see in her gaze. "You used my son, you betrayed him!" she screams. I shake my head and open my mouth to deny her claim but then another car comes speeding toward us with others following behind it. Roberto shifts and uses his body as a shield. I begin to panic, I'm terrified but something about what I'm feeling doesn't feel new, it's like old feelings are resurfacing.

"Knox," I hear Roberto breathe out a second before the sound of guns cocking silences him.

"You should have stayed dead." The deathly cold tone has a shiver working its way down my spine. "You won't walk away this time." Knox sounds like a cold blooded killer. Fear keeps me rooted to my spot.

"Let me explain—"

Knox cuts Roberto off. "I don't owe you a fucking thing—"

"No but you need to hear what I have to say," Roberto pleads. I shift only for my attention to be snagged by something glimmering on the guard rail. I feel this tugging sensation inside my chest forcing me to go to it, I don't realize I've moved until I'm gripping the railing. I hear someone shouting my name but it becomes white noise as I bend down and take in the sight of faded artificial flowers, moldy teddy bears, and a small cross that is tied to the railing, but it's the gold necklace wrapped around the cross that holds my focus. It's covered in black and green spots, I lift it off the cross and turn it over in my palm, I spot an inscription on the back and use the hem of the jacket Roberto gave me to wipe it.

I'll always choose you.

"Lakeland!" I jolt and jump to my feet spinning around to find Roberto by my side and Knox, Clara, Taylan and Xander as well Knox's men standing there with their guns pointed at me. "What the fuck are you doing with him?"

Knox roars but something feels off, I drop my gaze to the necklace then back to him.

"I'll always choose you," I say quietly, something about those words has a strange feeling swirling inside me.

"What?" I lift my gaze back to Knox, suddenly I feel dizzy and sway on my feet stumbling back a step, Roberto reaches for me but a shot rings out, he slams into me from the force. I scream as I fall backward, I meet Knox's fear stricken gaze a second before I feel myself falling over the railing.

This is how I die.

This is the end.

Those are the thoughts running through my head as screams tear from me. I don't want to die! Before I can fall to the river below my ankle is gripped and I grunt from the jolt. "Help me!" I scream as my hands dangle above my head. Fear isn't an adequate word to describe how I feel right now, this is a feeling I can't even name. It's worse than terrified, worse than numb, this is a feeling of certain death and knowing there is not a goddamn fucking thing you can do to stop it from happening. But the pain in my head never leaves me, it stays there taunting me, reminding me I am going to die without knowing the full story. "Knox!" I don't realize I have screamed his name until he answers me.

"I got you, Lay. I got you baby. Hang on." A whimper escapes me as the pain in my head grows so does the feeling of Deja Vu, it's so fucking intense it robs me of air and I begin to hyperventilate. "I won't let you go baby, this fucking bridge won't take you from me as well. Do you hear me, Lakeland. I fucking choose you, *I'll always choose you!*"

A tsunami of pain explodes inside my head hearing those words from him. I've never felt this much pain before, it's blinding. I feel like I am being ripped apart from the inside, my head exploding with excruciating pain that robs me of breath. I pray to black out, God, I fucking beg for the numbness that passing out brings. My eyes are open but I see nothing, I can't even hear a single sound, all my senses are gone. I can't see, I have no sense of smell, I can't even feel my limbs. If I wasn't in so much pain I would swear I was dead.

But suddenly, the pain vanishes and I'm hit with everything all at once.

"Lay, I have to tell you something." Nerves course through me as I stare up at the boy I have had a crush on for year., Knox Bronson has always seemed so far out of reach. He isn't like any of the boys at my school, he doesn't spend hours worrying about what he looks like or how much money he will inherit.

I dart my tongue out and moisten my lips as I peer up at him through my lashes. "Y-yeah?"

That sexy half smirk he only reserves for me makes its way to his perfect face and my heart stutters in my chest when he reaches out and grabs my waist. I suck in a sharp breath as he draws me in so I'm flush against him.

"Today's your birthday and I've waited a long fucking time for this."

My heart is pounding inside my chest, warmth spreads

through me like an inferno and the sundress I currently wear begins to feel too restricting, my nipples push against the material begging to be touched.

"A long time for what?" My voice sounds breathy to my own ears but I don't care, I have dreamed about this moment for years. So many nights I have dreamed about Knox holding me like this and looking at me like I'm his person, the only person in the world that he needs.

"For you to finally be mine. I choose you, kitten." Before I can say anything, he meshes his lips to mine, kissing me so deeply that my brain short circuits and I forget to breathe. Who needs oxygen when you can breathe in Knox?

I can't stop touching my lips, ever since he kissed me and claimed me as his I haven't been able to take my eyes off him. I watch him like a stalker from across the room as he, Xander, Taylan and River all crowd around the pool table and laugh at something Taylan said. I can't keep the smile off my face.

"Argh, you're making gooey eyes at my brother!" I jolt in surprise and spin to see Wave standing there looking disgusted, I panic. What if my best friend hates the idea of me loving her brother? Oh my God, what if she makes me choose between them? "Why do you look like you need to poop." I scrunch my face which just causes her to laugh.

"Wave, I have to tell you something—" She shushes me and places her hand on my shoulder with a smile on her face and nothing but love in her eyes.

"I know, Lake. I've known for years that you have had a thing for Knox." My face slackens, was I that obvious? "I also know he has been infatuated with you for years as well." My mouth pops open in disbelief.

"What?" I squeak.

"Lake, you are so blind sometimes."

"Am not," I defend in a huff.

"You really are. Knox doesn't care about anyone except for his boys, River, my mom and me. He doesn't care for anyone which is why I know this isn't a fling for him, he wants it all with you, Lake, and if you can't give him that, let him go." I gape at her.

"Wave, I would always choose him."

Chapter Thirty-Two

Knox

Her blood-curdling screams shred my heart to pieces.

"Pull." I snap my head to the side and glare at Roberto. I want to beat his fucking face in and stomp on his skull until I feel it crush beneath my foot but if it wasn't for him catching Lakeland when she went over... I push that thought away. We each tighten our grips on her ankles. Taylan and Xander each wrap their arms around our waists, helping to anchor us. Suddenly out of nowhere her screams stop, causing panic to flow through me as I heave her up. The second Roberto and I have her over the edge, I pull her limp form to me and hold her close. She's cold and her face is etched in pain, she writhes in agony, whimpering every couple of seconds. "What's happening to her?"

I cut a glance to Roberto and sneer at the fucker. "You stay the fuck away from her!" I roar. The bastard ignores me and keeps his gaze on my girl. I brush her hair back from her face and place a kiss to her lips, they're cold and have a purple hue to them.

"Come on, I'll patch up your wound," Xander says to Roberto who shakes his head.

"It's a flesh wound, it'll be fine." I grit my teeth telling myself that he isn't the priority, Lakeland is.

"Come back baby, I can't lose you too," I whisper.

"She needs a doctor." Concern is clear in Taylan's tone.

"No. It's too open and it will be easy for Giovani and Percy to get to her there." I fucking hate to admit it but the bastard is right, a hospital isn't safe for her.

"What do you suggest then?" Mom hedges. Roberto looks up at her and it angers me to see longing in his brown eyes.

"She wanted to come here, she said she wanted to go back to the beginning and I think her being here has triggered her memories—"

"No," Xander says, cutting Roberto off and drawing all our attention to him. He meets my stare with a guilt ridden look in his eyes. "She only started screaming when she heard you say you choose her, hearing those words from you broke down her walls." I tear my gaze from him and look down at the only girl that has ever given me butterflies, the only girl to ever make me feel like I was something more than a street rat. I brush my knuckles along her cheek, hating that her skin feels so clammy to touch.

"I'll choose you always, Lakeland." A whimper escapes

her as her face contorts in pain a second before she gasps loudly. "Come back to me, Lay."

"Waverly!" she screams my sister's name so loud that I jolt in shock. Tears leak from the corners of her eyes. "Wave, come back!" The anguish that laces her words is felt deep inside me, I hear her pain and feel it like it was my own.

Chapter Thirty-Three

All I want is to get the fuck out of here and run to Knox, if anyone can make sense of what's happening it's him!

I need my person.

I run out the front door, not even bothering to question why the hell Xander was here, all I know is I need to get to Knox and tell him everything his father told me. I refuse to marry him, I can't. I just need to get to him and explain everything, then he can help. But if what Roberto says is true, then I'll just be putting him in danger. I yank the car door open and climb inside.

"What the fuck is going on?" Wave snaps.

I slam it in drive and peel out of my driveway. "Your father is inside my house and wants to marry me, he says it's the only way to protect you and Knox."

Wave splutters. "What the fuck? That is not what I was expecting."

"What did you expect?" I snap, then cringe as I realize I'm taking my anger out on the wrong person, "I'm sorry," I add as I lean forward and try to see out the windscreen better, the rain is obscuring my vision.

"Xander called and told me to get out of the house and wait for you in the car." I chance a glance at her and frown.

"What was Xander doing at my house?" She bites her lip and shakes her head.

"The better question is why was my father there and what the fuck is your dad doing with him? You know he is the fucking mafia, right?" I nod.

"I have to leave, Wave. If I stay here, Percy will make me marry your father and I can't do that. I won't. Knox is my person, I choose him," I choke out.

"You won't marry that scum, I'll make sure of it," she growls as she pulls her phone out. "Shit, the storm must have taken out the power lines or something because I have no cell service."

"Fuck." I feel hysteria rise inside me as I plant my foot, needing to get to Knox. I have a horrible feeling in the pit of my stomach like something bad is about to happen. Tears of injustice flow freely. I knew Percy hated me being with Knox but I never thought he would go this far. He warned me that if I didn't break up with Knox I would force his hand but I didn't think he meant something like this.

There is nothing worse than not feeling chosen and I will never allow Knox to think I wouldn't choose him. I place my hand over the gold heart pendant I wear around my neck to remind myself Knox loves me, he never says those three words but I know he does. That's why he had the pendant engraved with his own version of those three words. Our love has created this miracle growing inside me, I will never allow Percy or anyone to harm our baby. I need to tell Knox about this, I haven't even told Wave or anyone yet.

I'll always choose you.

"Slow down, Lake!" I swipe away the tears that continue to fall and try to see through the haze of my tears as the rain continues to pelt down like bullets against the windshield.

How could my father do this to me?

"He's never chosen me, not once in my entire life, it's always been about his company and what he can earn," I manage to grit out before another sob tears its way out of me. This isn't how tonight should have gone. An hour ago, I was happy and getting ready for an amazing night out with my best friend to go spend the night with my boyfriend and our friends but instead, here I am running away with a broken heart because of my father. "I won't marry him!" I scream.

"I know!" my best friend shouts. "Now slow the fuck down or we won't make it there, the storm is bad and you driving like Dominic Toretto doesn't inspire me to be calm." Despite my depressed state and spiraling inside my own mind, I manage to laugh at her stupid joke. That's the thing with her, she knows me better than I know myself, she can bring me out of the dark space I retreat inside when life gets too hard. She is my person.

I ease off the accelerator, earning a relieved sigh from Wave. "I can't do it, I can't marry him." She reaches over and places her hand on my leg, offering me her support.

"I know. All we need to do is get to my house and then we pack our shit and go." I nod, unable to speak as my tears cascade down my cheeks.

"How do I say goodbye to him?" I choke out. The thought of leaving him behind because I can't marry his father in order to keep him safe is tearing me up inside—I hate my life. I hate that I am being forced to make this fucking choice. All because my father got involved with the wrong family and is using this to punish me for falling in love with a nobody as he calls him.

"You never have to. He won't let you go without a fight and he loves you so fucking much, Lakeland, that he even breathes in sync with you when you two are together. He is the person who will always choose you! Never doubt him, he will always find you and make sure you choose him, because without you, his soul would be shattered."

"Wave, I need to tell you something—" The words die on my tongue as the car is hit from behind. We both scream and I tighten my hold on the wheel, managing to keep the car straight without having a panic attack. Fear grips me when the car shunts us again. Wave screams as I bite down on my lip and jerk the wheel to keep us from spinning out and going over the bank. Rain continues to pelt down and obscure my view through the windshield.

"Lake, what the fuck is going on?" Wave screams. I chance a glance at her and the fear that is etched into her beautiful features spears me.

"I don't know!" I call back as I glance in the rearview mirror to see the headlights of the other car coming at us *again.* "Hold on!" *I scream as I plant my foot, I just need to cross the bridge and then we will be safe. He knows we're coming and he'll be waiting, they won't let whoever the fuck is doing this hurt us.*

"Lake, go faster, they're catching up!"

"I'm going as fast as I can! We just need to get over the bridge—-" Everything happens in slow motion, the car manages to hit the back left fender which sends us spinning out. We have no traction on the road and it feels like we are aquaplaning. I try to correct the car and get us straight but I overcorrect, slamming on the brakes does nothing. Our screams fill the inside of the car as we near the guardrail of the bridge, fear gripping me in its clutches the closer we get to the edge.

"Lakeland!" Wave screams as the front of the car smashes through the rail and the nose of the car hangs over the edge. I try to remain still but Wave thrashes in her seat trying to open her door. I feel the car shift as the back wheels begin to slip. I lift the handbrake and keep my foot on the brake hoping that will stop the car from going over the edge and plummeting us into the water below.

"Wave, stop fucking moving or we're going to fall over the edge!" I scream loud enough that she hears me over her own screams. She slowly begins to calm and turns to me with tears trekking down her cheeks but it's the look of terror in her eyes that sparks my anxiety. I have no idea what happened or why this is happening to us, but I know we can't stay here as the headlights from the car creep toward us slowly. "We need to

get out of here." She attempts to move so I rush to add. "Slowly."

She nods. I see it in her body language and the way her hands shake that she is in fight or flight mode. "My door is jammed, I can't get out." Panic is evident in her tone but I remain calm to try to ease her worry.

"Okay, can you climb over the back?" Her bottom lip trembles as she shakes her head.

"Lake, you climb out and I'll follow you."

I shake my head. "No. I need to stay on the brake so the car won't move."

"It's front wheel drive Lakeland, your foot on the brake isn't doing shit, now fucking move before they come back." I look out the window and the car is coming toward us but what scares me the most is the fact they are just crawling toward us at a snail's pace.

"Okay, once I'm out you climb straight over and we run."

"Okay," she says barely above a whisper. I fight through my fear and gently grip the handle and ease it open but freeze when the car slips forward. "Slowly!" My heart is racing so fucking fast and it is taking everything inside me not to break down and cry. This time when I open the door, the car doesn't move.

"Unclip my seatbelt slowly." Wave does as I ask and we both wait with bated breath to see what happens. When nothing happens, I slowly ease my foot off the brake and shift my body. The car creaks and slips forward when I'm halfway out.

"Tell my brother I love him!" Wave screams, then I'm

pushed the remainder of the way out landing on my hands and knees. I push to my feet and spin around to meet the terrified eyes of my best friend who is slipping over the edge. I grab onto the car and try to hold it so she can escape but it keeps slipping.

"Jump out now!" I scream as the front of the car begins to tilt toward the water.

"My leg's stuck. I love you, Lakeland. Now fucking run before he finds you." Gut curdling screams tear out of me as the car slips through my fingers and goes over the edge, leaving behind the ghost of my best friend's screams.

"Waverly," I cry out, then attempt to move toward the edge but the sound of the engine revving behind me draws my attention. I manage to spin around in time to see the headlights coming straight at me. I'm paralyzed by fear and unable to move, my legs won't work. I stand here welcoming the end, the only regret I have is not telling him. I should have told him earlier but I was scared and now he will never know. Closing my eyes I stand here and brace for what is to come. A scream rips from me as the car collides with my body, sending me sailing through the air. Pain courses through every inch of me when black spots dance in my vision. Before the darkness can take me, I look up into the eyes of a man I never thought would betray me.

"I'll make sure he knows what you did tonight, you took the love of my life from me," Xander spits. I welcome the blackness and pray I never wake up to live in this fucking nightmare.

Chapter Thirty-Four

Knox

Sobs claw their way out of her. I hold her tight, wishing I could take away her pain. I have never felt so fucking helpless in my life. I lift her hand but pause when I feel something clasped in her palm. I pry her fingers open and still at the sight of the necklace. I haven't seen this fucking thing in years. I turn it over and read the words I had inscribed on it.

I'll always choose you!

I gave this to Lakeland on her sixteenth birthday and haven't seen her with it this whole time. Was this the thing she grabbed by the railing? I shove it in my pocket as she jolts in my arms and gasps for air. I wrap my arm around her back and help her sit up. She snaps her eyes open and looks around at everyone but the moment our gazes lock, I see it. My heart pounds in my chest, I try not to hope but I can't stop it from rising inside me.

"Knox," she whispers as she reaches out and cups my cheek, fresh tears trail down her cheeks. I remain still barely able to breathe past the lump in my throat. "I'll always choose you." Her eyes shine with love. I tentatively reach out and cup her face in my hands as I bring her in close resting my forehead against hers.

"I choose you, Lay." A sob escapes her a second before her lips are on mine and she is pouring everything into this kiss, telling me without words that she loves me and feels everything I do but I need the words. I push her back. We're both panting, my heart pounds like a drum inside my chest. "Do you... did everything—"

She shushes me and smiles. "I remember everything. I'm so sorry, Knox. I wish I could take it back. I shouldn't have been driving but I was so upset—"

"Shhhh, calm down, baby. I need you to take it slow, okay?" She nods and swipes away her tears.

"We need to get out of here." Lake darts her gaze to the side and reels back at the sight of Roberto like she forgot he was here. When she reaches out to him, I yank her back.

"Shut the fuck up, you don't speak," I snarl at him. Lakeland ignores me and shifts out of my hold until she is kneeling in front of my father. She hesitantly reaches out and grabs his hand. I fight the urge to haul her away from him and shoot him right in the fucking head.

"Thank you." Now I reel back in shock. Why the fuck is she thanking that useless piece of shit for?

"You owe me no thanks, I wish I could have done more

that night." I hear the bitterness in his tone and wonder what fucking night he is speaking about.

"You need to explain everything to him and Clara, they need to know what happened. If they had known the truth..." she takes a shuddering breath and gives her head a shake before continuing, "Things may have worked out differently." The sadness I hear in her voice pisses me off, he isn't worth wasting her feelings on.

"I made my choices," he says firmly.

"Yes, but you had good reasons and when you tell him about how you tried to save me and... our baby—" I jerk back in shock. "Trust him, without his help that night my father would have killed me."

I can't take this shit any longer. Pushing to my feet, I grip her arm and yank her to me. "What the fuck are you talking about, Lakeland?"

She stares up at me with pity in her blue eyes and it fucking pisses me off, I don't need that shit from her. She is ruining this fucking moment. For years I thought the girl I was in love with had killed my sister, only to find out she didn't and had lost all her memories of our past. She got those fucking memories back and here she is comforting the cunt that wanted to pimp my sister out. She places her hand on my chest trying to comfort me and ease some of the anger inside me, but it doesn't do shit aside from making me want to fuck that pitying look out of her.

"Roberto only tried to marry me to save *you* and Wave." Her voice catches at the mention of my sister's name.

"That is a lie," my mom shouts as she points at Roberto.

"He is a liar. He never cared about us." Tears leak from her eyes, I always knew deep down she loved my father but I didn't realize just how much until now. "You pushed us away, treated me and our children like they meant nothing." Roberto climbs to his feet and winces in pain, he tries to step toward my mom but freezes when all the guns turn on him. The distraught look on his face is clearly not an act.

"You three mean everything to me!" he grits out. I scoff and shake my head in disgust.

"You mean my little sister meant so much to you that you wanted to put her on a corner to turn tricks?" Roberto flinches but I don't give a fuck and ignore Lakeland when she tries to plead with me to listen to him. I push her behind me as I get right in the fucker's face. He doesn't back down as I push my forehead against his. "You are nothing to me, I didn't bat an eye when I put a bullet in your fucking head because you were already dead to me." Pain etches his features, good because I want this cunt to hurt. I want him to feel the pain he inflicted on my mother.

"I wanted you to hate me, I needed you to." I keep my mask of indifference in place even though his words confuse me. "You three being as far away from me as you could was the only way I knew how to keep you safe. Gio tried to find you. I made sure to mask your trail for years until the night you showed up at my house and shot me."

"You are so fucking full of shit." I yell, fuck this cunt.

"Knox, he's telling the truth." I whirl around on Lakeland and pin her with a look, daring her to continue to defend this motherfucker.

"You don't get to take his fucking side," I roar. She recoils but I'm too angry to care.

"Knox, that's enough." Tay steps around me and comes to stand beside Lake. "We need to move, it's too fucking open here." Gritting my teeth I look around and see my men with their guns raised and focused on Roberto. I see my mom standing there crying silently and Lake who looks like she would blow over if a gust of wind came and decide Taylan is right.

"Fine, I want him taken to one of the cabins. I'll deal with him later," I order as I grip Lake's hand and wrap my arm around her shoulders, then lead her back to my car.

A huge part of me is elated that Lakeland's memories have returned, I'm more than fucking happy about it but when I look at her, I feel like she isn't. She hasn't said a word since we left the bridge. I lean against the wall watching her as she stares out the window with her arms wrapped around herself as if she is afraid if she lets go she will fall apart. I know she's angry with me because I wouldn't listen to what Roberto had to say, but she doesn't understand what it was like growing up watching my mom struggle while that fucker lived a lavish life and never had to worry about where his next meal would come from.

"Knox?" Turning around I see Xander and Taylan at the entryway. I shoot one last look over my shoulder at her, she hasn't moved an inch. Sighing, I lead the guys into the kitchen not willing to go any further away than the next room. I won't let Lakeland out of my sight after what happened today. Just thinking about her being alone with that piece of shit has my blood boiling and the need to fucking strip his skin from his body thrumming through me. "We set him up in Cohen's cabin. He's tied to a chair," Taylan adds.

Nodding, I cock my hip and lean against the counter so I can keep an eye on Lake through the doorway. "I'll deal with him later."

"What are you going to do with him?" I flick my gaze toward Xander who stands there tense. I can feel it in the pit of my gut that he's hiding something huge, I just can't find it within myself to care enough right now to push him for answers—I have too much on my fucking mind.

"I'm going to make him suffer," I answer.

"What did Lake mean when she said he tried to save her and your baby?" Tay asks.

I scrub a hand down my face feeling fucking tired and wrung out. "I don't know and I don't care what he did. One good deed doesn't own up for him being a piece of shit. I want you to send Mase and Floyd out with a team to scout the area and find out if Gio and Percy are here. Chaos promised to keep Karl and his men at bay. Without the extra help we have the advantage. If they find them, I want the rest of our men here by midday tomorrow. This shit needs to end," I snarl. Both my boys nod, I see it in their eyes, they are both ready to go to war and end this shit.

"I need to talk to you." Xander tenses at the sound of Lake's voice. I turn to her and nod.

"Okay."

"Not you, *him*," she says, flicking her chin toward Xander. I dart my gaze to him and frown. He looks conflicted, but without uttering a word, he nods his head and stalks out of the room with Lake following after him. I chase after them when I hear the front door open, but she spins around and pins me in place with one look. "I need to talk to him alone. Don't follow us."

"I'm not letting you out of my sight," I snap.

"I got her," Xander clips out.

"Yeah, right," she mutters as she steps past him and waits outside.

"I'll bring her back, I swear," Xan promises before he closes the door, leaving Taylan and me standing here.

"What the fuck was that?" I grit out.

A whoosh of air escapes Tay before he answers, "I got a bad feeling that your girl remembered something about Xander and it isn't good." I look over at Tay, he looks uneasy and slightly worried.

"Come on, I'll come with you to tell Mase and Floyd, it will help me to not go after them." Taylan chuckles and shakes his head.

"Now that she has her memories back, you won't be able to boss her around."

I scoff as I grab my coat off the hanger. "She'll do as she's fucking told."

"Bullshit. She had you by the balls before you even

emptied them inside her, that girl has always controlled you without even trying."

"Fuck off, dickhead," I bite out but my words lack heat and his answering laughter has me fighting back my own smile. He isn't wrong about Lake owning me.

Chapter Thirty-Five

Lakeland

I don't stop walking until we reach the edge of the lake that I spotted earlier when I was looking out the window. It's stunning with only the moon lighting the area. I had no idea this place even existed, it's surreal and like something out of a movie. Xander comes to stand beside me staring out over the lake. I can't even look at him. When my memories came flooding back I thought I would be happy, I wanted to be happy but I'm not. How the fuck could I be?

"You remember that night, don't you?" he asks in a monotone voice.

I keep my gaze ahead as I answer him. "Yes," I force out through clenched teeth. "When do you plan to tell Knox I didn't lose my memories because of his uncle and my father?" I hear him suck in a sharp intake of breath, the anger burning inside me at the fucking injustice that I was dealt has me feeling murderous.

"You gonna rat me out?" The fact he has the audacity to sound smug stokes that flame of anger inside me higher.

"This isn't a fucking game!" I scream as I whirl around on him only to find his gaze already on me. "You did this," I shout as I wave my arms around.

"I didn't do shit! You fucking left her in that car! You killed her, not me!" he roars, causing me to stumble back a step, shaking my head. His fists are clenched at his sides as his breaths come in rapid pants.

"You dumb fool! I tried to get her out first. I begged her to get out of the fucking car but her leg was stuck. If I had of known she was stuck, I would never have left her. I love Knox with my whole fucking heart. People think your significant other will become your soulmate but that wasn't the case for me, my boyfriend's sister, my best fucking friend was my soulmate." He recoils at my words but I'm not done. "I would have gone over that fucking bridge with her. I would never have left her, I loved Waverly."

"Yeah you *loved* her but I still fucking *love* her." Gasping, I stare at Xander with wide eyes.

"Oh my God, you came to my house that night because she called," I whisper aloud as I try to filter through my thoughts. "She called you because she saw her father, you didn't come to help Roberto." His jaw locks as I continue to piece everything together. "You came because Wave told you she needed you to help me." His nostrils flare and his eyes darken just as realization crashes into me. "Holy shit—"

"You keep your fucking mouth shut," he warns but I ignore him.

"Does Knox know you were in love with his little sister?" Xander slams his eyes closed and drops his chin to his chest. I study him for a moment as I try to recall more details about that night and what Wave had said. "Oh my God, she was in love with you too." A strangled sound leaves him and I know without him needing to say it that I'm right.

"I was out getting food that night when she called. I was only around the corner so I raced there to find her in the car looking scared. I pleaded with her to let me take her home and I would send Knox back for you but she refused, she said she wouldn't leave you behind." His tone is hard and guilt ridden but all I feel is love and sadness—love for the fact she wouldn't leave but sad because if she did she would still be here with us. "I told her to get her ass in my car and that I would get you and we'd leave but when I got inside, it was worse than what I thought. After you ran, Percy and Gio managed to get away from us. I left Roberto behind as I chased after you and Wave. I wasn't far behind Percy's car but the rain was so fucking heavy that night I could hardly see. I didn't... I thought that..."

I nod knowing what he's trying to say. "You didn't see them run us off the road, you thought I crashed and tried to escape not caring that Wave was still in the car." He slowly lifts his gaze to mine, the immense pain I see in his eyes robs me of air for a second.

"Their car was gone when I got to the bridge. I stopped and just stared for a second afraid if I drove any closer the car would fall but then I saw you jump out, then heard Wave scream and I... I fucking lost it. I thought you just left her." I may understand his reasons but it doesn't change what he did. His resentment cost me six years of my life and the life of my child! I stare up at him in astonishment, in his head he thinks he was right to do what he did.

"You didn't even try to speak to me, you just planted your fucking foot on the gas and mowed me down like I was a dog in the street!" I scream at him hysterically, with tears streaming down my face but I don't care, not remembering was easier, I didn't feel this crippling fucking pain in my chest. "You killed my baby," I choke out. Xander's face drops as he stumbles backward, shaking his head, trying to deny my claim but he already knows it's true. "You took every-thing from me... My life, my baby and... Knox. God dammit, Xander, if you had just fucking let me explain what had happened, my sister would still be alive!" Xander's actions from that night have had a ripple effect. Waverly lost her life and so did my sister. I can't stand the sight of him, I turn to walk away only to freeze at the sight of Knox and Taylan standing at the edge of the pathway. "Knox," I breathe out. At the mention of his name, Xander spins around. I can feel the anxious energy wafting off him, he and I both know there is no way Knox didn't hear what I just said. The murderous look on his face sends a chill down my spine. I am furious with Xander but I also don't want Knox to live with the guilt of killing his best friend.

The longer Knox just stands there staring at Xander without saying a word, the more uneasy I become. I see he's struggling to comprehend what he just heard. I want to wrap my arms around him and hold him close, telling him that we'll get through this but I'm scared. I have so much guilt inside me over that night, he didn't just lose his sister, he lost his baby he didn't even know I was carrying and he also lost... *me.* It's so strange feeling nothing for someone one minute only for a tidal wave of memories you didn't know were missing to come back to you, then for you to feel this overwhelming amount of emotions toward someone you thought you hated but slowly grew to care for. Then *bam*, you realize you're so deeply in love with him that you don't understand how you could have survived six years without remembering who they are.

I look to Taylan next, who looks torn. These are his two best friends and here he is being put in the middle and no doubt he will be forced to choose. These three have grown up together, forged a bond that blood brothers can't even manage to obtain, yet one night has ruined that. One night has changed everything they have ever known and there is no way to repair it. Xander took away that chance to make things right when he hid the truth from all of us and fed the demon inside Knox that thought I wronged him. He whispered words of hatred and blame about me, leaving Knox no choice but to believe his *brother.*

"What have you done?" Taylan speaks so softly I almost miss it, but the anguish and confusion is evident in his tone. Xander stiffens further but he doesn't get a chance to reply, out of nowhere, red lasers begin to cut through the air, then Knox is tackling Taylan to the ground as the first shots ring out. The air is knocked out of me when Xander knocks me to the ground and pins me there with his body. I scream as more shots ring out.

"Knox?" Xander shouts over the gunfire. I can't move my head thanks to his weight but I spot Knox and Taylan trying to crab crawl toward us but shots keep hitting the ground near them. I watch in horror wanting to scream at them to go back but then by the grace of fucking God, Knox's men come bounding down the path with their guns drawn. Some return fire toward the woods behind us while the others rush forward and haul Knox and Taylan back. Knox struggles in their hold, fighting to get free so he can come for me.

"Lakeland!" he roars, the fear in which he says my name sends a fresh wave of panic through me. As the shots get closer to where Xander and I are, screams tear out of me. I feel his arms wrap around my waist and then without warning he rolls us and I shriek only to sputter and choke when I swallow water. The freezing lake water is a shock to my system. Xander keeps an arm around my waist as we break the surface. I cough and try to tread water as terror grips me. I may not have had my memories for six years but a subconscious part of me has been terrified of open water for reasons I can't explain, but now I know why. I try to swim to the bank but Xander yanks me back against him and swims further into the middle. I scream for Knox who is still fighting to get to me but I can't move. I can only hope Xander doesn't succeed this time in killing me.

"Shut up. We need to get out of sight and you screaming like a fucking banshee keeps alerting them to where we are." Snapping my mouth closed, I quit fighting against him as I register he is right, since he threw us into the lake we haven't been shot at. Knox must come to the same realization because I see him stop struggling and nod to his men before they all break apart and go in opposite directions. I bite down on my lip to keep my teeth from chattering but the bite of the freezing water makes it difficult. When Xander reaches the opposite side of the bank he shifts me so my back is to the edge and he plasters his front against mine. "You stay here, stay low and don't make a fucking sound."

"You can't leave me here, please," I beg him, the thought of being alone in this body of water has me gasping for air. Xander grabs my face in both his hands forcing my head back so I can meet his stare.

"I'm unarmed, your father and Gio are out there with their men and I can't risk you getting captured or shot. Knox will never forgive me for what I did to you and I will never forgive myself for that, but if you get caught or killed, he will hate me for the rest of his life and I can't live with that. Stay here, Lake, please." His eyes implore me to do as he says. I'm so furious with him but even I can admit he is right. If Percy was to find me, he would use me against Knox, so would Gio, which is the only reason I nod my head. "I'll find Knox. Do not come out unless Taylan, Knox or I call out to you, got it?"

"Y-yeah," I say before I grit my teeth to stop them from chattering. Xander nods his head and propels himself out of the water, leaving me clinging to the side and staying low so no one can see me. I feel like a coward hiding out here. River wouldn't be scared, she would be out there fighting alongside Knox and his men. I'm not stupid, I know how to use a gun but I'm no sharpshooter. I whimper when I hear more shots and screams of pain but it's the sound of voices close by that has my throat closing with fear. If I stay here they are sure to find me. I shrink down lower and plaster my back to the bank as I scan the area, hoping to find somewhere safe to swim to until Knox can come for me but everywhere else is illuminated by the moonlight and now I get why Xander chose this spot because it's shrouded in darkness.

"I want all of them dead. Save me that little prick of a nephew of mine, I want him for myself." I stifle a gasp at the sound of Gio's voice above me. I hunker down further, praying to God they don't spot me.

"Find my daughter, I want her alive." I inhale sharply through my nose at the sound of my father's voice.

"What if she remembers?" Gio asks as shots continue to ring out around us, we're so secluded out here that no one will be able to hear the gun fight and report it to the police.

"She won't, the drugs she's been taking for years will make it almost impossible for her to recall a single thing from back then. She thinks Knox tried to kill her that night after we drove off." The carelessness in the way he speaks about that night is like a punch to the gut. A father is supposed to love their children and cherish them. Percy Deveraux never cared about me or my sister, we were just pawns for him to use and marry off to gain more real estate and money.

"Someone took her down that night but it wasn't Knox, whoever it was did a fucking good job. Not killing her was the best fucking torture for that little prick, I hope it kills him inside knowing the bitch he loved doesn't even remember him." Gio and Percy laugh and it sickens me to my core.

"Boss, we got one." My breath hitches when I hear more footsteps above me, then someone grunts in pain. I pray to whoever the fuck is listening for it not to be Knox.

"Ah, would you look at that, Percy." The gleefulness in Gio's tone is alarming me, he has to have someone Knox cares about.

"Kill me because I will never tell you where my son is." The lake water doesn't seem cold anymore compared to the ice filling my veins at the sound of Clara's voice, those sick fucks have Knox's mom.

Chapter Thirty-Six

Knox

Cohen tosses me a magazine and a gun. Stu appears out of thin fucking air strapping me with a vest. I look over to see Taylan strapping up and barking orders at our guys to spread out and form a perimeter to block these fuckers in. It's our best plan until Floyd and Mase get back with the rest of the men. These cunts have been watching us and waiting for the perfect time to strike.

"Lance, I want you, Jordan and Cash to get my mom the fuck out of here." They nod their heads and rush off to do as I ordered. Looking to Sel and Paul, next I order both of them to get Roberto out, if he is a part of my camp being attacked then his end won't be swift, it will be drawn out and painful. Once I'm strapped up, I nod to Cohen and Taylan to follow me as I instruct Stu to lead the rest of the guys out to close in on these cunts. "How far out are Mase and the others?" I ask Cohen.

"Soon as I heard the first shot I called him back, twenty minutes tops, boss." Grinding my teeth, I give him a curt nod. In twenty minutes we could all be dead, in a gunfight all it takes is a second for you to die so twenty minutes may as well be three hours.

"We move to the eastern side of the lake. Xander took Lakeland there to shield her from sight. Once we get her, you take her and get the fuck out of here, clear?" I can see Cohen wants to argue that he should be staying behind while Taylan and I run with her but not this time, this shit ends tonight.

"Yes, boss." I push in front of Taylan and crouch low to peer around the side of the cabin and immediately jerk back when a shot whizzes past my head. A whoosh of air escapes me as my adrenaline kicks in, I fucking live for this shit.

"Two on the corner, three on the right and one on the left. On my count we go." Taylan and Cohen grunt their agreement as I push to my feet. "Three... Two... One!" The three of us run out from around the side, Tay takes the three on the right, Co takes out the single fucker while I take down the duo on the corner. Both of them are hot on my heels as I rush to the next cabin plastering my back to it, we just need to get around this cabin to hit the woods and can use the cover of the trees to get to Lake without being seen.

"Knox!" Taylan hisses garnering my attention. I turn and follow to where he is pointing. My eyes widen at the sight of Xander stripping the guns off one of our fallen soldiers behind the cabin we have taken cover beside. I rush past them. At the sound of my approach, Xander lurches to his feet and points the gun at me. When he realizes it's me, he quickly drops it just in time for me to press up against him.

"Where the fuck is she?" I snarl.

"I left her in the lake. I wasn't armed and couldn't risk her getting taken—"

"But you could run her fucking down with our car and kill my kid?" Xander stumbles back a step and shakes his head. He opens his mouth but I refuse to allow him to speak. "When this is finished, you're gone," I grit out, making sure he can hear every ounce of hatred I feel toward him for taking her from me and robbing me of the chance to watch a life we created together grow inside my girl. Xander snaps his mouth closed and nods, looking pained. He has no fucking right to look that way!

"Move!" Cohen shouts just as men round the corner and open fire. We're forced to sprint for the cover of the woods. This is the worst possible situation to be in, we're in the open with no cover. The four of us run in a zigzag pattern making it hard for anyone to get a shot. A couple of feet from the covers of the trees I dive forward and roll along the ground until I take cover behind a tree. I peer around it and open fire when I spot Gio's guys. Shouts ring out from either side of me and I loathe to fucking admit it but I'm relieved when I hear the sound of three other guns firing from my side.

The five guys drop to the ground but I hear more shouts from behind them. "I found the Don, this way!" the cunt calls out to the others.

"Fuck," I snarl. Now that they know where I am they are

all going to be coming for me. I can't get to Lake with all of them on my ass.

"Go to her, I'll lead them away." I snap my head to the right and stare at Xander. He implores me with his eyes to trust him, years of brotherhood bonding has me wanting to accept his offer but after learning he betrayed me it gives me pause. "Go, Cohen and I will lead them away. Take Taylan and get her out of here."

"If you fucking—"

He cuts me off before I can finish threatening him. "I swear, I won't fail you now, go!" Xander takes off with Cohen on his tail. "This way, Knox!" he calls out, creating a diversion so those pompous cunts think it's me with him. Taylan and I wait behind a tree until the sound of the guys chasing after them fades, I chance a glance around the tree and when I spot the coast is clear, I nod to him and we take off running, pausing every couple of seconds to take cover behind trees until we deem the coast is clear. We push closer to the edge of the tree line and hunker down behind a large oak tree on the eastern side. I slide down the tree and pop my mag out, two rounds left and I have three more clips strapped to my side. I shoot Tay a look and motion toward his gun, he holds up four fingers and then points then two. He's got four rounds in the clip and two spare mags.

Resting my head back against the tree, I take a couple deep breaths and block out the sounds of all the shouting, gunfire and cries of pain as I get in the zone. To get to Lakeland we have to cross through an open space of land with no cover, we'll be sitting ducks until we reach the edge of the bank. Tay shifts and peers around the tree as I scan the area around us, making sure we aren't about to be ambushed before looking back at him only to find his panic stricken gaze on me. I feel the color drain out of my face as I take a look and crippling fear like I have never felt before in my life threatens to hold me immobile.

"Mom," I mutter her name as if it's a prayer and that the sight in front of me is nothing but a bad dream. At least six guys that are heavily armed form a semi-circle around Percy and Gio, while four more stand by my mom who is on her knees with a gun pressed to the back of her head. I feel my heart pumping inside my chest but I'm struggling to pull in any air—I can't fucking lose her. I won't lose another person I fucking love. I turn to Taylan ready to tell him to head back to get the others but the words die in my throat at the sight of him standing. He tosses me his gun and the spare mags, I catch them on reflex.

"You fucking get us out of this, you are better than your father ever was. Save Lake and change the fucking game, I won't let our mom pay the price for our fuck up." Before I can climb to my feet or utter a fucking word, he darts out of the cover of the tree as I watch. The moment they spot him, all their guns except for the one on my mom turn to him. Taylan holds his head high and raises his hands spinning around in a circle to show them he isn't armed. My heart aches, this is the worst fucking situation of my life. Taylan and Xander aren't just friends, they aren't just some kids I grew up with, they are my fucking brothers and losing one of them would be like losing my sister all over again. "You want to fuck with Knox?" he shouts. "Come get me and make me an example. That woman means nothing to him, he left her unguarded. I'm the better bait."

"Motherfucker!" I snarl as I try to think of a plan, something that will get them both out of this alive. Goddammit, Lakeland is still in the water and I have no way to get to her either. I'm fucking powerless. I took this family from my father because I never wanted to feel powerless again, yet here I am, with more money than I can spend in three lifetimes, a bunch of loyal men ready to die for me but I still don't have enough power to save the ones I fucking love. A branch snaps and I draw my gun, aiming it and ready to fire, but hesitate at the sight of Roberto coming toward me with Jordan, Stu, Mika and a few others. He uses hand signals to direct *my* men to spread out along the tree line before coming to me. I don't lower my gun.

The fucker doesn't stop even when the barrel of my Glock is pressed against his chest, his brown eyes boring into mine. The stubborn set of his jaw does nothing to sway me from dropping my gun, I don't trust this cunt.

"Come on you motherfuckers!" I flinch at the sound of my best friend's voice, followed by the sound of flesh hitting flesh. I slam my eyes closed, hating that he's out there getting his ass beat because of me.

"Look at me." Without consent my eyes snap open and meet my father's. "You're a fucking Don, you are the head of this family. You have the power and the control to turn this shit around. Your men that have returned, are laying waste to rest of theirs. Man the fuck up, Son, and do what needs to be done." I fucking hate that, hearing him call me son has that stupid little boy inside me that longed for their father when he was younger to rise up. "Save your family." His words fan the flame of determination inside me. I hold his gaze as I think for a second before nodding.

"Hands behind your back, you're going to trade your life for my mom and Taylan's." His eyes shine with pride. He nods his head and turns around, placing his hands behind his back. Stu comes forward and offers me a cable tie. I look from it to Roberto's wrist and ponder it for a second before snatching the fucking thing and placing it around his wrists, but I don't tighten it. I shove Tay's gun into my waistband but keep my own in my hand. I grip Roberto's shirt in my other hand and heave him forward, Stu and Jordan following me out. "Hey!" I yell, drawing all their attention to me. Anger burns inside me at the sight of Taylan on the ground in a ball as five cunts stand over him. My boy lifts his head and the sight of his face bloody and bruised has me gritting my teeth. The fucker smiles but then flinches in pain. Tearing my gaze from him I look back to Percy and Gio, ignoring the cock suckers who turn their guns to me.

"Knox Bronson, come to surrender?" Gio says cockily. I look at my mom who is sobbing and covering her mouth with her hand as she stares at Taylan on the ground before darting her fearful gaze to me. "Ah, the scum brother who has been a thorn in my fucking side for years," Gio spits out. Roberto remains silent as I continue to force him forward only stopping ten feet away from the cunts. I may have men scattered around in the trees ready to strike at any moment but Gio and Percy know they both hold the power here with a gun trained on my best friend and my mom.

"Surrender?" I say menacingly. "Never," I snarl. Percy's face contorts in disgust at the sight of me so I decide to taunt the cunt, I just need one of them to snap and break formation so I can strike. "Percy, still a spineless cocksucker I see." The fucker's eyes widen in indignation.

"You filthy, fucking gutter rat!" he screams bringing a smile to my face.

"A gutter rat your daughter loves to fuck nightly." His face turns beat red. I hate using Lake to get at him but I don't have a choice. I just hope if she can hear me she knows I'm full of shit. "Fuck, even without her memories she still loves my cock inside her."

"You little bastard!" He tries to come to me but Gio holds him back as Stu and Jordan cock their guns, ready to fire. I shake my head, telling them to stop when the fucker holding the gun to my mom's head pushes the barrel against it harder. "Get on your knees and surrender or your mother dies." I keep my face blank not showing these fucks that Percy's threat has me on edge.

"I don't kneel," I say in a cold tone. "You want my surrender? That won't happen but I will trade you Roberto for Clara and Taylan." Percy laughs but my focus is on Gio and the way he is eyeing his brother, they may only be half-brothers but you wouldn't think it with how similar they look. I decide to take a huge fucking risk and use what Roberto told me. "I know this fucker has been causing problems for you, *Uncle*." Gio's mask falters for a second but it's long enough for me to see the look of bloodlust, he wants Roberto dead more than I do. As long as his older brother lives, his claim to being the head of the family will always be challenged.

"He means nothing to us, we have you by the fucking balls you—"

Giovani cuts off Percy's pathetic threat. "You get your mother back but we're keeping your friend." My nostrils flare and I grind my teeth.

"No," I force out. "I told you my terms," I roar, spying out of the corner of my eye a dozen or so of Gio's men coming from the woodlands behind them. Fuck! I shift slightly behind Roberto and discreetly drop my hold on him and pull Taylan's gun from my waistband and place it in his hand. I look between the both of them and know they are never going to give up either of them, I see it in Gio's eyes.

"You have four seconds before I kill them both," Gio clips out. I look between Taylan and my mom and panic. Fuck it, I open my mouth to tell them to take me instead but terror renders me speechless as I watch Lakeland leap from the water. The guy holding a gun to my mom's head turns toward Lake, without hesitating I lift my gun and fire. The men behind them begin running forward as more shots ring out. Gio pulls his gun and aims it at me just as I turn and shoot the cunt who holds a gun on Taylan, while Stu and Jordan fire off rounds.

"Knox, no!" my mother screams. I turn toward her in time to see Lakeland charge her father just as Gio fires his shot at me. I stand here waiting for it all to end. They say you see your life flash before your eyes when you're about to die but I see nothing except for the heartbroken look in my mother's eyes and the gut curdling scream that comes from Lake. I hate that I will never get to hold them again, but at least I'll finally get to see my sister again, I think as I close my eyes and wait.

Chapter Thirty-Seven

I feel nothing as I launch out of the water and run at my father, I won't allow these bottom feeding cockroaches to harm the man I love. I haven't even gotten a chance to speak to him or hold him since my memories came back and I won't allow these bastards to take that chance from me. Percy spins around and his eyes widen, but he has no time to prepare as I jump at him, the momentum taking us to the ground. I scream as I hit, punch and claw at his face.

"Fuck you!" I scream. When I hear Clara scream, I snap my gaze up, forgetting all about Percy as Knox stands there looking from his mother then to me before closing his eyes, waiting for his end as Gio fires his gun. I scream, wanting to look away but unable to. My stomach drops as I wait to watch another person I love die before my eyes but at the last second Roberto spins around covers Knox with his body, taking the bullet to his back and taking them both to the ground. That's all I see before my father punches me. I fall to the ground groaning.

I hear shots over the buzzing in my ears and try to shake away the dizziness and push to my feet, but I'm sent sailing backwards when I'm kicked in the side. I cry out only to have the cry silenced when I'm robbed of air by another kick. I lay on my back gasping for breath as I stare up at my father. The cold, callous look in his eyes reminds me of all the years I had forgotten about when he would take his anger out on me, only for River to swoop in and save me, she took the beatings meant for me. Percy kicked her out because she refused to allow him to hurt me. She also wanted to tell me the truth about the accident but the monster we call *Dad* told her he would kill me if she did. Percy lifts his foot and presses his boot down on my throat, cutting off my airway. I claw at his leg and thrash beneath him trying to get free.

"You ungrateful little cunt. You spread your fucking legs for the wrong member of that fucking family!" My head begins to pound from the lack of oxygen, I feel my arms turning sluggish, the sounds of gunfire are drowned out by the sound of my blood pumping in my ears. In a last ditched effort to save myself, I reach up and grip the inside of his thigh with my fingers and pinch the fuck out of it. It's a pussy move but I don't care. The moment he removes his foot and stumbles backward, I suck in lungfuls of air. He roars in anger as he comes at me again but this time he rips my head back by my hair and punches me right in the mouth. The metallic taste of my own blood is the first thing to register before pain explodes in my face when he delivers the second hit.

I fling my arms, trying to shield my face from his punishment. "Why are you doing this?" I scream. The hits stop and I chance a glance through the gaps in my arms to see my father looking down at me with nothing but malice in his eyes. I see the real him, the angry jaded coward of a man I am forced to call my father. He is the only living relative I have left and yet I still know I would be better off without him.

"It was never about you to begin with, then you caught Gio's eye and I made a deal but that fucking prick Roberto ruined it, or so we thought, until you had no memory of your time with his bastard son."

"What the hell does Knox have to do with any of this?" His lip twitches in a snarl and I tense in preparation for him to strike me again, but he doesn't.

"The night his sister died he changed. I could control Roberto with the help of Giovani until Knox ruined it and took out his father. Keeping you alive and away from him kept our family safe, we knew he would never harm us so long as we had you. The bastard thought he hated you but he could still never bring himself to kill you because your sister made a deal with him that kept you alive. Things changed when he took the chair as the head of the family with the other Don's. We knew marrying you off to Gio would force him out of hiding, all we had to do was wait for him to come for you and now look, this is all because he fell in love with a worthless bitch. Hurting you meant hurting him which in turn led to us getting the upper hand on his father. Once he's gone, you will be sold to the highest bidder and finally make yourself worth something to me."

I almost wish I hadn't asked why he had done any of this. How could a monster like him ever share blood with me and my sister? He rears his arm back ready to strike me again and I don't bother to lift my arms to ward off the blow. I know Knox was outnumbered and I would rather be beaten to death like Riverland than face a reality of living in a world where Knox no longer does or being sold to some sadistic fuck.

"You're right." The husky sound of his voice has my head jerking upward to see Knox standing there with a gun pressed to Percy's temple. My father pales and freezes with his arm still raised. "All of this is for *her*. I stayed away because of a deal I made with one of my best friends but the second you broke that deal I came for what is mine." The conviction and the way he says I am his, I feel it in my soul.

"Pull the trigger then." Percy tries to sound unaffected but he can't keep the quiver out of his voice.

Knox tsks him. "Now, where would the fun be in ending a piece of shit like you so quickly?" Percy pales, he begins to ramble and plead for Knox to kill him as Mase and another guard grab Percy's arms and haul him off me, kicking and screaming. The moment he is gone, Knox drops to his knees beside me and I take in the sight of the blood covering him as he reaches for me and crushes me against his chest. I cling to him like he is my lifeline, being in his arms chases away all my fears. I feel safe, loved and protected.

I pull out of his embrace and gaze up at him. His eyes scan my injuries and darken at the sight but I don't care about that, I need him to know how I feel. "You never had to be anything more than who you were for me to love you." Reaching out I push to my knees and cup his cheek, loving the way he nuzzles into my touch. "I choose you, Knox, in every life I'll always choose you!"

The heated look that enters his eyes at my words has my breath hitching and my heart racing for a whole new reason. Knox leans down and rests his forehead against mine, we breathe each other in and all the sounds around us fade to white noise and nothing else exists in this moment except for me and him.

"I'll choose you always, Lay," he says softly before sealing his lips to mine. This kiss isn't like any of the others, there is no urgency or rush to it we take our time getting reacquainted with the feeling of each other. I know for him this must be too slow because he has been kissing me for weeks but this is six years in the making for me as the woman he has been kissing wasn't the real me. Not the me who is madly in love with him and has been since I was child, he was kissing the *me* that had no control over falling in love with him even when he was an asshole.

"We got to move, I got a crew coming to scrub the scene now, we need to get out of here, Knox." We pull apart at the sound of Taylan's voice. I look up and my chest clenches at the sight of his battered face. I push to my feet and wrap my arms around him, he's stiff for a second before he finally returns my embrace. "I knew calling you kitten would jog your memory." I snort out a laugh and shove him back, he flinches and I feel like a bitch.

"I'm so sorry–"

He raises a hand stopping me as Knox wraps an arm around my waist. "You and I both look about the same right now, kitten." I purse my lips and glare at him.

"You don't get to call me kitten, you get to call me Lay or Lake." Tay and Knox both chuckle.

"It's good to have you back, Lay." Taylan's words have warmth spreading through me, then I take in the scene around us and gasp.

"How?" I breathe out.

Knox picks up what I'm putting down without me having to elaborate. "Once you attacked, Roberto took a bullet for me just as Mase and the others got here and joined in on the fight, that gave us the upper hand."

"What happened to Gio and Percy?" I spit out.

"They will be taken back home where I can take my time with them and... enjoy not having to rush." A shiver trails down my spine at his sinister words. Knox leads me back toward the cabins. I take in the sight of all the bodies on the ground. These men gave their lives for a cause they thought to be noble but how fucking wrong were they, they fought for an evil fucking monster and they paid the price with their lives. "Hey." Knox draws to a stop and turns me to face him, a couple of guys try to draw his attention but he waves them off keeping his focus on me. That, what he just did, not ignoring me to deal with someone else is the reason I will always choose him. He showed me for years before my accident when he professed his love that I could always count on him to be there for me. "What's wrong?"

Stepping into him I crane my neck back and hold his gaze as I wrap my arms around his waist allowing his warmth to soak into me. "Promise me that we will always find our way back to each other, no matter what."

His eyes soften as he leans down and kisses me. "I will always find my way back to you, kitten." I breathe him in, needing to be close and reminding myself that this isn't a dream and he is really here.

"Knox, I never want to miss a day with you. We lost six years together and I don't want to lose another second. I don't want anyone else to die so we can be together—"

"Shhhh." I clamp my mouth closed and fight back the tears that want to fall. "These men around us knew there was a possibility they wouldn't return home. The men who fought for *us* died fighting to end a sex ring leader. With Gio and Percy gone we can now end that fucking app. The moment Karl steps a single foot out of line, I'll be there taking his ass down. All of that aside, I would go to war with God for you any day of the week because that's what you mean to me, Lay."

"Knox!" At the sound of his mother's cry, I step away from him as she comes bounding toward her son, crying. He pulls her in close and assures her he's okay repeatedly. I shiver and rub my hands up and down my arms, trying to get some warmth into my bones. I decide to slink off back to the cabin so I can take a hot shower before we leave and get out of these wet clothes before I catch a cold.

I feel horrible for feeling happy and like a weight has been lifted off my shoulders when so many have lost their lives. I pause at the bottom of the stairs of our cabin and tilt my head back looking up at the night sky, the stars shine brightly. I spot three bright ones and I allow myself to think of them as the three women I love most—Waverly, Riverland and my mom. I hate that the three of them aren't here with us, with *me*. My best friend and sister died so I could live, how the fuck do I live with the weight of their sacrifice?

Chapter Thirty-Eight

Knox

After I managed to convince my mom I wasn't going to drop dead, I took off trying to find Lake. It's stupid that her not being in my sight makes me panic, thinking she'll be taken from me again. I know we have a lot to talk about but right now, all I want is just to hold her until my mind can finally catch up with the fact that she is really back, *my* Lake is back for good!

"She's in the cabin." I halt at the sound of his voice. Xander steps out of the shadows and comes toward me with his hands stuffed in his pockets and guilt stricken look plastered across his face. The rules of the Re Della Strada state that another family member can never be harmed by one of our own and he broke that code when he hurt Lake and by default killed our baby. I can never forgive him for that.

"Why?" That one word holds so much fucking weight.

Xan takes a shuddering breath and drops his gaze to his feet. "I was in love with your sister, Knox." I recoil.

"What?" He slowly lifts his gaze back to mine and I see it in his eyes. "You son of a bitch," I snarl taking a step toward him, only for Taylan to appear out of thin fucking air to get between us and push me back.

"It's not what you think," Xan snaps.

"Then explain it, motherfucker!" I shout.

"I loved her." Pain laces his words. "Waverly meant to me what Lakeland means to you, she loved me too."

I shake my head denying what he says. "My sister would have told me—"

"She tried!" he screams, cutting me off. "She tried to tell you so many fucking times but you just brushed her off every time she tried to talk to you. I even told you that I loved her and you laughed, smacked me on the back and said *good one, fucker.*" I scrunch my face not recalling that happening. "Unlike you, we had to hide our true fucking feelings because neither of us wanted to risk you hating us for falling in love."

"She's my little sister and you were screwing her behind my back?" I roar, my anger is burning hot inside me now.

"It was never like that with her! Why do you think I never joined in on your three way with Lakeland?" He doesn't give me a chance to answer. "Unlike Taylan, I wasn't available like him because I was in love with your sister. Wave knew about it and said I could if I wanted to and acted like she didn't care but I knew she was full of shit. I would never hurt her, Knox. I fucking ran to her that night when she called. I begged her, I fucking begged her to come with me and I would send you back for Lake but she was so fucking stubborn and wouldn't leave without her best friend. I got Lake out and they took off but Percy and Gio followed them. I got there too late." His voice catches on the end part and his eyes fill with anguish.

"What happened, Xander?' I grit out through clenched teeth. I feel my mom come up beside me and look around to see some of my men have stopped to watch the showdown between us.

"I saw Lakeland get out of the car and heard..." He growls and tugs on the strands of his hair as he tries to get the words out. "I heard her scream, that fucking sound haunts me every night when I close my eyes. I blacked out and before I knew what was happening, my foot was on the gas and then I mowed Lake down." Taylan presses against my chest harder, sensing my need to break Xander in half rising with each word. "I jumped in after the car and tried to find her, I couldn't see anything it was too fucking dark. I don't know how long I searched for her, I just remember the cops dragging me out of the river and then we were home and telling you what happened."

"You saw my baby?" my mom chokes out. Xan darts his gaze to my mom. He may be angry with me but he would never disrespect my mom. He stands taller and nods. "You went in after her?"

"Yes."

"Thank you," Mom chokes out, shocking us all.

"Huh?" Xan rasps out.

"You tried to save my baby girl and for that I will never be able to repay you, Son. You could have died that night as well." All emotion is wiped from Xander's face as he looks at my mom.

"I did die that night, Mom. My heart fractured and stopped beating when hers did. I loved your daughter so fucking much. Fuck, I still love her."

I scoff earning a glare from my *former* best friend.

"Knox, please don't—" I cut my mom off before she could continue to beg me to spare Xander's life. I shove Taylan away as I step forward, leaving an inch of space between me and Xander.

"Alexander Grayson." His features harden at the use of his full name as he braces for his punishment. "You broke the code of the Re Della Strada by hurting a member of our family and taking the life of my unborn child from me." Saying that shit burns my chest, it fucking hurts like a bitch. "Punishment is death."

"Knox."

"No, Brother." I ignore mom and Taylan and continue.

"But given who you *were* to me and what you tried to do for... my sister." I take a deep breath and fight through the onslaught of emotions that rage inside me. My heart breaks over the loss of my child and the years I missed with Lake but it also fucking breaks me knowing this is the last time I will ever see one of my brothers. "I hereby banish you from the family." Gasps sound out around us. "You are hereby stripped of all titles and rank. You are to leave my country and never return or you will be met with death at my hands and my hands alone." Unshed tears gather in his eyes, he swallows audibly and nods. A lump forms in my throat hating that this is how things are ending with us but I can't forgive him for what he did, he lied to me and hid the fucking truth for years.

"I'll prove to you that I am worthy of your forgiveness. I'll show you, even if it takes me the rest of my life, I'll prove it to you because I am not dying without my family by my side." He snaps his arm out and grips the back of my head pulling me to him where he presses his forehead against mine. "I won't give up. I broke your trust and fucked up badly, Brother, but I'll make this right somehow. I swear it on my life, I will fix *us*." I don't let it show but I fucking hope he is right but right now, I can't think of anything aside from needing him away from me before I shoot him and have to live with the guilt of killing my brother.

He releases me and brushes past to go to my mom and Taylan. I stay as I am with my back to him. It takes him a few minutes before he returns to stand before me, his face is void of all emotions and his mask is firmly in place. I look him over one last time cementing his appearance to memory.

"This will be the last time I speak to you, if there is ever another time you hear my voice it will be the last thing you hear before I send you to join my sister." His jaw locks but he remains silent. "Take a car, you have twenty-four hours to cross the border and get the fuck out of my territory. If you are caught after that, you will be executed like a traitor." He eyes me for a second before a whoosh of air escapes him and he nods.

"Understood." He turns and walks away but before he can get too far I call out to him. "Yeah?" he says as he looks back over his shoulder at me.

"Go get em killer." A glint enters his eyes as the corner of his mouth lifts in a smirk before he stalks off.

Entering the cabin I go in search of Lake, needing her to distract me from what just happened but I can't find her. I head upstairs and push open the master bedroom door and I'm greeted by the sound of the shower running from the adjoining bathroom. I don't think as I strip off in the doorway, closing the door quietly behind me and locking it so we aren't interrupted. I slink across the room and nudge the door open. Immediately, steam hits me in the face, and as I wait for it to clear, I drink in the sight of her. Her back's to me and her perfect ass is only displayed through the glass doors. Fuck, the sight of her naked with droplets of water trailing down her flawless skin has my cock hard and ready to be buried inside that tight, wet little cunt.

Without making a sound, I cross the room, grip the handle and slowly open the door, then slip inside. Before she can react, I plaster myself against her back and have her throat in one hand and the other gripping her waist. She doesn't fight, she just leans her head back against my shoulder and looks up at me with a lustful look in her eyes.

"Make me forget about what happened tonight."

Bending down I nip at the soft skin between her neck and shoulder, drawing small moans from her. I shift and suck the lobe of her ear into my mouth before releasing it with a pop as I brush my lips over her ear when I speak.

"I'll never allow you to forget another thing, but I'll make you feel so fucking good that you won't even think about what happened tonight while I'm buried so deep inside you that you have no fucking idea where you begin and I end." Her eyes close as a moan tumbles free.

"I remember how it feels when you show me how much you love me." She lazily blinks her eyes open to meet my gaze, her blue eyes are filled with heat and longing. "Refresh my memory on how it feels when you show me what it's like to be owned by Knox Bronson." My breathing turns ragged, she is definitely fucking back. Lake's always known how to taunt me and have me eating out of the palm of her fucking hand like a starved dog. Spinning her around, I push her back against the wall, loving the sound of the hiss that escapes her as she arches her back off the cold wall. I don't have it in me to go slow, I need to be inside her more than I need my next breath.

Gripping the backs of her thighs I lift her. She locks her legs around me as I capture her lips. She opens for me instantly, swirling my tongue around hers I moan at the taste of her. She wraps her arms around my neck and pulls me in closer so there isn't a sliver of space between us. I grind against her, teasing us both, I do it once more before she breaks the kiss, panting and breathless.

"Knox, I need you. Don't make me beg I've waited too long for this." I smirk at her neediness.

"Baby, I just fucked you—"

Her eyes narrow. "No. You fucked wannabe me and now you have the real thing back and I want to be reminded what it feels like to have my man's cock deep inside me. Don't play hard to get, baby. You got to pull me around by my hair before, but you and I both know if you tried that shit now, you would be the one crying yourself to sleep on the hardwood floor." I cringe at the reminder of how much of a cunt I was to her.

I shift and guide my cock to her entrance as I hold her gaze and slowly push inside her as I speak. "I didn't mean to hurt you—"

"Yes, you did," she rasps out before moaning. "You were hurt. I get it but we're past that now so don't bring it up again." I pause halfway inside her and scowl at the little shit.

"*You* brought it up!"

A fiery look enters her eyes and I fight the smile from breaking free. I've longed to see that look in her eyes for weeks now. "Are you trying to start a fight?" Knowing how to win this without saying a word, I slam the rest of the way inside her, relishing in the scream that tears out of her. I don't give her a chance to recover before I pull almost all the way out of her before thrusting back inside her, moaning when I feel her greedy little cunt quiver around my cock.

"You take my dick like a good girl don't you, baby?" I praise as she locks her ankles and braces her hands on my shoulders, then begins to bounce up and down on my cock.

The feeling of her fucking me is the best fucking high I have ever felt but the sight of her perky tits in my face pulls a feral growl from me. As I lean forward and capture one of her nipples in my mouth, she throws her head back and cries out when I bite down on the hardened peak.

"Oh fuck, just like that, Knox." I switch sides and bite down harder on the other side as I grip the globes of her ass and slam her down onto my cock. "Fuck yes, don't stop, please. I need to come on your cock." I pull back, meeting her hazy gaze.

"Come on, baby, come all over your fucking cock, show me how much you missed it," I grit out as I slam inside her ruthlessly without a pause, keeping my tempo the same.

"Yes, it's mine," she screams out just as her pussy walls clamp down on my cock. "Knox!" My name is shouted like a prayer from her sinful lips as her orgasm rips through her. Unable to stop myself, I come a second after her but instead of roaring out my release, I capture her lips in a heated kiss. She swallows my groans and rides me, drawing out my high as I empty everything I have inside her.

I break the kiss and bury my face in the crook of her neck as we both try to catch our breath. She runs her fingers through my hair absentmindedly, I fucking love it when she plays with my hair. We stay like this for a long time, not wanting to let each other go but I know everyone is waiting on us and it's that reason alone that I reluctantly release her with a peck to her lips and smack to her ass, earning a squeal from her.

"Hurry up, we need to get out of here." She pushes her

lips to the side not liking my demanding tone, so I ease the sting with a promise. "The quicker we get home, the quicker we get to spend the whole day in bed." She pouts, earning a raised brow from me.

"Only one day?"

I snort. "How about I finger fuck you in the backseat on the ride home." Her eyes turn glassy as she pictures what I'll do to her in her mind. "But, if you make a sound and Taylan or my mom catch onto what we're doing, I'll leave you on edge and you'll be sucking my cock the moment we get back home. Deal?" A sly smirk tugs at the corners of her mouth as she slowly trails a finger down my chest. I tense knowing she is up to something. The moment she grips my cock in her hand I jolt. "Lakeland," I warn her through gritted teeth when she pumps me.

She bats her lashes and smiles up at me trying to act innocent. "I think you need to punish me now since your best friend just walked in on you fucking me like a savage a minute ago." Fucking Taylan picked the damn lock! Before I can say a word or do anything, she drops to her knees and peers up at me through her lashes as she wraps those fucking perfect lips around my shaft. Throwing my head back, I groan. Fuck yes, I missed this shit. I fist my hand in her hair and hold her in place as I thrust my hips.

"Hands behind your back," I bark. She eagerly obeys and opens her mouth wider to take me further inside. "You like that cock in your mouth don't you, kitten?"

"Hmmmm." Her moan sends vibrations up my cock and I shudder, fuck she sucks my cock so good.

"You want to touch that pussy, baby?" Her eyes light up with need.

"Hmmm," she moans as she bobs her head up and down on my cock. Gripping her hair I halt her movements. She flicks her gaze to mine.

"You don't get to come until I say, now suck that fucking cock and make me come, then I'll finger that greedy little cunt in the backseat while Tay watches me do it the rearview mirror." At the mention of Taylan watching me finger fuck her, she moans and her eyes roll backward. I would bet good fucking money that her cunt it dripping fucking wet and clamping down on air.

Chapter Thirty-Nine

Lakeland

One month later...

Since arriving back here four weeks ago, Knox has been doing damage control. I had to give a statement to the police and make it known that my father lied and Knox never kidnapped me. The police are still hunting for Gio and Percy but they won't find them, they're still chained up in Knox's basement. He and Tay refuse to kill them, saying death is too easy and they need to suffer. I choose to not think about what happens down there and turn a blind eye to the times Knox saunters into our room covered in blood.

The one time I didn't mind being present for the brutality that this life displays was when Tristan, the dirty fucking traitor that sold us out to Gio and my father, was forced to walk the line of the families of the men and two maids who lost their lives while every other member of

Knox's crew was present to dish out their beating. I watched them slice, hit, spit, throw things and scream at the scum. That motherfucker was responsible for my sister being beaten to death. I wanted to take part in it but Knox wouldn't allow it, saying that the guilt would eat me alive at night. Watching Tristan die filled me with a sense of justice knowing that my sister can finally rest easy now that she has been avenged. We got River's ashes back a week after we got here and I know I need to take her to where our mother is buried but I can't, not yet. I'm not ready to let go of my hero just yet.

Chaos Murdoch agreed to help us take down the app Percy created to sell women and children. When Taylan showed me the app and how it worked, I threw up at the sight of the young girls on there. Chaos shut it down so no one could bid or buy from there but he didn't close it because they want to track the IP addresses of the people who purchased off the app and free the women and children who have been sold. Not sure how else I could help them with the rescues, I pledged all the properties my father owned as safe houses for the men to take them to. Knox and the Murdoch's as well as the Memento Mori have agreed to allow each other to cross into each other's territory at any time if it is for a rescue. Knox said the Russian leader has agreed to this as well but the Greek, Irish and English have not been let in on what we are all doing.

All the money Percy made from the app I have donated to Koby and Anya Murdoch's shelters they run for women. There is no way I could have kept that money or spent it knowing where it came from so it only seemed right that I give it back to the women. I wish I could do more but I don't know how! Knox has been so supportive of my wish to go to nursing school. I told him about it last week, saying I wanted to do something meaningful with my life and when I pitched him the idea he thought it was great. He said Chaos's cousin, Amelia, is a doctor and might be able to help me with some of the studies or just be there to answer any questions or concerns I may have.

I toy with the heart pendant around my neck as I stare down at Amelia's contact details in my phone. Knox gave me back the necklace I found at the bridge. He said he had gotten it for me before the accident but never got a chance to give it to me so he had it cleaned. Ever since he gave it to me I haven't taken it off because it's a reminder that no matter what he will always choose to love me.

I hit dial and wait with bated breath, feeling nervous. After the sixth ring, I lose hope and move to end the call but she answers.

"Hello?"

"H-hi." I'm met with silence, I clear my throat and push on. "My name is Lakeland Deveraux and Chaos gave me your number." I chew on my bottom lip nervously.

"Yeah?"

A woosh of air escapes me and I deflate. "I'm sorry, I'm totally blowing this. I'm calling because he said you might be able to help point me in the right direction of a good nursing school."

"You want to be a nurse?" I bristle at the disbelief in her voice.

"Yes," I snap. "Is that a problem?"

"Not at all. It's just a shock because anyone who knows my cousins usually don't really take too well with saving people." I can't help the snort that bursts out of me.

"Sorry. I understand that. When I told my boyfriend, he looked shocked but he supports me. The rest of the guys think I'm crazy." Amelia laughs.

"Get used to it. Given the fact you know my real name I'm gonna take a wild guess here and assume you know who my father is?"

"Yeah, I do."

"My father thought having a daughter as a doctor would benefit the family, if you catch my drift, but I didn't train for years to patch men up long enough for them to torture others. I became a doctor to save innocent people and restore some balance to the world since my family constantly tips the scale." I can't explain how much I resonate with her.

"I want to do this because my father drugged me after my accident." I spent the next forty minutes filling Amelia in on what happened to me and how my father drugged me. She was sympathetic and kind. She offered to send me through some information about nursing schools she knows of that are really great and offer online classes, but I would need to complete the practical parts of the assessments in a hospital.

I flop down on the bed and sigh, I never thought I would find my calling in life. I always thought I was destined to spend my life holed up in my father's house, alone and always wondering what was missing from my life.

"Kitten, why are you smiling?" I lull my head to the side and smile at my snack of a man. The black shirt he wears clings to him like a second skin, those jeans hug his thick thighs perfectly. "Keep making fuck me eyes and we won't make it to dinner with Roberto," he scolds me playfully. I groan and pout but the pout quickly disappears when he crawls up my body and nestles his way between my legs. He rests his elbows on either side of my head and stares down at me with nothing but love in his green eyes. Knox has been working hard to heal from the loss of his sister. He and I share a random memory of Wave each day, this helps us think that she is still with us and eases some of the pain her loss has left inside us. I know Knox has been hurting over Xander's betrayal, I can't begin to imagine how he feels.

"Are you still tracking Xander?" I ask. He releases a loud exhale and shakes his head.

"No, he slipped the men I sent after him. He's gone." I cup his cheek trying to comfort him.

"I know it hurts but I try to think that our baby is with your sister and she is looking after him or her until we get there." He smiles sadly and nods.

"One day I may be able to think about it like that but right now, I can't. Xander knew the truth about what happened that night. He let me hate you for something you didn't do." My face softens.

"I'm right here, baby. I'm not going anywhere." Knox constantly checks in on me daily and if I'm not in my usual spots he panics until he finds me. He's trying to get over his fear of losing me but I secretly hope he never does. I love that he needs me close always.

"Well, if you didn't agree to this stupid fucking dinner with Roberto then you wouldn't be leaving this bed but since you did, you need to get your ass up and change."

"I don't want to!" I whine.

An evil glint enters his eyes. "I'll let you sit on my face before I fuck you tonight." Heat pools low in my belly and my eyes become hooded. I feel myself growing wet at the thought of his wicked tongue plunging inside my pussy as I—.

"Can I watch you fuck his face?" Knox leaps off me and I scramble to sit up at the sound of Taylan's voice.

"Don't you ever fucking knock?" Knox snarls. Taylan screws his face up and shakes his head.

"I would have knocked but your door was wide open and I was honestly enjoying the show." Knox takes a single step toward him but Tay takes off laughing. I can't stop the giggle from coming out of me, earning a scowl from Knox.

"You fucking encourage him!"

"I do not! You were the one who let him sit in the corner and watch us fuck the other night." He opens his mouth and then clamps it shut, Knox knows I like being watched when he fucks me so we have allowed Taylan in a few times to watch and let me tell you, looking into the eyes of another man while you're being fucked by your boyfriend is so fucking sexy. Try it and thank me later.

"Fine. From now on he isn't allowed in until he fucking learns boundaries." I snort.

"Boundaries? I think you need to learn what those are as well since you let him eat my pussy as your cum dripped out of me." A smug look crosses his face.

"Yeah, maybe you're right. How about a raincheck on dinner and we get Tay back in here so he can eat your greedy little cunt while I fuck your ass to teach you a lesson?"

I swallow and lick my lips as I try to act unaffected by his offer. "Your dad is going to be upset." My voice is breathy to my own ears, my argument weak at best. When Knox yanks his shirt off and pops the button on his jeans, I clench my thighs together to try to alleviate the ache he has caused.

"Please, my mom thinks I don't know that after each of Roberto's visits, when he pretends to leave, that he parks his car around the side of the house and sneaks back in through the kitchen door so he can take the back stairwell to my mom's room, where they bump uglies." I gape up at him.

"Oh my God!" I squeak out. "Your mom and dad are fucking?" Knox recoils in disgust and shakes his head.

"Don't say that shit out loud again. He's fucking lucky I haven't shot him yet." I roll my lips over my teeth to keep from smiling. Clara gave Roberto a chance to explain everything when we got back and she forgave him. Knox is still warming up to the idea and agreed not to kill him for his mother's benefit but two weeks ago at dinner, Roberto made the mistake of sitting next to Knox and calling him *Son*. That ended with Roberto having a fork impaled into the top of his hand. I think they are bonding in their own way, kind of, well I'm hoping they will. Deciding not to push him, I open my legs. His eyes drink in the sight. I'm wearing a denim skirt sans panties with a knitted off the shoulder sweater. "Fuck, we're not going to dinner." I bite my bottom lip and lift my skirt, teasing him. He groans at the sight of my bare pussy. I feel my arousal coating the inside of my thighs.

"Fuck, I need you inside me," I moan.

His eyes narrow slightly. "Fuck, you're perfect, Lay."

Warmth explodes inside me at his words. "I choose you, Knox."

"I choose you always, baby."

Epilogue

Doxy

Eight years later...

Time is a meaningless commodity in my life, nothing changes here except for the amount of cocks that force themselves inside me each day. Unlike before, where I was chained to the table and raped repeatedly, I'm a good whore now. I can walk freely around the house so long as I keep my head down and obey everything the master tells me. For fourteen years I have busted my ass to gain the trust that I have. I never complain when the master and his men fuck me, I take it. I know what each of them like—some like it when I fight, others like it when I scream but Nolan is the worst. He only fucks me when I have to relieve myself. He loves using my mess as lube so he can fuck my asshole. Master only allows him to do that once a month since I kept getting infections from it.

At the sound of the front door opening, I quickly shuffle to the edge of the table. I quickly spit on my hand and rub my pussy before I bend over. If the master has been away for a long trip he needs to be relieved as soon as he walks through the door. I fight the shudder of disgust that rolls through me at the sight of others walking in behind him, they all stare at me. Master says nothing as the men claim their seats and begin to speak in hushed tones. I feel him behind me and wait. I hear his belt and then his zipper before I feel the tip of his cock pressing at my entrance. He groans, thinking I'm wet for him. I've learned ways to make this bearable like spitting rather than it feeling like sandpaper.

I whimper when he slams inside me. "See this, this my fucking whore," Master calls out as he thrusts inside me. "Look at the sight of her, waiting and willing to take any cock like a good fucking bitch. I trained the cunt well," he grunts out as he continues to pump inside twice more before coming. He never lasts long and I am always grateful for it. Once he pulls out I stand and ready myself to leave, but he grips the back of my head and slams my face down on the table. I cry out and regret making a sound instantly when I hear his dark chuckle. "You know the rules, Doxy, you made a sound so now they all get to take turns instead of just me." Slamming my eyes closed I will my tears not to fall, if he sees me cry it will be worse.

I force my mind to go blank as I hear them all leap out of their chairs. I barely register them raping me until one of them shoves his cock inside my ass without any lube. I bite down so hard that I bite my lip through, tasting my own blood. Tears gather in the corners of my eyes but I swallow my cries and think of something, anything to distract me from this fucking pain.

Soon, you will get your chance for revenge! Hold on, you can take all these fuckers out and then you can finally go after those fuckers in Canada! They will all pay for their part in this fucking nightmare I have lived in for fourteen fucking years.

"Karl?" someone shouts. The guy behind me stills as a man I have never seen enters the room. He takes one look at me and pales. "What the fuck is this?" he roars. The guy with his cock in my ass laughs.

"This is called—" He doesn't get a chance to finish before the man pulls a gun, fires a single shot and his cock rips out of me as his body drops to the floor. I hear someone come up behind me and fight the urge to gag, his buddy just got shot but that doesn't put him off? These cunts are all fucking sick! Every single fucking one of them!

"You lay a single fucking finger on her and you'll join your friend." The menace in his tone is clear.

"What the fuck do you want, Trevante?" Master snaps. The man keeps his gaze on me as he speaks. It's unnerving to have him looking at me, he doesn't see me as a hole to fuck like the others, he sees me as a... person.

"The Americans have aligned themselves with the Canadians and now the Greeks. They even have the fucking Russians and you can't even get Ian back on your side?" My eyes widen at the way he speaks to the master. I have never heard anyone speak to him like that before.

"Watch your fucking tone, boy."

"The Re Della Strada is going to come for you now that Ian isn't backing you and is putting his hat in the ring with the Greeks. You're on your own!" the man shouts.

"That little cunt Knox won't do shit to me," Master snarls smugly. Hearing his name has a deep-seated hatred rearing inside me. I'll have my vengeance against him one day soon, I fucking swear it. They will all pay for the fucking injustice I have suffered for over a decade, for the losses I have had to go through.

"How the fuck can you be so sure?" the man snaps angrily.

I feel master lay a hand on my bare back and remain still, fighting not to flinch away from his touch. "Because, eight years ago, Gio managed to drive a wedge between him and his best friend. Alexander Grayson is gone and no one has seen him." This is news to me, I had no idea they weren't together anymore, what happened? "And I have a golden ticket that ensures I break him worse than the loss of his best friend."

"And what exactly is that, *Dad?*" My mouth parts on a silent gasp, the master is his father. Any hope I had of this man helping me flees and I'm back to feeling despair and praying for the fucking devil to come snatch me and take me to hell.

"I have her," he says, patting my back. "She has been my hidden gem for years, knowing that when the time came for that little prick to try and come for me, I could finally shove it in his face and show him I won the war years ago." The smug tone of the master's voice has the man studying me intently for a moment.

"Who is she?" he asks quietly but never takes his gaze off me.

"She only responds to Doxy."

The man's face contorts in disgust. "You call her an abbreviation of the word slut?" I slam my eyes closed and fight off the wave of shame.

"Before I named her Doxy, she was known as Waverly Bronson, meet Knox's twin sister that he thought drowned fourteen years ago, Son."

The motherfucking end!

For now....

Pre Order your copy Fractured Heart now!
https://mybook.to/fracturedheart

Book 1 is finished, done and dusted I tell ya!

Writing Knox and Lake was a mindfuck but in the best possible way. I love these two so much and I truly hope you feel the same way.

I know you hate me for the cliffhanger but I swear book 2 is already being written and will be live soon. BE WARNED, book 2 will be the darkest book I have ever written and will come with a list of triggers as long as the phone book. It won't be a sappy love, love story, it will be a book about a woman who has been through hell and she doesn't need a man to fucking save her.

I cannot thank you enough for reading *Shattered Soul*, it means the world to me that you have taken a chance on reading one of my books!

If you would leave a review that would be amazing!

<u>Shattered Soul</u>

<u>Fractured Heart</u>

<u>Tainted Essence</u>

<u>Fairytales With A Twist</u>

<u>Condemned Beast</u>

Secret Society/ Bully

<u>Filthy Few</u>

<u>Forever Filthy</u>

<u>Filthiest Of Them All</u>

Sports Romance

<u>Playing For Keeps</u>

<u>Offside</u>

<u>Touchdown</u>

<u>End Game</u>

<u>Hail Mary</u>

<u>Blindside</u>

RH Sports

<u>Hate Us Like You Mean It</u>

MM

<u>Love Me Like You Mean It</u>

Paranormal Romance

Well, firstly I have to thank my husband because he is the real MVP for letting me play him like a fiddle and use his disco stick to try out all these positions. I also have to give him a shout out for letting me drag him around by his hair so he could describe the pain for me, it helped so much writing those scenes where Knox dragged Lake around.

My gremlins, fuck I love you both more than you know but you both need to learn really quick to get right with the Lord and play with Jesus and not me because my nerves are fucking frayed from your fighting. Our house is not a WWE ring, goddammit.

Leah, babes these books do as well as they do because of the covers you create. I couldn't do any of this without you, not only are you my designer, you are my friend and I cherish our friendship so much. It's because of that friendship why you know me so well and I never have to give any input into these covers, haha.

Jaye-*the bitch from Waterford,* if you fuck with my shit again we are done! Thank you for formatting my books but quit fucking with me woman, I'm tired of you laughing at me!

My alpha's, Debbie, Clare and Sarah, you three are my Musketeers! None of these books would be what they are without you, I mean that shit. You three make my job so easy and polish these books to perfection. Thank you from the bottom of my heart, I love you.

My beta girls, Erin, Rizzo, Morgan and Patti, you ladies are the core of this whole book journey, without your hype, love and constant support I don't think I would be where I am today. I love each of you so fucking much for all you have done and continue to do for me.

My Army: Alicia, Amber, Angel, Ash, Barb, Charlotte, Cyndi, Debbie, Jasmine, Jen, Kahanna, Katelyn, Lakshmi, Lora, Lyndsey, Sarmi and Tess. Thank you ladies so fucking much for being the best freaking team an author could ask for, I owe you all so much for the love and dedication you give me.

Lizz, Thank you from the bottom of my cold dead heart for always fitting me in and making these books what they are. You are a miracle worker and I would be fucked without you!

My darling dark delicious readers, you are the most amazing bunch of humans I have ever had the chance to interact with and also being able to meet some of you has been the highlight of my year. Thank you so much for taking a chance, reading these crazy motherfuckers and loving them as much as I do.

Sam xxx

ABOUT THE AUTHOR

Samantha Barrett is originally from Auckland, New Zealand but now lives in Brisbane, Australia.

Sam writes all things dirty dark and delicious with a side of twisted mind fuck.

She is a lover of all things red flags and an anti-hero is a must.